IT WAS COMING OVER HIM NOW . . .

That feeling he always got, just before it happened. A coursing of his blood, his heart pumping great volumes of the liquid through his veins making him feel as if he were vibrating with energy. He felt a sensation of great, almost supernatural strength.

He motioned the little girl inside, then pulled the cover closed. It was dark. The chirping of a cricket was magnified in the small enclosed space. Cool and moist, he could feel the chill coming from the walls. They were always afraid at this point. Some had even tried to leave, crashing against the closed entry. But by now it was too late.

"Don't be scared," he said, his hand on her shoulder, using the voice he knew the little ones liked to hear. "We're going to play a little game."

PRAISE FOR MARC BERRENSON'S PREVIOUS NOVEL *L.A. SNITCH:*

"A rapid-fire procedural . . . Action-packed . . . Compulsively readable"
Publishers Weekly

Other Ben Green Mysteries by
Marc Berrenson
from Avon Books

L.A. SNITCH
SPECIAL CIRCUMSTANCES

BODILY HARM

MARC BERRENSON

AVON BOOKS NEW YORK

BODILY HARM is an original publication of Avon Books. This work has never before appeared in book form. This work is a novel. Any similarity to actual persons or events is purely coincidental.

AVON BOOKS
A division of
The Hearst Corporation
1350 Avenue of the Americas
New York, New York 10019

Published by arrangement with the author
Library of Congress Catalog Card Number: 91-92451
ISBN: 0-380-76613-2

First Avon Books Printing: May 1992

AVON TRADEMARK REG. U.S. PAT. OFF. AND IN OTHER COUNTRIES, MARCA REGISTRADA, HECHO EN U.S.A.

Printed in the U.S.A.

RA 10 9 8 7 6 5 4 3 2 1

For Kare:
Everything that is good
comes from you.

For my parents:
Esther and Manny,
Josephine and Murray.

ACKNOWLEDGMENTS

As always, I am indebted to my editor at Avon Books, David Highfill, for his skill in smoothing out the rough spots, and for the TLC he gives to both author and manuscript.

CHAPTER 1

It was unfair, the way she always talked to him like he was a little kid. He was ten, wasn't he? Ten years old! Old enough to ride his bike, the chrome Mongoose that his dad had bought for his birthday, down the street, even around the corner if that's what he decided he wanted to do. After all, he was ten, not a little kid anymore.

Josh Gordon made sure his wraparound Oakley sunglasses were secure, then pushed himself up over the seat of his bike so that he could stand and pedal at the same time. He started pumping the pedals as fast as he could, rocking from side to side as he sped down the street toward the corner.

Stay on the side of the street, dear. And don't go off our block. His mother was always telling him that. Josh figured she'd be telling him that when he was fifteen or even sixteen, really old. *And don't ride that bike of yours anywhere near Mulholland Drive, mister. It's much too busy.*

About a block away, Josh rested, sitting on the seat, letting himself coast the rest of the way down the block toward Mulholland Drive. He figured he was way old enough to be out by himself, no matter what his mom said. Mothers were always that way, not wanting you to do anything, afraid you might get hurt or something, when he hardly ever did. Josh figured that as long as he kept circling the block, riding close to the curb like she wanted, his mom would never know.

It made him feel good to be out in the street, doing

something that he knew the big kids did all the time. His mom was too old to know about those things. Things had changed since she was a kid. She was a real nerd the way she talked about it. Kids were different now. They knew what was happening. At least the cool kids did. And he was one of them. With his T&C Surf T-shirt, his fluorescent Nike Air high-tops, and, of course, his Oakleys, he looked like one of the big kids. Way cool.

Josh was thinking about how radical he looked the first time that the truck with the camper passed him. He was on Mulholland Drive, where he wasn't supposed to be, riding close to the curb, because the traffic was pretty heavy and the last thing he wanted was to have something happen and have to explain to his mom that he was riding his bike on Mulholland, and then have to wait all afternoon until his dad got home, knowing that she'd tell his dad, who'd start yelling. Then his bike (and who knew what else) would be history. Grounded for life. Maybe longer.

He didn't notice the bearded man driving the camper the first time. When he did see him, Josh thought the guy was lost, with a weird, confused look on his face. Maybe he wanted to ask him about a street name or an address? Josh tried to pedal the bike straight, not wanting to crash into the curb, and not wanting to wander any further into the center of Mulholland. But the man in the camper was right up beside him, pacing him, looking over at him, then at the road, then back at him.

Whadya want? Josh wanted to say, though he didn't. The guy looked a little scary, like he was looking at him but at the same time not looking at him. Josh wondered why the man didn't say something. For a second he remembered what his mom and dad had said about not talking to strangers. They were always telling him that sort of stuff. Then there was that movie at school about the same thing. All the kids thought it was funny. Some guy in a raincoat asking some little girl to yank on his weenie or something like that. He and his friends got a big kick out of that one, and even the girls in his class had started to giggle. Like he'd really let some weirdo do something sick like that to him. Fat chance, man!

But the man in the camper wasn't trying to talk to him. Instead, he just kept staring, like they knew each other. Josh thought the man looked like someone he'd seen before, but nobody that he knew. He decided he'd turn off at the next corner, wondering if the man would follow him in his camper. Not like he was scared of the man or anything like that.

About the time Josh decided to turn, the camper swerved back into the center of the street and sped off ahead of him. Josh could see some writing on the back of the camper near the door, and a picture of two fish, blue and green, with hooks in their mouths, jumping in some sort of fake-looking water painted on the door.

See, he was okay. No big deal. He knew what to do, how to handle himself. Nothing for his mom to worry about. He was a lot older now than he had been. One of the big guys at school. Josh decided to ride a little further than he had before, feeling that he had everything under control. He knew his mom wouldn't say anything, unless she didn't see him pass in front of the house for a long time. Josh continued pedaling up Mulholland, instead of turning where he usually did. Another two blocks up the street he knew there was a turnoff with a steep hill. The hill was hard work, but once at the top it was a fast roller-coaster ride down to his house.

Josh turned off Mulholland. About halfway up the hill he spotted the camper. It was parked on the other side of the street, ahead of him near the corner. Josh stopped pedaling, resting at the curb, keeping his attention focused on the camper. The man, the one who had been giving him the weird looks, was out by the side of the camper, near the sidewalk, talking to a little girl. Josh recognized the girl from school, but couldn't remember her name. She was a lot younger than he was, he thought. Maybe seven. In one of the lower grades. Josh was surprised to see her there because he didn't know that she lived so close.

The man was talking to the girl. Josh was amazed to see how tall the man was. He couldn't tell when the man was sitting inside the camper driving down the street. But now he could, and the guy looked like some sort of basketball player, except too old. His beard, black, covered the bottom part of his face. Josh could see the white where his teeth poked out from the center of his beard as he smiled at the little girl.

They were talking now, the man and the girl. Josh thought about getting back on his bike and making his way up the hill. But something told him to stay put. He kept looking at the man and hearing his mother's voice, though he didn't realize what was happening until later, after he had had a chance to think about the man and the girl, and what he saw.

The bearded man was now kneeling down on the parkway next to the little girl. She was drawing with chalk on the sidewalk, and the man, all bunched up but still taller than the girl even down on his knees, was helping her, smiling and showing her what to draw. Then the man stood and he put his arm on the little girl's shoulder and led her to the back of the camper. The girl stood on the curb while the man opened the door of the camper and went inside. A second later, Josh saw one of the man's long legs coming backward out the door, reaching for the rear bumper. Then he was outside, standing in the street, holding something in his arms, showing the little girl. It was a doll. Almost as big as the little girl. With blonde hair, just like the girl's. And when you pulled a string in the doll's back it said something. Josh could hear the faint sound of the doll's voice every time the man pulled the string. Another voice, one he later recognized, was repeating to him not to ride his bike in the street, and whispering to him about not talking to strangers.

The man was motioning with his outstretched hand now. He was standing by the open door of the camper, looking around quickly, then looking right at the little girl, who was holding the doll and pulling on the string. The man was waving his hand toward the girl, trying to show her something inside the camper. The girl kept looking to her side, then back at the man. Josh had the feeling that the girl didn't know the man. That she was trying to decide whether to look inside the camper at whatever it was that the man wanted her to see.

Then the man took the doll from the girl and placed it inside the camper, on the other side of the open door. He was still motioning for the girl to come closer. Josh could see the man's smile, like a white hole in the middle of his black-bearded face. When the girl stepped off the curb, the man laughed and said something. He placed his arm around the girl's shoulders again and helped her up over the raised bumper. Within a second, the girl was inside the camper out of sight. The man closed the camper door and hurriedly ran to the other side. A few seconds later Josh heard the rumble of the truck's engine and saw a few puffs of black smoke come from the rear of the camper as the truck slowly moved up the street, turned, and was out of sight.

Josh walked his bike across and up the street to where the girl had been. All that was left of the little girl was a few pieces of colored chalk, and the drawings she had made on the sidewalk.

CHAPTER 2

"Don't be frightened, Erin. It's just a private place I have to keep all of my . . . good things. You want to see the good things, don't you?"

He watched as the girl nodded her head, unsure, thinking.

She's thinking that she's made a mistake, he thought. Probably about her mother telling her about strangers. I'll have to watch her closely, make sure she doesn't bolt.

"I'll just be a second," he said, gently maneuvering the girl to an area a few feet from the entrance. He would have to put his back to her while he removed the plywood and the boulders. At least where she was, she'd have to brush against him if she decided to run. Screaming was something else, though. Probably nobody would hear, not at this time of the evening, but better not to take the chance.

"I brought this for you," he said, removing a large pack of Skittles candy from his jacket pocket. She took the candy, and he could hear her shaking the pieces in the package as he opened the entrance. It was coming over him now. That feeling he always got, just before it happened. A coursing of blood, his heart pumping great volumes of the liquid through his veins, making him feel as if he were vibrating with energy. He felt a sensation of great, almost supernatural strength.

He motioned the little girl inside, then pulled the cover closed. "Don't be scared," he said, his hand on her shoulder, using the voice he knew the little ones liked to hear. It was dark. The chirping of a cricket was magnified in the small enclosed space. Cool and moist, he could feel the chill coming from the walls, in the blackness, before he could light his lantern. They were always afraid at this point. Some had even tried to leave, crashing against the closed entry. But by now it was too late. The feeling was upon him. A life force within him of such pure divine power that there was nothing anyone could do to stop what he was meant to accomplish.

"I'll just light this lantern," he said, removing the glass cover, adjusting the propane, and touching a match to the fabric wick. The wick burned blue and orange. He replaced the glass and turned up the light, which cast a ghostly, uncertain illumination on the inside of the mountain walls.

"There, that's better." He looked at the girl. She'd dropped the package of candy at her feet. He could see her shaking, heard her whimper. Something about "Mommy." That wasn't unusual. Always, right about now, except with the boldest of them, they wanted their mommy. He tried to remember feeling that way himself. So long ago . . . What came to mind was not the same, though. His memories of his mother were different, always filling him with sadness and regret.

He placed the inner piece of plywood over the opening and secured it with the leather straps. The large rock in the center of the space had been cleaned and scrubbed since the last time he'd been there. He'd learned that lesson the hard way, once not being as tidy as he should have. It was amazing how resourceful wild animals could be once they smelled it. But it was a lesson well-learned. Now he was more careful, scrubbing the great stone and the interior of the space when he was done.

"We're going to play a little game," he said. He removed the leather fasteners from where he had placed them. Just the feel of the sinewy straps brought back images of the last time. The last one had talked to him. Called him Daddy. And he'd learned that her real daddy was gone and rarely came to visit. He'd felt sorry for the beautiful little girl. She had even agreed to play with him, smiling at his size and the way her slightest touch made him gasp with pleasure.

But this one would be different. He would need to help this one along. But in the end, it would be the same. A vindication of his being. Delivering that pure face of sweetness to Eternal Heaven. For Him. For His greatness and glory. It caused him to feel slightly faint with happiness—and anticipation.

"Do you believe in God?" he whispered into her ear, close enough that he could see the fine hairs on her delicate lobe highlighted against the darkness as if they were on fire. "God will take care of you," he said. "God has selected you, through me, Erin. You should feel honored."

He had a sense that she was scared, not listening. It didn't matter, though. He was doing the Lord's work now. He was filled with His power, throbbing within his body, directing that His will be done.

He moved away from her, just a few feet so that the light stood between them, illuminating her face. He wanted to make sure she was watching. She was. Shaking, and crying, but riveted to his every move. It was good. The way he'd intended. The way he'd seen himself doing it a thousand times.

Slowly he removed his shirt, carefully folding it and laying it to the side, under the piece of clear plastic. Then his shoes, socks, and pants in the same place. He then slipped his underwear down his legs, carefully folding and placing them with the rest of his clothes. He now stood before her, hands on his hips, watching her eyes attempt to avoid coming to rest on the one spot that she tried not to look at. He knew she would see him, though, see his mounting power, be transfixed by it.

"Erin," he said, softly, "I want you to take off your clothes."

She shook her head violently back and forth, crying. The others had done the same. He came closer to her, standing over her so that the physical manifestation of his power jerked up and down with a life of its own. This was the part he savored. What he would remember later, when he was by himself. He forced himself to pull away, still looking at her face. He then turned, reached down, and carefully removed the others from the corner. He held them up for Erin to see.

"See, Erin. You're not alone. My dear, you're not alone." He wondered if she understood what she'd seen. Perhaps she had, because she stopped crying for the moment. With unblinking eyes she followed his hand. He hung the chain on the wall, lightly caressing the cool surface of their eyes. He turned each of them so that he could see them reveling in his power, his glory, as he brought yet another beautiful child within his fold.

"Let me help you," he said, approaching the stone. He began to remove her clothes. First the tiny pink shorts, then the knit top. Then the pretty little panties with the hearts in rows around the waist. He loved those. Would have liked to have kept them, but he knew better.

"There," he whispered, barely able to control his joy. She was beautiful. Perfect. He sat her down on the stone. "You are very beautiful," he said, no longer aware of her tiny protestations. Her tears dropped onto him as he secured the leather strap loosely around her ankles.

He reached over into the bag he had brought from the camper. From inside he removed his tape recorder, checking that the batteries were still there. He then lifted the cover of the recorder and removed the cassette, checking the notations he'd made on the label, then replacing it. He had tried to use those newer, voice-activated tape recorders before, but the sound wasn't what he wanted. Too much static on the stop-start, when the microphone picked up the sound just a split second too late. He found listening to those tapes disturbing, with parts of sentences, usually the first word or first syllable of the first word, missing or distorted. And the girls' crying wreaked havoc with the voice-activation mechanism. So he went back to his old Sony. He had a ninety-minute cassette, and he'd decided to just let the tape run. Catch everything.

He removed the first of his Vise-Grips pliers, the smallest one, from his toolbox. It was his favorite. Miniature, like a toy, a childlike version of the original. It was almost as if the company had designed this size especially for him.

"Don't be frightened," he said, adjusting the screw at the end of the Vise-Grips. He moved toward her and she scooted back away from him. It made him smile. Leaning over her now, his face only inches from her soft pink nipples, he placed the nose of the pliers against the skin. He looked at her face, no longer crying, her mouth open. "This is for the grace of the Lord," he whispered as he squeezed the handle. For a moment, the entire space was silent, except for the whoosh of the young girl's breath, out of control.

He looked to make sure the tape was working. Feeling his head swim with pleasure. A lightness of being that was like an electrical current to the brain.

Erin Dailey saw something flash, and it reminded her of something familiar, but she couldn't think of what it was. Starbursts. Through hazy eyes, like finding someone underwater, she saw the man with the beard, looking at her. She remembered those eyes, wondering how he did that, seeming to look at her while looking someplace else. Her mother's face was there now, scolding her, telling her she'd done wrong, that she hadn't listened. She was a bad girl. And still that flashing. She was a bad girl. And bad girls get punished. Her mother had told her that. There was a weight tugging at her chest. When she looked, she didn't believe it. It didn't make sense that something like that would be there.

He placed the still undeveloped pictures inside the lid of the tool chest, then set the camera aside. From inside the chest he removed another pair of Vise-Grips, slightly larger. He adjusted the set-screw, aware that the girl was almost gone now.

His mind drifted back to another scene. He was small, not much older than the little girl. His mother was there, in the tiny room with him, telling him what to do, giving him directions. *That feels so good,* she would tell him. *You're Momma's little darling,* she purred. *Momma's little helper.*

He pushed the memory from his mind, concentrating on the soft pink spot between the little girl's legs.

She said, "Mommy," her faltering voice making the word into four syllables, then fell backward against the stone. He stood over her motionless body, grasping himself, thinking of his power.

When he'd recovered, he lifted himself from the stone and looked at the girl. Placing two fingers on the side of her neck, he checked the pulse that he knew was there. Her eyes were closed, the lids flickering in minute up-and-down movements. He glanced at the tape, then at his other children, noticing their smiles and the interest with which they were watching his every move.

When everything had been made ready, he stood back for a moment, feeling the electrical anticipation of what he was about to do. He felt himself stirring again. That would have to wait, he told himself. Later, with the tape and the pictures it would come again.

From inside the oiled leather sheath, he removed the knife.

"Honey, did you hear about the missing Dailey girl?"

Josh listened to his mother yelling from the kitchen to his father, who had just returned from work and was changing clothes in the bedroom. His father didn't answer. He didn't like yelling conversations across the house.

"Did you hear me, dear?" His mother started to move out of the kitchen down the hallway, holding a spoon. His parents' bedroom was right across the hall from his, and his door was cracked open while he played Nintendo.

"Little Erin Dailey is missing," she said. His mother was using her high worrisome voice, the one she used on him when he forgot to do something important that she'd reminded him of. There was a silent pause, after which Josh heard his mother say, "You know, dear. The little girl from down the street. She goes to Joshy's school. We met her parents at the last P.T.A. book drive." Another short silence, followed by a grunt of acknowledgment from his father.

"I'd think you'd be more concerned," his mother scolded.

"I am, dear. I'm sorry. My mind's still at the office. How long has she been gone?"

"Since yesterday. She was playing in front of her house one moment, the next she was gone. It's scary, something like that happening so close."

Without being able to see them, Josh knew that this was the part where his dad would hug his mother, patting her on the back, telling her not to worry. They always did that sort of stuff.

"Do they have any idea where she might have gone?" Josh heard his father's voice becoming louder as he left the bedroom.

"None. The police were out scouring the neighborhood, asking if anyone might have seen her."

"She's in Josh's grade?"

"Younger," his mother answered.

A recollection appeared in Josh's mind. Something he hadn't thought about until then. The camper, and riding his bike on Mulholland Drive, where he wasn't supposed to be. And the man with the beard helping the little girl draw her pictures.

"Are you ready for dinner?" It was his dad sticking his head inside his room.

"Yeah."

"Turn off Nintendo, then. We'll be eating in a few minutes."

Josh mumbled something unintelligible and continued to manipulate the Nintendo controls, his eyes glued to the television screen. He was aware that his father remained a moment at the doorway to his room, then clucked his tongue in frustration and left.

Were they talking about the same girl? Josh wondered if the girl's name was Erin. He couldn't remember. He'd never heard her last name. Maybe it was somebody different. Sure, that was it. He didn't have to tell his parents about the bearded man. It was probably nothing. Not the same thing that they were talking about. After all, the girl had gotten into the truck on her own. Nobody forced her.

She was smiling. The bearded guy was probably her father, coming home from work, seeing her playing too far from home, and giving her a ride. Yeah, that was it. Josh wondered if the girl might have gotten into trouble for playing where she wasn't supposed to be. It made him think of what his mother had told him about not riding his bike on Mulholland. So far, he'd kept that one a secret.

"Josh, did you hear your father? It's time to eat." His mother now, standing at the door, poking her head inside. "Do you know little Erin Dailey?" she asked. "She lives a couple blocks down the street."

Josh shook his head. He punched at the control box, turning off the game. The screen went dark.

"You see what can happen when you stray too far from home, Josh?"

He mumbled an "Uh huh."

"The police say she was drawing pictures on the sidewalk in front of her *own* house. See, Joshy?" She put her arm around his shoulders and ruffled his hair, pulling him close to her stomach. He could smell the spaghetti-sauce smell on her apron. "You can never be too careful. If something were to happen to you, I'd just never forgive myself!"

They both walked into the kitchen. His dad was seated at the table waiting for them.

"Too careful about what?" he said.

"I was just asking Joshy about the Dailey girl, dear."

His dad, talking to the bowl of spaghetti that he held in front of him: "Well, you didn't see anything, did you, Josh?"

Josh shoved the broccoli to the side of his plate and shook his head.

CHAPTER 3

"Picture this, Benny. The guy's charged with rape by means of a foreign object, right? And he's just arrived from Iran, I mean straight off the boat. The first thing he does, now he's in America, home of the Whopper, demolition derby, and pay-for-view anything, he goes to one of those sex joints where you'd have to have not gotten your rocks off in about a million years to wanna touch the kinda women they got there. He hooks up with this broad, who, seeing the three-inch, thick wad of bills all wrapped up nice and neat in the guy's gold money clip, figures why settle for a quick fifty when she could string the guy out all night and walk away with the whole wad."

Ben Green sat at the counsel table, calmly listening to Antoine LeDoux's whispered story, while at the same time trying to keep track of the testimony from the Mexican gang-banger on the witness stand. He, along with the rest of the lawyers, was beginning to lose sight of why they were trying the case in the first place. Ben felt a buzz, audible only to him, in the front part of his head, somewhere inside and just above his right eye. He found himself daydreaming about being out on the deck behind his home that overlooked the canyon, the cool evening air numbing the buzz in his head, helped by his second frosty Absolut.

"Everything's going just fine," said LeDoux, "at least until my client pulls out this sexual device he decided to buy at the local sex emporium. Ya know, Benny, they don't have many of those places in Iran. Can you imagine the Ayatollah and all the robed brothers throwing quarters in the machine watching Debbie do Dallas?"

Ben smiled. The image amused him momentarily. Took him away from the tedium of the courtroom. He looked down the length of the counsel table at the other defense attorneys on the case, each seated next to his Vietnamese client. Next to LeDoux sat Bernie Saltzman doing a crossword puzzle that he had hidden under the first few sheets of his yellow legal pad. On the other side of Bernie was C. Randall Jeffries, working on answers to a set of interrogatories in a bankruptcy case. Next to Jeffries was Harrold "the Hammer" Richler, whose main practice was personal injury. Richler was programming his brand-new pocket computer, one of those computerized personal secretaries that made it impossible to forget a birthday or important event, or so the advertisements claimed. Richler hadn't quite mastered his new toy, hitting the wrong key every now and then and creating an audible electronic beep, which resulted in a scowl from the judge and titters of laughter from C. Randall Jeffries, who was bored with both the interrogatories and the juvenile court trial that he was supposedly involved in.

LeDoux continued, "So this Iranian decides to be creative. He's got this enormous plastic penis that he bought at the local sex shop. You've seen 'em, the ones that run on batteries with the head that vibrates. He tries to stick it up this poor girl's you-know." LeDoux started to chuckle quietly, placing his hand over his mouth. Ben noticed LeDoux's trademark diamond-encrusted gold Rolex highlighted against the smooth coffee-colored skin of his wrist. As usual, Antoine "Lucky" LeDoux was immaculately tailored, from his navy shoes of soft Italian leather to his twelve-hundred-dollar custom-made suit. All of his shirts were hand-tailored especially for him, with his initials monogrammed on the cuff, along with some sort of crest of arms over the shirt pocket. Ben had never gotten around to asking LeDoux what the crest of arms meant, since, as far as Ben knew, Lucky was the seventh in a family of eleven kids, all born and raised in Brooklyn.

"Well," continued LeDoux, "the girl sees this huge pink

plastic dildo coming her way and decides she wants no part of it *or* the crazy Iranian. By that time my client's practically frothing at the mouth." LeDoux began chuckling once more.

"Benny, ya know what the Iranian says to me in court, after they read him the charges? He hears the judge say the words 'rape by use of a foreign object,' and he starts to get all upset. I ask him what's up, and he says to me, 'This is America, Mr. LeDoux. Everybody the same in America. Everybody got same rights.' And I say, Yeah, that's right. So what? And you know what he says to me, Benny? He says the judge is prejudiced against him because he's from Iran, a foreigner! Ya get it, Benny? The Iranian thinks *he's* the foreign object!" With that, LeDoux broke into a loud belly laugh, causing the witness to pause in his testimony.

The judge looked impatiently down at LeDoux, who had turned his back on the court proceedings in an effort to hide his laughter.

"Mr. LeDoux," he said, "I know we've been at this trial for the last five days, and I know that it seems like it will never end." He paused, trying to maintain control. A smile, as if its appearance had surprised him, flashed across his face, then quickly disappeared. The judge added, "I'm sure that we all have more interesting, more pleasant things we'd like to be doing right about now, like maybe sticking pointed needles into our eyeballs . . . but *please,* have a little respect for Miss Thurber who is trying very hard to get this witness to give her the answers that she wants."

Thomas Boynton was the judge. He'd graduated from Harvard Law School at the top of his class and was the assistant editor of the law review in his senior year. After law school, Boynton entered the U.S. Attorney's Office, prosecuting high-grade white-collar crime and handling certain high-publicity organized-crime prosecutions. One of the rising stars, or so the newspapers had said at the time. Then Boynton's wife decided to leave him after sixteen years of marriage and two kids. His oldest daughter joined the Holy Temple of the Followers of the Most Holy Joe Don Baker, a commune that lived in tents on a small piece of land somewhere in Oregon, and followed the teachings of an ex–country-and-western singer. Boynton's son, at the age of fourteen, ran away from home, was placed in a group boys' home by his mother, who had obtained custody in the divorce proceedings, and was later arrested for sales of cocaine to an undercover narc. Thomas Boynton, finding that the chaos his once-ordered life had become was too much to handle, quit the U.S. Attorney's Office, but not before using his political pull to secure an appointment to the Los Angeles Superior Court bench, where he now sat, day after boring day, listening to juvenile court cases.

"I'm sorry, Your Honor. It won't happen again," LeDoux apologized, still sporting a small grin.

"Should I stop, man?" The question was from the witness, one 'Little Rascal,' who was testifying as to the events of a gang fight between the members of his gang, who for the purposes of this case were alleged as the victims, and a rival gang. "I mean, that black dude keeps laughing and making noise, man." The witness pointed at LeDoux. "Jesus, it's hard to think, ya know what I mean?"

Boynton smiled. He seemed to enjoy the young Mexican's comment about LeDoux.

"It ain't right, man." The gang-banger seemed to be losing control. LeDoux's interruption, or his own inability to articulate his thoughts and feelings in answering the D.A.'s questions, seemed to have frustrated the young man. Little Rascal looked at the judge as if for assistance. Then, his attention still focused directly on Boynton, the young man extended his hands at his sides, palms upward in frustration, and blurted out, "I mean, Jesus . . ."

Boynton leaned toward the witness, peeking at the young man over his round tortoiseshell glasses, his Adam's apple bulging over a red, white, and blue bow tie. Ben noticed a sly glint of anticipation in Boynton's eyes. "Young man," said Boynton, stifling a laugh, "A simple 'Your Honor' will suffice."

The attorneys, those who had been paying attention to the repartee, started to laugh. Even the Vietnamese clients, who had remained quietly seated throughout the trial, emotionless, inscrutable in expression, cracked smiles.

"And Mr. Richler," said Boynton, changing gears, "if you would be so kind as to program your computer on your own time, the Court would be forever in your gratitude."

Richler looked up, seemed to think for a moment about what Boynton had said, then placed the computer back inside his coat pocket.

"Richler just settled a giant malpractice case," whispered LeDoux. Ben was only half-paying attention. He, like the other attorneys at the counsel table, was representing a client charged with various counts of felony assault with a multitude of martial arts weapons that would have made Bruce Lee envious. All of the minors charged were members of the Vietnamese Crazy Boys gang. Day after day they each came to court dressed in dark slacks tapered at the cuff, black canvas-soled shoes, billowy white silk-like long-sleeved shirts buttoned to the top. They all wore their hair in a sort of bouffant with a large wave in front. A throwback to the fifties. A kind of Asian Elvis look.

All of the alleged victims were Mexican and members of the Langdon Street Boys gang, with nicknames like Sleepy, Shok, Little Rascal, Spider, and Monkey Man. Each sported the homemade tattoo of the Langdon Boys on the back of his hand, and each was dressed in a pair of oversized khaki trousers and a large, freshly ironed, perfectly white T-shirt.

LeDoux resumed whispering as the Mexican gang-banger on the witness stand continued to testify. "Richler's client went in for a simple prostate operation," said LeDoux, "and came out with a permanent hard-on. Jesus, can you imagine something like that? Damn thing wouldn't go down. Now maybe, for a stud like myself, that wouldn't be such a bad thing. But this guy was in his early seventies!"

Ben didn't listen to the rest of LeDoux's story. Between the Spanish-language interpreters for the victims and the Vietnamese-language interpreters for the minors and their families, it was like the Tower of Babble, and Ben was having a hard time following the thread of the prosecution's case. To compound matters, the D.A.'s office had assigned a brand-new deputy, Clarise Thurber, to handle the trial, and she had not the slightest idea of what she was doing. Everybody realized she was in way over her head, even at this low level.

"Miss Thurber," said Boynton, rubbing the palm of his hand over an obviously tired and somewhat impatient face. "Perhaps this would be a good time to take our mid-morning recess."

Before the D.A. could answer, Sam, the courtroom bailiff, an elderly black man whose khaki sheriff's uniform had been laundered so many times it was practically see-through, jumped up from behind his desk and began moving toward the minors.

"All right," said Sam, moving quickly toward the counsel table. "All you gentlemens please have a seat outside in the waiting corridor until your cases are called, *comprendo?*"

"They're Vietnamese," said LeDoux.

"Yeah, well, I don't speak no Vietnamese, and no Chinky either. But these boys understand me, don't you, boys?" Sam smiled, showing a row of gold-filled teeth jutting out at different angles. Sam had been a courtroom bailiff for as long as anyone could remember. He'd been Boynton's bailiff for the last couple of years. He'd almost lost that job, though. Sam was a very religious sort. Taught Sunday school at the local Baptist church. One day he got it in his head that he'd look more magisterial, more biblical is the way he put it, if he had something like a robe to wear when he taught school. He figured that the judge wouldn't miss his for one day, and it was just hanging there in his chambers all weekend, so what was the harm? As it turned out, one of Sam's students threw up on the robe and Sam had to explain the entire incident to Boynton, who was less than amused. Sam wasn't fired, but he was watching himself just a little bit more closely since the incident.

"Any of these Ornamentals gonna testi-*ly?*"

Ben turned at the question. Behind the clerk's desk, Trixie Cash, Boynton's courtroom clerk, sat cracking her gum. Although her jaw moved like a finely tuned machine, the rest of her face remained motionless, vacant. Ben felt like making a comment about the hair-sprayed helmet of lacquered red hair that rested like an overturned bowl with handles atop her head, but he thought better of it.

"You mean Orientals, don't you," said Ben, knowing that Trixie meant exactly what she'd said.

"Yeah," she said. "Ornamentals, just like I said." She smiled.

Ben didn't feel like returning the smile. He'd sparred with Trixie Cash countless times over the years, and if there was anything he'd learned from their encounters it was that Trixie's mental development had for some mysterious reason been arrested at the age of sixteen while a teenager somewhere deep in the Appalachian Mountains. The only thing Trixie seemed to understand these days was the truncated communication of long-distance truckers over the CB radio. She kept hers under her clerk's desk and was known to strap on a set of headphones even while court was in session.

Ben's client, Minh Luu, one of the group of five who were on trial, stood next to him. Minh understood perfectly what Trixie Cash had said, and did not seem amused by her comment. Minh had an A- average in school. The combined grade-point average of the entire group on trial was a B, which, Ben knew from experience, was not unusual. Through some quirky overlap of intercultural priorities, the Vietnamese Crazy Boys were not just the only gang in Los Angeles whose members would actually graduate from high school—they were the only gang with a cumulative grade-point average above a 3.0.

Ben told Minh to have a seat with his parents out in the hallway. It was quickly turning into one of those days that made him wonder about the wisdom of his decision to return to the practice of law.

The case resumed later in the morning, and after another hour and a half of testimony, Boynton recessed the trial until the next week. Ben headed for his car. Minh Luu, his fellow gang-bangers, and the juvenile court case quickly receded from his thoughts during the drive home. Before leaving the courthouse, Ben had called for his messages, and was surprised to hear his ex-wife's voice on the tape. He hadn't heard from Sara since Julie's funeral nearly three years earlier. The last image he had of his ex-wife, standing across from him at their daughter's burial, was something akin to the way boxers glare at each other during the pre-fight instructions.

But he couldn't really blame her for that. Sara needed somebody to hate, and the demented psychopath that had ravaged their daughter's life, and much of their own in the process, was conveniently not around to accept her scorn. Considering how things had happened, it was, Ben thought, little to ask of him: to volunteer for his time in the stocks, and, if not welcoming, then at least accepting of the pillory.

So now, apparently, there was something of interest to them both, which was about to intercede into the cavernous space between them, stretching like warm caramelized sugar, its frail weblike tentacle, for the instant, precariously connecting them once again. And what was this thing, this reason for her reaching out after so long a time? Sara had said only that she needed to speak to him, and her voice, its normal separation-monotone, had not betrayed her feelings.

It struck him, suddenly, that he had just assumed it was about Julie. That Sara's message had something to do with the only reason for their communicating since the divorce. But Sara hadn't mentioned anything about that, and he wondered, with a sliver of hard-fought optimism, if perhaps, after such a long lapse, Sara had found herself thinking about what they had been through together, and merely wanted to maintain some semblance of relationship between them, no matter how tenuous.

The red message light on the machine was blinking as he entered. He played back the messages, not leaving the room, just in case she tried to call again. The last message on the tape was from Sara, saying that she had mailed something to him three days ago, and asking did he get it. Sara said for him to call if the letter hadn't arrived, and she'd try to explain it to him on the phone, as a last resort, or so the tone of her voice made clear. So much for optimism and relationships.

Ben inspected the floor near the door. In his haste to check the tape machine, he'd stepped over the pile of mail, mostly advertisements, that lay just inside. Shuffling through assorted envelopes and multicolored advertising flyers, tossing them onto the kitchen table like a Vegas blackjack dealer, he found the plain white envelope with Sara's return address in the corner.

He set the envelope aside for a moment, glanced out the kitchen window, past the wood deck to the canyon below, which was presently swathed in twilight shadow. The mountains appeared as if highlighted with fluorescent fire. It was, under normal circumstances, his favorite part of the day; still light enough to catch the undulating nuances of the canyon and hillside, like loose skin of different hues of brown, black, and green.

The letter cried out to be opened. He knew that very soon he would lift the envelope into his hands and slip his finger beneath one corner of the flap, working it open carefully. Then he'd remove whatever it was that was inside, what Sara had not wanted to speak of on the phone, what he knew would be unpleasant, perhaps even worse. He saw himself going through those motions as he held the envelope in his left hand, staring at Sara's return address, as if that would afford him some concrete clue as to the contents. He'd felt less intimidation opening the grocery-bag-brown window envelopes from the I.R.S. He'd gotten used to those, he supposed. Always the thought of an audit—he had made very little in the last few years and in reality had nothing to fear from the prying eyes of the government—causing him to hesitate and hold the contents at arm's length, distancing himself from the expected bad news.

Whatever was inside was very lightweight. Ben opened one corner of the envelope then ripped the edge and shook out the contents. A clipping from a newspaper. One of the local papers back east where Sara lived. Attached to the clipping by means of a paper clip was a short handwritten note. He read Sara's barely legible scrawl:

> Thought you would want to see this. You may have heard already. Needed to replace the stone due to the damage. I've taken care of it. Sorry.
>
> Sara

The newspaper article was less than three full paragraphs. It dealt with an incident of anti-Semitic vandalism at the cemetery where Julie was buried. Certain of the grave sites had been defaced with swastikas and other anti-Semitic symbols and slogans. The local police had no leads as to the identity of the perpetrators. It was, according to the article, the third incident of anti-Semitic vandalism in the city during the last month.

Ben felt the wetness of perspiration from the drive home on the back of his shirt and the elastic of his underpants. A deathly cold stretched its frozen fingers up his back, reaching around his neck, standing his hair on end. Anger was part of it, but not the main ingredient. Disappointment, hopelessness, and despair began to take over.

Not that he was a stranger to such feelings. It had come over him before, this sense of ultimate failure, when he had been told of Julie's death, and during the time afterward when people had expected him to learn how to deal with it. They never said as much, these people who observed his every move. But he knew what they were thinking. Their unspoken impatience. Enough is enough. A respectable period of grieving is only natural—healthy as a matter of fact. But he had gone beyond that. Exceeded the limits of good taste in such matters.

He was past that now, or so they thought. He had any one of a number of non-grieving faces that he showed to people to make them feel comfortable. Nobody wanted to deal with the real Ben Green, he was aware of that, though no one had actually told him as much. He didn't have to hear it to know that it was true. He could see it in their faces, in his own. It was something that continually echoed in his mind. And for a while, even he was convinced, at some median level of consciousness, that he had things under control, that the grief that had rendered him helpless, that had almost killed him, had subsided.

Now this . . .

The first swallow of vodka punched him and made him wince. He took another. This one went down easier. Cold and numbing. Still some time away from the desired effect, though. He was seated on the chaise in the back, overlooking the other houses suspended from rock and earth, like undesirable growths, clinging to the canyon walls, adding their predictable human angles to the otherwise wild and ever-changing terrain.

It always made him feel vulnerable, his rather precarious position in all this. And that feeling of vulnerability, in the past, had given him a perspective on things. It had helped.

But now it seemed to aggravate his sense of hopelessness. His mind was running at its own pace now, no longer subject to his control. Scenes of the past, without order, randomly flashed their images for a second behind his eyes, then yielded to the next, and the next, and . . .

Ben rested his elbows on his knees and pressed against the sides of his head with his palms. Pressed until the physical pain obliterated the past into darkness.

After some time, he wasn't sure how long, he found himself in a different position, only somewhat disoriented, his cheek chaffed by the rough redwood flooring of the deck. The sun was still there, highlighting the ridge of jagged mountain, except different. Shiny, like silver against utter darkness. He blinked, and in a moment realized that he'd been deceived. It was dark. Nightfall. He was on the ground, gazing into the reflection of the moon on the polished aluminum leg of the chaise. He rolled gently on his side. A three-quarter moon lolled indifferently overhead, casting a faint iridescence over the patio.

He'd been dreaming. Nazi storm troopers coming to his door and pushing him aside. Grabbing Julie and Sara and removing them from the house. He'd tried to fight, but was struck by the butt of a gun. Lying on the ground, through watery eyes he watched the military truck carrying Sara and Julie pull away from him. He was transfixed, paralyzed, unable to move. Julie was crying, calling out to him. He couldn't help.

Then there was another part of the dream: seeing her again, still, unmoving. This time on a pristine slab of some cool material, perhaps marble or a thick piece of glass, like ice. *Yes,* he told the man in the white coat, *that is her, that is my daughter.* And the man pursed his lips in a quick smirk, grabbed the end of the slab on which his daughter lay, and shoved it on invisible tracks into an invisible wall, causing the slab and Julie to disappear. In the dream, it didn't shock him that Julie had disappeared so magically. Later, while awake, he had the recollection that he had expected it. Ben remembered looking at the forearm of the man wearing the white coat in the dream and seeing a faint blue tattoo, the SS symbol. Then, as if he hadn't as yet noticed the man's features, Ben suddenly became aware that he wore the same face as the Nazi guard that had taken his family away.

Think it through, Ben told himself, hunched over the small glass-and-metal table, rubbing a hand over his face and massaging his eyes. The newspaper article, Sara, his identification of Julie at the morgue . . . Amazing how his mind worked. He hadn't had one of these dreams in months. Now the nightmarish images of his past had been set free once more to torment him. To perhaps finish off what had been started almost three years earlier.

Ben heard the sound of the automatic garage door and the creaking of the hinges. Claire. Home late. For an instant he considered not telling her. Run into the kitchen, grab the newspaper clipping, smile, offer a drink, and act like nothing happened. He'd gotten as far as flexing his hands on the armrests of the chair, readying to hurry to the kitchen, then decided against it. Claire would see it in his eyes, hear the truth in his voice, his thinly disguised bonhomie. Doomed to failure. He could never fool her.

And if he did tell her?

She would watch him, acting like she wasn't. Closer this time than the last. That for sure. And he'd go through their days together knowing that she was thinking thoughts that she couldn't reveal. Something else added to the pile of subjects that would remain undiscussed.

"Ben, are you back there?"

She appeared at the sliding-glass door, looking for only the briefest of moments at his upturned face. Then she knew.

"Something's happened," he said, dropping his chin to his chest and starting to cry.

CHAPTER 4

Ezekiel Thibodoux let the line play out, guiding the translucent eight-pound test from the spool with his left hand, feeling it in the crook below the first digit of his index finger. The line drooped loosely, with only the slightest pull, disappearing a few feet from the tip of his rod into the stream's sandy bottom. Just a few more feet, he told himself, careful not to let the hook travel too far over the rocks. That's where they were, just beyond the rushing water, in that quiet pool near the bank, under the shallow spreading roots of the alder.

Thibodoux remained focused on that one spot, waiting for the line to go taut, the pull on his finger. In that split second, he took in the scene: his line, corkscrewing from the end of his rod, stretched loosely across the width of the small stream. He stood a few feet from the mossy bank, each foot on a small rock partially buried within the streambed. The sun came at him from downstream. That was something that he always checked before starting, not wanting to cast a shadow over the water that might reduce his chances. He waited quietly, knowing they were there.

Suddenly, the tip of his rod bowed down toward the water, a slight tug, then more twitching, and the line ripped taught against his finger. Instinctively, he jerked the rod up, setting the hook. With the fingertips of his rod hand, he adjusted the drag, lifting up on the rod to reduce the slack. He could barely see it now, a small shaft of silver in the water where the once-silent pool was now bubbling with activity. He moved back, cranking the line in, cautious about getting tangled in the overhanging branches. He could see it clearly now, a rainbow, his eye catching the yellows and pinks, watching it slither its way toward the bank, the battle almost over. A plant, he thought. The naturals had more fight in them.

Thibodoux kept his eye on the fish, watching as it made preparations for one final jump. He moved the rod from his right hand to his left, keeping the line taut, his eyes riveted on the silvery sliver that wiggled just a few feet below. Carefully he bent closer to the water, sliding his hand quickly under the belly of the trout and firmly cradling it in the palm of his hand.

Once on shore, the trout appeared diminished. Not just in size, for Thibodoux knew that the water magnified the size of the fish. But there was something lessened, almost sad, he thought, about seeing its shining body wiggle and thrash awkwardly in his hand, when just moments before its grace and beauty in the water had been unequaled.

Thibodoux carefully removed the hook from the lip of the trout. This would be the last one of the day, he decided. He lifted the chain stringer from the bank of the stream, inspecting his catch. Opening one of the unused metal clothespins of the stringer, he inserted the wire through the trout's mouth then back out one side through the gill. He then snapped the wire shut, tossing the stringer back into the stream. The trout, once back in its natural habitat, thrashed quietly for a few moments, perhaps believing it had been set free.

Thibodoux stretched out on the bank, on his back, resting on his elbows. If he craned his head slightly to one side, he could catch the sun filtering through the branches of the alders, warming his cheeks. He closed his eyes, listening to the quiet hiss of the stream, birds chirping in the distance. This was the best part. Not the actual catching of the fish, though he did like that, but in a different way. It was the peacefulness of being within himself, alone, that he treasured. For as long as he could remember, it was this part that he'd appreciated the most. The reason he'd come back.

After a time, he found himself fuzzily recollecting a dream he'd just had. Then he realized that he'd dozed off near the bank of the stream. The sun no longer cascaded through the branches of the trees. It had moved to some lower point in the sky. What was left was cloudless space. An infinity of pure sky-blue that made him dizzy to look at. There was nothing to mark his position, no cloud or airplane, or mountain range at the edge to denote his place in the universe.

Thibodoux jerked himself up onto one elbow, thinking that it was time he returned, but not wanting to leave. The stringer of fish was still there, the silver chain attached to the shore, spreading out into the cool dark water of the stream its necklace of fish-charms.

With hands that worked without thought, Thibodoux quickly gutted each of the trout, a sure-handed slice up the belly, removing the entrails, then sluicing the gutted fish in the stream before placing it in his ice chest. When done, he carefully wiped the edge of his knife on a rag and placed it back in the sheath. This ordinary task brought to him other thoughts, which he didn't try to avoid. He knew it was useless. All the years, before and after, the memories were there to stay.

Thibodoux had just climbed inside the cab of his truck when his beeper sounded.

They couldn't really be that mad at him now. After all, he was just a kid. How was he to know that it was so important?

Josh Gordon sat at the kitchen table where his mother had told him to sit and not move. She didn't look mad, more excited than mad.

"Yes, Officer." His mother was talking into the phone, and he could tell she was upset. Josh hoped she wasn't upset with him. He hoped that whatever it was that his mother wanted to hear from the person on the phone, she heard it. Otherwise, Josh knew his mother would be mad and probably take it out on him.

"I did call early this morning, Officer. This is Mrs. Gordon. It's my son that saw the little girl, not me."

Josh watched as his mother listened, nodding her head.

"Yes, Officer. He's here with me now. I'll keep him home from school if you want." His mother seemed to be calmer now. Josh liked the idea of missing school. Things were working out better than he expected.

"Well, don't you want to speak with him? Yes, well, all right, if that's what you think. Yes, you've got my phone number and address. You'll call first, right? Good."

His mother placed the phone back on the hook. "Time to get ready for school," she said.

Josh groaned. "What'd they say, Ma?"

"They'll send someone by the house later."

Josh saw that she looked upset, but still on the excited side.

"They're notifying the detective who will be handling the case," his mother said. "He'll want to talk with you, Joshy. But I'll be there with you, so don't worry."

He wasn't worried. Josh was just glad that he wasn't in trouble for riding his bike on Mulholland. He'd talk to whoever they wanted as long as he didn't get grounded for that.

"Now you just put this out of your mind for now," his mother said, patting him on the head. He was glad to see that. He was definitely not in trouble on this one. It was like the time he had figured out the video recorder for his mom after being told not to go near it. Both his mom and his dad had looked at him with that look that he knew came right before getting yelled at. And then, when he explained what he'd done, they couldn't believe that he had figured out all the wires and cables dangling from the back of the box. Then his dad tried the VCR, and saw that in fact it did work. He'd been a star after that. They weren't mad at him at all. Just the opposite. They looked at him differently, like he was some sort of genius or something.

And now, this business with the little girl was almost like that. When he told his mom what he'd seen, she wasn't at all interested in why he wasn't supposed to be there on his bike. She hadn't even mentioned anything about that. She had that same my-little-boy-is-a-genius look on her face. He realized that he knew something that they thought was important. Important enough for them not to bother punishing him for riding on Mulholland. And afterward, he could hear his parents whispering to each other about what they should do. That was last night. This morning, his mother still hadn't said anything about his riding his bike where he wasn't supposed to. She still had that look, treating him real nice, like she did on those days when he had to go to the dentist.

Josh had watched enough TV to know that this talk he had to have with the police would be better than going to the dentist.

The Sexual Assault Division of L.A.P.D. occupied a corner of the detective room at Parker Center. About a half dozen desks, a six-drawer filing cabinet, and the part-time use of a secretary who shared the rest of her time with Bunko/Forgery and Metro Traffic.

Ezekiel Thibodoux had accustomed himself to not being in one of the glamour divisions. Robbery-Homicide always got a lot of attention, the detectives getting their names splashed across the local papers on a regular basis. He could remember when the Sexual Assault Program, or S.A.P., as it was called, was first formed. All the women's groups had joined forces with the anti-child-abuse organizations to bring attention to the newest of the chief's boutique divisions. But shortly after it was formed, and the hoopla died off, it quickly became no more special than any other division of L.A.P.D. Other community-interest groups came into vogue, and S.A.P.'s supply of manpower and secretarial support, that the chief had boasted about earlier, began to dwindle.

Thibodoux decided to stay, though. He'd passed up the various promotional exams, even though he had a performance rating that would have warranted promotion.

He liked what he did. If he took a promotion, it would mean transfer to another division. And he did not want that. He was good at what he did, and the others in the department, despite their jibes at his lack of sociability, his keeping to himself, respected him at least for that.

Thibodoux stood over his desk, reading the report prepared by the officers who were first at the scene. Another child had been murdered, under twelve they'd estimated, though they weren't sure since the child's head had been sliced off. The body had been found by some construction workers, foundation men, in a shallow grave on a remote hillside near Newhall. They'd called the cops, the sheriffs who worked that part of the county. The sheriffs contacted L.A.P.D. as soon as they saw that the small toe on the child's left foot was missing. Only four toes. Thibodoux wondered if there was a person left in Los Angeles who by this time hadn't heard the story of the missing girl, Erin Dailey, and the fact that she'd been born with only four toes on her left foot.

So they'd called him. The girl had been abducted within the city limits, making it an L.A.P.D. case, and the sheriffs, having more than their share of grisly homicides to handle, were very happy to dump the whole thing in his lap.

No head?

The report stated that a search was performed of the surrounding area, but the head could not be found. Scientific Investigations had been called to the scene. Thibodoux figured they were all still out there, combing the area for something, anything, that might give them a clue as to how Erin Dailey's body, what there was left of it, found its way to the shallow grave on a hillside near Newhall.

Thibodoux felt his back start to spasm. He figured he must have strained something. At six foot six inches, he'd spent most of his adult life accommodating his height to that of others, cramping and contorting himself into squad cars and behind desks built for shorter people. Rubbing at the base of his spine, massaging with his fingertips, he wondered if the pain was caused by that, or maybe something else entirely.

He was almost out the door, on his way to Newhall, when he heard his name paged. At the front desk, a sergeant held up the telephone receiver in his direction. "Captain Tanner," the sergeant said, without interest.

"Thibodoux."

"Glad I caught you," said the captain. "You're on your way to the scene, I assume."

"Yes, just on the way out."

"Good. Listen. West Valley got a call earlier. A citizen. About the Dailey girl."

Thibodoux was aware of his heart beating a regular rhythm. It was something he hadn't noticed until then.

"Her son supposedly saw the girl with some guy, maybe the day she was nabbed. Don't know for sure. Might not even be the same girl. I didn't want to send any uniforms out there. You know those guys. Probably spook the little kid. Anyway, it might be nothing, but we told the mother you'd be in touch."

Thibodoux murmured his thanks, took down the witness' name, address, and telephone, then handed the phone back to the desk sergeant.

A witness. Maybe a witness. Thibodoux had been in this business for close to twenty years. The last ten in S.A.P. Child murders and molestations were his specialty. He had a way with kids, or so they said. Knew how to talk to them, get them to remember things they probably would've been better off forgetting. But the courts didn't have special rules when it came to children. They still had to make the long walk to the witness stand, and sit there in front of a courtroom filled with critical adults, reliving what for most of them would be the most traumatic experiences of their life.

But Ezekiel Thibodoux had a way with kids. That's what he was thinking as he headed for the parking lot, his heart still beating a regular thumping rhythm in his chest, only slightly faster now.

Thibodoux eased the truck along the curb in front of the school. It was quiet. He thought, looking at his watch, that in a few minutes there'd be the sound of bells, children screaming, and the bark of deeper, adult voices trying to control them.

Thibodoux wondered if this was the best way to approach it. He thought about waiting, perhaps confronting the situation in some other surroundings. He knew that the boy's home, with his parents nearby, was not the atmosphere he wanted. The school would be better. No parents around to influence the young boy, feed him answers, make suggestions.

He flashed his detective's shield to the teenage girl who worked in the main office. She seemed mesmerized by the shiny gold. An older woman came up behind her and Thibdoux explained who he was and why he was there. Without hesitation, the woman retreated to her desk and lifted the telephone. Thibodoux could hear her speaking to someone and requesting that Josh Gordon be brought into the office. After she hung up, the woman scribbled something on a piece of paper, grabbed a large piece of laminated wood with the words MAIN OFFICE PASS carved on one side, and handed the paper and the pass to the girl.

Thibodoux took a seat on the wood bench that spanned the width of the office. He was about to pull a cigarette from his jacket pocket when he remembered where he was. He would have to watch that, he told himself. Careless. After so many years he was beginning to take certain things for granted. He told himself that he would have to be much more careful in the future.

What would the boy do? It used to be that kids were afraid of him when they first saw how tall he was. And his face . . . It was the sort of thing that made them stare, at first. Then he'd make it work for him, getting their attention, then getting them to open up. Tell him all about it. Pretty soon, they came to believe that he was their friend. The tall man with the Abe Lincoln beard. Just like on the pictures at school. They learned to trust him, do anything for him. That was helpful when it came time for court. The D.A.'s would just let him handle the child witnesses. Thibodoux would sit at the counsel table, next to the prosecutor, and with his face, the face that they'd come to trust, he'd let the children know that it was all right. That everything would turn out okay.

But this was the awkward moment. This first meeting. Again he had a surge of anxiety, wondering if it would have been better to meet the boy elsewhere, without so many pairs of eyes looking on. Thibodoux removed his detective's shield and slid it onto the outside of his coat breast pocket so that the shiny badge was clearly visible.

The final bell rang, and within seconds the office and the corridors outside were filled with throngs of children, running, screaming, and jumping on one another. Thibodoux took it all in, wondering if Josh Gordon was among the streams of miniature bodies passing by the office door. He wondered what the boy looked like.

"Detective Thibodoux?"

Thibodoux turned his head. He'd been daydreaming and hadn't seen the woman enter.

"Yes," he said, hesitating a split second before locking on the boy's eyes. There it was. Thibodoux saw it in the child's expression. He knew. Thibodoux removed his badge and showed it to the boy.

"Josh," he said, speaking softly, "my name is Detective Ezekiel Thibodoux. But you can tell me Zeke, if you like." Still no answer. The boy held the badge with both hands, staring at his reflection, not looking up.

"Perhaps there's a place, a small room," said Thibodoux, "where we might have a little privacy."

The woman from the office said of course, and showed Thibodoux and the boy to a small room adjacent to the rear of the building. Thibodoux entered, then turned, expecting to see Josh Gordon follow. The boy still had his badge clutched with both hands, staring into the mirrored finish.

"Go ahead, Josh." The woman was behind the boy now, gently pushing him into the room. The boy moved a few inches, then refused to go further. He still had his head down, gazing fixedly at the shiny piece of brass in his hands.

"Go on now, Josh." Again the woman, impatiently. "Detective Thibodoux won't hurt you. He just wants to ask you some questions."

Josh Gordon refused to budge. He turned away from Thibodoux and the office door and sat down, still not looking up. Thibodoux came around and stood behind the woman whose tone had now taken on an admonishing quality, quickly losing patience with the young student.

"Do you want me to call your parents, Josh?" It was said as a threat, but it elicited the young boy's first overt response, which was a nod of the head. Thibodoux could see the boy's eyes becoming watery. It was just a matter of time, he knew, before the kid broke up. Then there was no telling what would happen. Things were not going well. Not as he had planned. Still, he'd been in this position before. He'd take care of it. He knew what to do.

"I think this is not a good time," said Thibodoux.

"I don't know what's gotten into him," said the woman. "He's one of the most talkative kids in school. In fact, too talkative." She tried a smile, but Josh was having none of it. His expression remained fixed.

"Perhaps I'll try the parents," said Thibodoux. "Not talking to strangers is something that we try to promote." The woman nodded. Attempting to smile, he realized that he'd blown it. His mind raced quickly over his options. There was nothing he could do here, not now, not with all these people staring at the two of them.

He left his business card with the woman and headed for his truck. The boy would tell his parents about this. Thibodoux repeated to himself, moving his lips without speaking, what he thought the boy might say. The words came out easily. He'd heard them so often before.

And if he told them everything? Thibodoux knew what would come next. He felt a slight queasiness in his stomach. Now he would have that cigarette. Grabbing the pack in his fist, he brought it to his mouth and pulled one out. He'd already punched the lighter in the dash. It glowed orange as he brought it to his lips, reminding him of another orange glow. He couldn't think of that now, though. It would cloud his mind, push him off course.

Thibodoux sucked deeply on the cigarette, holding the smoke inside, then slowly exhaling through his nose. There, that was better. Nothing was quite as bad as it seemed, once one could relax and step outside of the problem for a moment. He would work this one out, just like the others. After all, Josh Gordon was merely a little boy. And he was Ezekiel Thibodoux, veteran cop, specialist in child molestations and murders. It would all work out in the end. Thibodoux was sure of that.

Josh Gordon didn't want to leave the office. He could hear the sounds of the other kids outside beginning to grow quiet. The woman put her arm around him and walked him to the door. The man with the badge was no longer there.

The badge . . . How could that be?

"I don't know what's come over you," the woman said, kneeling down so that their eyes were even. "You tell your mom to give me a call if she has any questions."

Josh nodded, then started away. He was aware that the woman was standing in front of the school, watching him. He was glad of that, glad the woman had been there. The woman thought there was something wrong with him. She didn't know, and he couldn't tell her. After all, the man had a badge!

In the distance, Josh could see the truck. The one with the camper. The man's camper. And though the truck was too far away to see, Josh knew there was a picture painted on the door in the back. The two fish jumping in the water.

CHAPTER 5

Baruch atau adonai, elohenu melech ha'olam, ashar keedshanu b'mitzvotah vetzevano, laheetatau bah-tse-tseet.

"What does that mean?"

Ben leaned close and said, "It's the blessing over the *talis.* Part of the bar mitzvah ceremony. See, now he's put the *talis* on over his shoulders?"

"Oh." Claire seemed interested, having only the vaguest recollections of certain parts of the ceremony from her childhood. It had been over twenty years since her last bar mitzvah. Though she was born Jewish, the traditions were hazy at best.

It was Frank Chen's kid's bar mitzvah. Ben thought Frank looked right at home on the stage, beaming from ear to ear. Rhoda, his wife, sat next to him clinging for dear life to his arm, crying tears of joy. Or at least Ben figured they must be tears of joy. Maybe she had just remembered what this whole shindig was costing them?

Kenny Chen, the bar mitzvah boy, was in the process of racing through the *V'ahavta,* anxious to get to his party afterward. Ben and Frank, Kenny's dad, had known each other since before Kenny was born. Back in the academy days and the first few years thereafter. Frank had spent most of his career in Administrative Narcotics, so their paths continued to cross even after Ben became the legal mouthpiece for low-level drug dealers and assorted other criminal violators.

Baruch atau adonai elohano v'elohey avotano . . .

The *Avot,* Ben thought. Claire had stopped asking questions. She stared at the stage, eyes wide open, swaying slightly in her seat like a cork in water. Ben glanced around the room. Pretty good crowd. Lots of cops: Frank's friends. And lots of Chinese, old and young, no yarmulkes: Frank's family. Rhoda's family sat in the front of the sanctuary on the opposite aisle from Frank's. At least Ben thought they must be Rhoda's side since none of them were Chinese, and they sang the loudest, and seemed to know when to stand and when to sit even before the rabbi told them.

A far cry from the old days, Ben mused. When he had been bar mitzvahed it was in the conservative shul where his parents belonged, with folding card-table chairs on linoleum, one large floral arrangement in the center of the stage, a rabbi who wouldn't think twice about whacking you on the back of the head if you messed up, and no music, completely a cappella.

This, though, was an entirely different case of matzos. The pews—and there actually were beautiful oak pews, like in a church, stretching the width of the sanctuary—were bordered on each side by floor-to-ceiling stained glass windows. Ben thought he recognized a few familiar biblical characters depicted in the glass, but their names escaped him. The carpet felt like three inches of wall-to-wall insulation, a plush salmon color to match the velveteen cushions on the pews. Set off to one side of the stage, recessed into its own little cubbyhole, was a pipe organ, and behind the organ sat a matronly lady adding her somber tones to *"Mi Chamocha"* and *"Adon Olam."*

The parents, Frank and Rhoda Chen, sat on one side of the stage with the bar mitzvah boy. On the other side, there were high-back chairs, like thrones, for the rabbi, cantor, and a young man with a beard who played the guitar. The young man with the guitar was currently standing off to the side, partially hidden by one of the half dozen enormous bouquets of spring flowers that adorned the stage. In the center, above where the participants sat, hung the Eternal Light. Ben remembered that in the old days it was supposed to be an oil lamp, and members of the congregation were assigned the very serious task of making sure that there was always enough oil in the lamp, lest it should go out. These days, it was electric, like everything else. Ben wondered when the temples would catch up with the times and computerize the whole thing. Digital Eternal Flames . . . The thought made him smile.

"Is it almost over?" Claire had stopped swaying. She was pulling at her panty hose.

"Almost," he said, though he had no idea. It seemed to him that the boy hadn't read from the Torah yet, and he recalled that that was, or at least it used to be, the most important part. These days, the most important part was the party afterward. Ben had taken a peek at the reception room before entering the sanctuary. A Caribbean motif, complete with palm trees, sand, coconuts, a steel drum band, and fire-breathing calypso dancers. He knew this was Frank Chen's doing, since all Frank ever talked about was returning to the islands where he and Rhoda had spent their honeymoon. Ben couldn't remember anything like this when he was a kid. He wondered if there was a bar mitzvah prayer to cover the fire-eating calypso dancers.

Barchu et adonai hamvorah . . .

This he remembered. The traditional trek of the relatives to the stage on the pretense that they actually knew what they were doing. The blessing prefatory to the reading of the Torah. Very serious business. It was written phonetically in English, next to the Hebrew. It was a gesture of honor by the family of the bar mitzvah to be called to the Torah. Various relatives took their turn coming up to the *bimah* and murdering the Hebrew. A few seemed to actually remember bits and pieces, an unforgettable rhythm, like riding a bike, wobbly, but definitely there, recognizable.

An old man, short, balding, his glasses drooped to the tip of his nose, slumped in one of the front pews, eyes closed, breathing heavily, on the verge of snoring. The ceremony was running long. Frank and Rhoda were at the *bimah* now, behind the wood podium, saying how much they loved, admired, treasured, and otherwise felt about little Kenny on this day of his becoming a man. Kenny smiled, and seemed to accept the whole thing in a fairly nonchalant manner: the reminiscences of when he learned to ride a bike, when he started school, when he became interested in girls—a titter of laughter on that one. Kenny turned red.

Then it was the rabbi's turn. He gave a stern look at the snoring man for a moment, then went on with a sermon on the meaning of Kenny's Torah portion, a subject Kenny had lightly touched upon in his speech, spending the greater part on the fact that he wanted to grow up to be an investment banker instead of a cop, no offense, Dad.

Claire's eyes were beginning to close. Ben had told her she didn't have to come. Even though they'd both been invited, Ben knew that Frank Chen would understand. But Claire had insisted. It would be a good experience for her to go to temple, she said. Though he didn't understand why, Ben saw no value in challenging Claire on this. Ben wondered whether she was getting to that age when one started thinking about making one's peace with God. He remembered that his parents, who never were very religious as he was growing up, suddenly became devout as they got older. A sense of their own mortality, he assumed.

Ben stood for the mourners' Kaddish. It startled Claire, because he hadn't explained. She gave him a look of understanding, though, when he sat back down. A look, and a knowing grip of his hand. She was good at that.

"This is it," said Ben, standing again. Everybody, at the rabbi's request, joined hands, swaying from side to side, and sang *"Ain Kelohanu."* Ben remembered loving this song when he was a kid. Snappy. At least as snappy as any of the temple songs got. Except here, he found himself stumbling to fit the words of the song to the tune. They'd changed the music. Some in the congregation, the kids, knew exactly where they were going, belting out the verse. Others, mostly the old Jews—the fact that he now fit into this category mildly depressed him—found themselves a few beats behind the melody, stretching the words, trying to follow along with the unfamiliar tune. It was like, Ben felt, singing the words from "Yesterday" to the melody of "Lady Madonna."

The religious part now over, everybody crowded into

the center aisle, making their way to the back of the sanctuary, where the Chens were shaking hands, but more importantly, where two white-shirted gentlemen wearing red bow ties were busy pouring drinks.

Claire said that she wanted to congratulate the Chens and started off without Ben. Ben figured as long as Claire was fulfilling their social obligations, there would be nothing wrong with him getting a little drink before the bar got too crowded.

"Absolut rocks," he said.

"Care for a twist?" The bartender seemed pleasant, but mechanical. He had a name tag on his shirt that read HI I'M TED YOUR BARTENDER. Ben figured he'd probably be the same or worse if he had to spend his Saturday nights pouring free drinks for this sort of crowd.

Ben took the small glass of clear liquid from the bartender, along with a square paper cocktail napkin, on which were printed the words KENNY'S BAR MITZVAH and the date. He was just about to turn to try and find Claire when he felt someone tap his shoulder.

"When you gonna start drinking a man's drink?" The gravelly voice Ben recognized immediately. Francis Powell, the chief of police, and Ben's close friend.

Ben waved at the bartender. "A Shirley Temple for the chief here."

"Shirley Temple, my ass. I'll have a Jack Daniels, neat." Powell watched Ted pour two fingers' worth, then motioned for him to pour more. Before leaving the bar, Powell tossed down half the drink, smacked his lips, and wiped his mouth with one of the paper bar mitzvah cocktail napkins. "Now that's a real man's drink."

Ben smiled. He hadn't expected to see Powell at the party. The chief rarely socialized with the troops, even though Ben knew that Powell would have liked to do more. It was too hard to pick and choose which invitations to accept and which to turn down, so Francis Powell had developed the policy of declining all such entreaties in the hope of not offending anyone. But Frank Chen and Francis had graduated in the same academy class, along with Ben, and Chen was a star of sorts in the department, albeit something of a loose cannon.

"I didn't see you inside," said Ben. They were standing under one of the palm trees that had been set up on the perimeter of the dining area around the dance floor. In the background, the steel drum band—three very dark Jamaicans—gyrated to their happy sounds. Ben felt like he was on a cruise ship.

"I was right there," said Powell. "Wouldn't'a missed this for the world." He pulled out a black yarmulke with the name of a mortuary stenciled in gold on the inside. "See, I even got my own little beanie. Carry it with me in the car." He seemed to go sour for a moment. "Funerals, you know."

Ben nodded. Across the room he spotted Claire, standing in the corner, still chatting with Rhoda Chen. While the room was decorated like some island oasis, the theme of the bar mitzvah was motorcycles. Kenny Chen must have been into bikes. On each table was a wooden model of a motorcycle, Hondas, Yamahas, BMWs, and Harleys. Instead of flowers, multicolored motorcycle helmets were positioned atop the wooden models, each helmet with a racing number on the side that denoted the number of the table. Nearby, at two of the twenty or so circular dining tables, were Frank's family, nearly a score of elderly Chinese, seated with hands folded, looking at each other, and pointing to the fire-eating calypso dancers. Ben wondered what they must make of all this.

"Chen told me you'd be here, Ben. I need to talk to you, in private."

Ben looked around. Most people were juggling plates of hot and cold hors d'oeuvres and glasses of booze. A few had found their seats and were looking on as the boldest of the couples tried to dance the fox-trot to the steel drum band while avoiding being torched by the fire-eating calypso dancers. In the corner, a caricaturist was drawing pictures of the kids. Next to the artist was a large glass booth in which dollar bills swirled. The kids were lining up outside the booth to take their turn inside, hoping to grab as much money as possible in their allotted time. The table of hot hors d'oeuvres stretched halfway across the room, with everything from cocktail weenies to wontons to tostadas, and even short ribs of beef. Another table, equally as long, sagged under the weight of two whole salmon, a huge vegetable platter with watermelon and honeydew cut in the shape of flowers, a dozen assorted cheeses, pickled and creamed herring, gefilte fish, assorted dips, and chopped liver molded in the shape of a Torah. Heartburn city. Ben figured that the last thing any of the over two hundred guests at Kenny Chen's bar mitzvah would be interested in would be eavesdropping on the conversation between himself and Francis Powell.

"Talk," said Ben, grabbing a piece of kishka from a silver serving platter before the waiter moved out of reach.

Powell looked around. "Yeah, I guess you're right." He slugged down the rest of his drink and motioned to Ted for another.

"You been busy, Benny?"

Ben had just taken a sip of vodka and let the glass remain at his lips for a moment, eyeing Powell over the rim. He knew that sound. Powell was up to something. He wanted something.

"Busy enough," said Ben.

Powell had that cat-that-swallowed-the-canary smirk. Ben had seen it before. Another orchestrated conversation with Francis Powell at the podium, baton in hand.

"Yeah," said Powell, taking the new drink. "I heard about that big-time juvenile case you've been trying. The Vietnam War all over, 'cept this time it's high-school kids, right?"

"You arrested somebody, Francis. I can't help it if you arrested the wrong gang."

"Wrong gang, my ass." Powell chipped away at his front teeth with his fingernail, making little sucking noises as he tried to remove a piece of food.

"Anyway, I'm sure that's not what this is all about, is it, Francis? A couple of idiots banging each other over the head outside the local high school is not the reason the chief of police drags himself on a Saturday night to a bar mitzvah just to talk to one of his employees. Ex-employees, that is."

On stage, the Jackie Rosen All-Stars were tuning up. Jackie Rosen, sporting a very bad toupee, was behind the microphone kibbitzing with the Jamaicans. It reminded Ben of seeing Jackie Mason making a fool of himself on TV at some awards show a few years back.

"Something's come up," said Powell. "If you can spare the time, I'd like you to do a little favor for me, Benny."

Powell's little favors often turned into full-blown investigations. Ben had been out in private practice again for less than a year, and here was Francis Powell parked at his doorstep asking him to return to Internal Affairs once more. Ben wanted to beg off, but he owed Powell. And Powell knew it.

Jackie Rosen was asking everyone to take their seats. The Jamaicans had disappeared; Ben hadn't noticed them leaving. The fire-eating calypso dancers were also gone. All they'd left in their wake was a partially burned limbo bar.

"It's something you don't want handled through Internal Affairs, right?" Ben knew the answer. He just wanted to hear Powell say the words.

Powell nodded, finishing off his whiskey. "It's like this, Benny . . ."

Jackie Rosen was yelling over the microphone. The band on stage behind him was playing the entry music for Jake and Elwood Blues, building up to the big intro.

"Ladies and gentlemen," Jackie yelled. Ben noticed Jackie's toupee, even from his table at the far edge of the dance floor. The All-Stars was a mixed group of musicians, half over sixty, the rest under twenty-five. The old guys looked serious, concentrating on keeping up. The young ones looked bored. A short blonde dressed in a sequined miniskirt and three-inch black pumps, Jackie's female vocalist, stood to the side clapping her hands. "Please stand and put your hands together," said Jackie, the music mounting, "for the guest of honor this evening. The bar mitzvah boy himself, *Mr. . . . Kenny . . . Chen!*"

Ben, along with the rest of the crowd, looked in the direction of the back of the hall. He spotted Francis Powell, who had returned to his chair a few tables away. From the rear doors came Kenny Chen in his tux, sitting atop a full-size Harley Davidson, a Hog, revving his way down the aisle between the tables onto the dance floor. Amazing!

Ben longed for the good old days when a bar mitzvah boy would be satisfied with merely a few run-of-the-mill fire-eating calypso dancers.

CHAPTER 6

Dr. Samuel Hirsch considered himself a fastidious man. He hadn't seen fit to marry, and at thirty-four, he had more than his share of women anxious to have a try at him. He lived by himself in a condo in Brentwood, near San Vicente. He enjoyed his morning jog, and on weekends stretched the run down San Vicente Boulevard to the beach. He had no responsibilities other than to himself and his patients. No dog, no cats, not even a goldfish. Animals were messy.

Dr. Hirsch had the boys in the garage detail his black Porsche Cabriolet, washing, waxing, and shampooing, every week, sometimes more often depending on the weather. On those rare occasions when he discovered a female companion with intellectual pursuits worthy of his interest, he'd take them for rides along PCH with the top down. Between the Porsche, his condo, and the fact that he was pulling in a few hundred thousand a year practicing psychiatry, he figured he didn't need good looks. Not that he was bad-looking. Homely was more apt. His mother had told him that, and he wasn't so vain as to deny it. But the women didn't seem to care. He could get married tomorrow, to a real looker, if he was of the mind.

So much good fortune had befallen him that he felt the urge to give something back. Something of himself. And to this end, he'd contacted a friend from med school who worked for a group of doctors servicing a contract with the city. The medical group provided a limited number of hours of medical service to city employees at a reduced rate as part of the perks offered by the city to pacify their striking employees during last year's labor negotiations. Dr. Hirsch had, magnanimously—his own estimation—offered his services as a psychiatrist, with strict limitations on the hours that he'd hold himself out to such patients. Of course. After all, he still had his upscale full-fee paying clientele to remember.

Ezekiel Thibodoux had been coming to Dr. Hirsch for nearly six months, and it was Thibodoux that occupied Hirsch's thoughts this afternoon as he prepared, by reviewing his notes, for his upcoming session with the L.A.P.D. investigator.

Hirsch found Thibodoux's case extremely interesting. Especially lately. The man was more reticent than most, but over the last couple of months barriers had fallen, and Hirsch was, for the first time in a long while, genuinely enthused about the progress of one of his patients.

Enthused, and at the same time concerned. With Thibodoux, disturbing references had been brought to the surface, references that had taken Hirsch by surprise. Hirsch wasn't certain what to make of them. He hoped to find out more, by placing Thibodoux once again under hypnosis. After each such session, Hirsch took copious and detailed notes of what had transpired, what Ezekiel Thibodoux had said. A hodgepodge of biblical references interlaced with ramblings about his mother and father. Then there was the stuff about the children. Hirsch assumed that was the result of job-related stress. He was well aware of what Thibodoux did for a living, and the nature of his specialty within the department.

Thibodoux's stream-of-consciousness conversation while under hypnosis had been filled with horrible scenes of children suffering, which, Hirsch assumed, Thibodoux had been forced to become a party to as part of his job. It was this stress that the doctor felt was at the root of Thibodoux's problems, not so much Thibodoux's perceived inability to deal with his childhood. Dr. Hirsch was considering recommending a medical leave for Ezekiel Thibodoux. He wasn't sure how the patient would react to that recommendation. Getting away from all the violence, Hirsch felt, would do a world of good for the man.

His phone buzzed and the receptionist advised him that Mr. Thibodoux was on his way in. Hirsch shuffled his notes back into the folder and placed the folder on the corner of his desk. When he opened his office door, Thibodoux was there, about ready to knock.

"Come in," said Hirsch. "Let's get started."

Thibodoux took a seat opposite the doctor's desk in a cushioned leather club chair. An identical chair stood a few feet away. Hirsch plopped himself down in the second chair and swiveled toward the patient, a leather-encased notepad resting comfortably in his lap.

"Is there anything you want to start with?" he said, looking down at the yellow pad, doodling in the corner. It was his practice, especially with Thibodoux, to try and low-key their sessions. Reduce the trauma of the inquiry in the hope of getting a more relaxed, more insightful response from the patient. Eliminate the patient's automatic defense mechanism. He realized that Thibodoux was used to asking the questions, having the roles reversed. Hirsch had handled similar situations before, with other police officers and certain of his colleagues.

Thibodoux pursed his lips, looked out the window at the buildings across the street for a brief moment, then said, "I have a question, Sam." Even now, using the doctor's first name felt tremendously uncomfortable for Thibodoux. He had mentioned this to Dr. Hirsch initially, when the doctor insisted that they be on a first-name basis. Thibodoux supposed that the doctor felt this was helpful, that it was just one of his psychiatric tricks to get his patients to relax, feel more at home. Thibodoux felt like telling him that it was unnecessary, that he wanted to tell him all he could, regardless of how familiar they each were in addressing one another.

For Thibodoux, the sessions had been important. He knew he had stepped way over the line, that he was floating, lost, out of control. When he wasn't there, doing it, the part of him that everybody else knew took over: the Ezekiel Thibodoux who was a deacon in the church, an experienced investigator with the Los Angeles Police Department. That Ezekiel Thibodoux was shocked and outraged at what the other Thibodoux had done. Beyond comprehension. And it was that shocked and outraged Thibodoux that had initiated the sessions with Dr. Hirsch.

But now something had happened. A blur or crossover was taking place. He found his two selves each vying to increase their turf, their control over him, like warring gangs wreaking havoc on one another.

He supposed it was the boy. With the first girls there had been no interest, no parents giving interviews to the newspapers about their missing children. Runaways or castoffs, whatever you called them, those two had been on their own. So they hadn't been missed.

But this last one had turned out differently. He should have known that. He of all people. He should have known. But the control was no longer there. He supposed this flip-flopping back and forth between selves was at the root of it. Wanting to do good, and not wanting. Knowing the evil he was unleashing, and, at the same time, wanting it to stop. It had moved outside of himself now, completely autonomous, with a life force of its own.

He let Dr. Hirsch play his psychiatric games. He'd even gone along with the hypnosis, in the hope that Hirsch, or somebody, would know what to do; figure a way of putting an end to the evil. He should have known better, though. Dr. Hirsch's well-intentioned efforts were too little, much too late. *She* had seen to that. His mother, and the man whom she slept with that she called his father. Thibodoux would never admit to that. He might be the result of his father's seed, but that's as far as it went. He'd never be like him. Never.

"I take it," said Hirsch, "that from your reticence, there is nothing pressing, nothing that you wish to unburden yourself of?"

Unburden. That was an interesting word, Thibodoux thought. A psychiatrist's word for telling all. And if he did . . . *could* . . . tell all? Then what?

"Nothing," said Thibodoux. Something had taken over him. Hirsch sat calmly, waiting for him to *unburden* himself, as he had before. Except now there was a red flag, a warning light blinking on and off inside his head, telling him of impending danger.

The boy had seen him!

The boy would be telling his parents that he had seen him. The parents would tell someone else, maybe go directly to the police. And then . . .

"Let's start with where we left off last time," said Hirsch. "You were telling me about going fishing with your father. Camping trips, that sort of thing."

Thibodoux's mind flashed back thirty years: A canvas tent, nighttime, deep in the woods. Just him and his father. The lantern inside the tent casting magnified shadows of his father on the canvas. The sound of broken glass, the smell of alcohol mixed with vomit and sour body odor pressed up against him.

"Yes," murmured Thibodoux. Get back to the boy, he told himself. There were steps to take here, matters to discuss.

"Doctor," he said, feeling his way, choosing his words with caution. He did not want to alarm Dr. Hirsch. Thibodoux said, "The matters we discuss here . . . Am I right in assuming they are strictly confidential?"

"Of course."

"And were I to say anything, whatever that might be, about my past or my job, something like that . . . It would remain confidential, correct?"

"Well, I . . . I can only say that what a patient tells his doctor in confidence is privileged. But then, you should be better versed in the legal technicalities of all that."

Thibodoux noticed for the first time that Dr. Hirsch seemed uncomfortable. "Yes, that's true," he replied. "Though, there are certain exceptions."

"You're speaking of the law that requires a psychiatrist or psychotherapist to report his patients to the authorities, in certain limited situations?"

"Where there are admissions of child abuse by the patient."

"Yes," said Hirsch, sounding less in control now, more uncertain of where this conversation was headed. "But—"

Hirsch cleared his throat, as if wanting to move on to another topic, "—we are not in that situation, Ezekiel. You have made certain disclosures to me, some of which I attribute to your reaching back into your past. The relationship with your mother, the camping incident with your father. Other things have been said during our sessions, some under hypnosis. I can only assume with these things, though they don't make complete sense at the present time, their true meaning will be revealed as we go along." Hirsch paused, seeing the concern still on his patient's face. "Rest assured, Ezekiel, that your disclosures here will be treated with the utmost secrecy. I do not want that to interfere with or hinder our efforts. I believe that we are on the very brink of opening some important areas, and I don't want anything of an extraneous nature clouding your thoughts."

Extraneous nature. Thibodoux wondered whether Dr. Hirsch would use those words if he knew about the Gordon boy. But Dr. Hirsch meant well. He tried.

Thibodoux cursed himself for allowing Hirsch to submit his medical bills through the union. A paper trail. It was supposed to be confidential, the business part of who paid for these sessions. Perhaps it was. It was too late now in any event. Thibodoux decided that he'd finish up with this session, then perhaps send Dr. Hirsch a note, claiming he wished to terminate their relationship. For personal reasons. Yes, that would have to do.

"I know," Thibodoux said, thinking about the Gordon boy and his next move, "that I can trust you, Sam. I know that my life and my secrets are secure in your hands."

CHAPTER 7

Jackie Rosen and the All-Stars were playing "The Wind Beneath My Wings" as Kenny Chen danced a slow dance with his mother in the center of the dance floor, the boy's head seeming dwarfed by his mother's substantial bosom. Frank Chen looked on from the head table, beaming with pride—or perhaps, Ben speculated, Frank was already slosh city. That was the thing about Frank Chen. He didn't drink much, except on rare occasions. He didn't smoke or whore around. He wasn't always bitching about pulling a bad assignment or getting shafted by his superiors. All in all, Frank Chen was not your typical cop. In fact, if you were to see him on the street, out of uniform, you'd never figure him for a flatfoot. That was what made him so successful. Someone in Administrative Narcotics had recognized Frank's worth long ago. They sent him undercover—the man on the street, the executive or shopkeeper who just happened to be into a little hash, perhaps some nose candy. Frank fit the part. After all, who'd expect a Chinese IBM type to be into doing dope?

And Frank Chen was in love with his job. He carried a cannon: a Smith & Wesson Model 586 Distinguished Combat 357 Magnum with an eight-and-three-eighths-inch heavy barrel in the nickel finish with checkered Goncalo Alves target grips. The damn thing weighed close to forty-six ounces and hung like a cast-iron splint between Frank's armpit and waist. It was always that way with the little guys. They always wanted the biggest guns. Not that

Frank Chen was exactly trigger-happy. He just liked to wave it around, let the coke-heads and pill-poppers see what he was packing. *You should see their eyes!* he'd say. A little gun just didn't get the same respect.

Frank Chen had taken a lot of flak at first, being the only Chinese narc in the city. But that all changed as soon as the other guys saw how hard he worked, and how, like a chameleon, he could weasel his way into places and situations that other undercover narcs couldn't.

Ben thought, Go ahead, Frank. Laugh. Enjoy. Best not to think of the bill for all this right now. Ben figured that Frank must be getting help, probably from Rhoda's side. Otherwise, there was no way he could afford to pop for a wingding like this on a cop's salary.

Claire had moved to Rhoda Chen's table, and the two women were in a lively discussion over something. The unsavory habits of cops, probably, and the trials and tribulations for the women who lived with them. Ben had danced most of the slow dances, and a few of the fast, but with the latter he felt very much out of his element. Like the kids were staring at him, wondering what the geek was doing on the dance floor. Claire clucked her tongue, swearing that she'd find a younger man to whisk her around the dance floor if Ben couldn't hack it. Ben, anxious to avoid further humiliation, and grateful for the relief, wished her the best of luck in that endeavor.

Ben caught sight of Francis Powell heading for the set of double glass doors that led out to the patio. Other than himself, there was only one couple left at his table, and they were in the midst of a heated argument over whether they should have given Kenny Chen a bigger gift. Ben grabbed another drink from Ted the bartender, and went out to join Powell.

It was one of those late-July San Fernando Valley nights when the temperature, at nightfall, dropped from 110 to 90. The air had a suffocating stillness that made it hard to inhale. Stale and thick. Short little breaths were best, and very little movement. Coming out of the air-conditioned reception hall, the climatic change hit Ben even harder. It reminded him of walking out of the casinos in Vegas at two in the morning, except more humid.

Powell was seated on a white wrought-iron bench that bordered the concrete patio. From out here, one could hear Jackie Rosen and the All-Stars, even make out the tune, though the lyrics were muffled. Powell had his legs crossed, was smoking a cigarette, looking out over the roof of the sanctuary at a crescent moon. The tip of his cigarette glowed orange-yellow, like a single firefly circling and swarming around his head.

"Nice party."

Ben didn't answer as he sat down next to Powell. Both men looked out on an expanse of lawn where, during the day, the kids from the temple day school played baseball and football. There was the hum of some sort of flying insect coming from the bushes behind them. Powell's cigarette smelled good, and though he didn't smoke himself, Ben could understand the attraction on a night like this, after a big meal, relaxing outside. Whether it was worth the heart disease and the cancer was another story, though.

"How long would this take?" asked Ben.

Powell threw his cigarette to the ground and twisted it out with the toe of his shoe. "Not too long," he said. "Depends."

"Yeah, that's what I was afraid of."

"It may turn out to be nothing."

"Who we talking about?"

"Zeke Thibodoux." Powell let the name hang between them without adding more.

"Rape squad, right?"

"Rape and child abuse," said Powell. "S.A.P. program. Experienced man. Helluva good investigator."

"So?"

Powell paused. "So he's been linked to the Erin Dailey murder."

Ben's gasp was barely audible, though Powell heard it clearly.

"Yeah," said Powell, "I know."

"Whadya got on him?"

"A witness. A little kid I.D.'d Zeke with the Dailey girl the day she was taken."

"A kid?"

"Ten-year-old. Lives in the neighborhood. Saw Thibodoux talking with the girl. Said the girl got into the back of Thibodoux's camper and he drove away."

A waiter came outside pushing a cart filled with dirty dishes in a gray plastic tub. He glanced their way, then continued to push the cart around to the other side of the building.

"How good is the I.D.?"

"Not sure," said Powell. "The kid's parents contacted Chen. Actually, a lawyer, friend of the kid's family, was the one who called Frank. The parents didn't know how to handle it."

Ben turned, facing Powell, who kept talking.

"Thibodoux went out to the kid's school to talk to him. As soon as the kid saw Zeke, he froze. When he got home, he told Mommy and Daddy everything about it. They called the lawyer, and he called Chen. The lawyer evidently owed Chen for a favor Frank did for him on a case."

"I was wondering," said Ben, "why you seemed a little short on space at your table."

"Yeah, Frank squeezed me in at the last moment." Powell laughed. "I told him I wouldn't eat too much."

Ben thought about Ezekiel Thibodoux. He knew who he was—almost everybody knew Zeke Thibodoux. Tall and lanky, with that Abe Lincoln beard of his and that crazy glass eye. Thibodoux kept his own counsel, though. Quiet and withdrawn. Very religious, or so Ben had heard. Extraordinary success dealing with child molesters.

From inside, Ben heard the sound of Kenny Chen's voice over the microphone, introducing various groups of friends and relatives. With each group, the band played a few bars of a different song. The candle-lighting ceremony, Ben figured. He should really be inside—both of them should.

"I want you to handle the investigation, Benny. I can't use any of the regular guys. They all know Thibodoux. If there's nothing there, with the kid, I mean, I don't want it getting out that I started tightening the screws."

"What do *you* think?"

Powell reached inside his coat pocket and pulled out his cigarettes. Powell was very methodical about the way he prepared to smoke. Carefully, as if he were removing a uranium fuel rod from a nuclear pile—and, Ben thought, perhaps Francis was doing exactly that, in his own way—Powell plucked one cigarette from the pack with his fingertips, placing the end between his lips while he replaced the pack in his pocket. With two fingers he then scissored the unlit cigarette from his mouth and held it to the side while he fished in another pocket for his lighter. Then back to his lips, holding the cigarette with his hand covering his mouth as the flame flickered at the end for a moment. The first toke was deep and steady, and Powell's eyes seemed to roll slightly in his head as he savored the flavor. Then the long steady stream from pursed lips, as he cradled the glowing little stick in loving hands resting on his lap.

"I think Thibodoux's a damn good cop," said Powell. "I think he's gotta helluva good record on child-abuse cases. Hell, ask any D.A. that handles those suckers. They're damn hard to put together, what with kids as the only witnesses. They all say Thibodoux's the greatest. He's got a way with kids. They trust him, and . . ." Powell paused.

Both men thought about what had just been said.

Powell continued, more slowly now, "There's always been something about him that's a little weird, Benny. The man never mixes. Stays by himself. Even the other S.A.P. officers don't know much about him. Not the kind to go out for a beer with the guys after his shift."

"He's religious, I hear."

"Yeah," said Powell, sounding unconvinced. "Let me ask you something, Benny. What would you think if I told you that Thibodoux's been seeing a shrink pretty regularly over the last few months?"

Not unusual. Ben had known a number of cops who had gone to shrinks. It came with the territory. "How'd you find that out?"

"I have my sources. Let's leave it at that."

"I'd say," said Ben, "that maybe he had something in his life that was bothering him, and he needed help to work it out."

"Yeah, I figured the same thing, until I thought about it a little more. It doesn't fit for a guy like Thibodoux. Too religious. You ever see his family?"

Ben shook his head.

"Like something out of *Deliverance.* Wife is this little bitty thing that never says a word. Jumps every time he even breathes heavy. Three kids, just like him. Hardly leave the house except to go to school."

"Sounds like you've already started the investigation."

"Just a few well-placed questions. Nothing to raise any eyebrows. But you gotta admit, for a guy like that, going to a headshrinker doesn't make sense. Did I tell ya he was a deacon in his church? One of those fundamentalist places. Holy rollers, you know what I mean." Powell shook his head, then inhaled quickly on his cigarette, blowing out the smoke in puffs as he spoke.

"I don't see it, Benny. Not a guy like that. Trust in God, that's what he'd do, but not in any headshrinker."

"So what do you want me to do?"

"Check out the shrink. We'll get a warrant, maybe see what's going on in Zeke Thibodoux's head."

Ben shrugged in disbelief. "A warrant? You gotta be kidding, Francis. We don't have nearly enough probable cause to get a warrant, even from a favorable judge. All you got is this kid, right? We're talking about searching a *psychiatrist's* office, for God's sake, not some sleazebag drug dealer living on the second floor of a flophouse in Lake View Terrace."

"Talk to the kid, Benny."

"And even if we do find some judge that owes us one, you think any of that shit'll be admissible in court? Jesus, Francis! Thibodoux's lawyer'll attack the warrant with motions to quash, motions to traverse . . . And even if he loses the motions, he'll claim the information is confidential, doctor-patient privilege. And I'm not sure that I'd disagree with him on that one."

Powell turned toward Ben and smiled. The cigarette was a mere stub now, glowing at the end of his fingertips. He stood, turned, and faced the bench where Ben still was sitting. He flicked the cigarette, like a sparkler, onto the grass. "Talk to the boy, Benny," he said. "Use Frank Chen if you want. He's already familiar with the facts and knows how to keep his mouth shut." Powell smoothed his tie against his chest, then buttoned his jacket. "I've gotta get going, Benny. You'll give my regards to Frank and the family?" He had his hand outstretched. Ben shook it automatically, nodding, and watched Powell retreat through the reception hall and quickly make his way to the exit.

Jackie Rosen and the All-Stars were hammering out a hora from inside the hall. The same refrain over and over. Faster and faster. People were screaming with delight. Ben knew Claire would be looking for him, her dance partner. He hated horas. Too dangerous. He always feared he'd step on some little kid's toes. Claire had mentioned it on their way to the temple. It was the part from *Goodbye Columbus* that she remembered. The wedding scene.

On the grass, Powell's cigarette stub glowed orange for a few more seconds, then disappeared.

CHAPTER 8

Ben and Frank Chen were seated in Ben's car on the street in front of Samuel Hirsch's office. Both men were reviewing the L.A.P.D. instructional manual's latest updates on the serving of search warrants on physicians. Francis Powell had pulled some strings with the D.A.'s office and found someone to draft a warrant for Dr. Samuel Hirsch's office relating to Hirsch's medical records on Ezekiel Thibodoux. The deputy D.A., when he had handed Ben the warrant, just shook his head in disbelief, saying, "I don't know what judge you're going to find to sign this thing." He then laughed, and returned to his office.

Powell had already taken care of that, though. Ben brought the warrant, at Powell's direction, to Judge Henry Davis Washington, who was coming up for reelection in the fall and desperately needed to claim the support of the chief of police to bolster his campaign. Judge Washington also happened to be an ex-cop and a former deputy district attorney. It was well-known in the legal community that Henry Washington was the prosecution's man.

Search warrants for doctors' offices were not all that common. The legislature, in an effort to respond to the spate of litigation that had arisen in the courts over alleged doctor-patient privilege violations by law enforcement—officers searching through patients' confidential medical records—had established special rules, Penal Code Section 1524, dealing with the procedure to be used for issuance of search warrants for documentary evidence in the possession or under the control of lawyers, psychotherapists, physicians, or clergymen who themselves were not reasonably suspected of engaging in criminal activity. Documentary evidence was defined to cover almost anything from blueprints and drawings to computer printouts, X rays, files, tapes, and papers of any type or description.

It was L.A.P.D.'s condensed summary of section 1524 that Ben and Frank Chen were looking over outside Samuel Hirsch's office. They had followed the procedure outlined in the code: Judge Washington, at the time he signed and issued the search warrant, had appointed a "special master," as directed in section 1524, to accompany them in serving the warrant on Dr. Hirsch. The special master, again pursuant to the language of the statute, was an attorney selected from a state bar list, whose presence at the premises to be searched was designed to ensure that decorum be followed in the search. Strict observance of 1524 mandated that only the special master actually perform the search, unless the subject of the search agreed otherwise. It was the special master who would direct the search of Samuel Hirsch's office, speaking with the doctor, advising him of their reason for being there. Ben and Frank could stand by, taking it all in, but unless Hirsch agreed to their participation in the search, they were to remain mere observers on the sideline.

"If Hirsch claims the privilege," said Ben, still reviewing the legal summary, "then that's it. The special master has to seal the record and return it to court for an *in camera* hearing to determine whether it's admissible."

"Yeah," said Chen. "That means everybody gets their lawyers, schlepping briefcases filled with motions for the judge to review in chambers. If we get lucky and win the motions, there'll most likely be appeals, and we'll be cooling our heels for weeks until those are decided. Meanwhile, Thibodoux is out there doing his number."

Ben thought Frank Chen was right. The whole procedure for searching a physician's office was unbelievably cumbersome. Especially when compared to the relative ease by which cops could get search warrants for other locations. From both sides of the counsel table, Ben had seen search warrants issued on the slimmest of probable cause. Some informant, seeking to cut his own deal with prosecutors, would rat on a confederate, with the agreement that his identity in the affadavit for the search warrant remain anonymous. Once the legal restraints against unlawful search and seizure were overcome by issuance of the warrant, almost anything found would be fair game. With a little creative report-writing, all matter of items found in the search would come within the purview of the warrant and thus be admissible in court.

Ben had filed motions on behalf of his clients seeking to overturn search warrants and render inadmissible the items found during the search. There were motions to quash the warrant on its face, claiming that even assuming the assertions in the warrant were true, they lacked the force to raise a substantial suspicion that the items to be found were related to criminal activity. Or motions to traverse the warrant, claiming that the assertions in the underlying affadavits were untrue, and the warrant was thus tainted and deficient. More often than not, such motions fell on deaf ears. The trend in the courts was moving away from the strong defense of the rights of the accused. In recent years, with the Reagan appointees and the conservative Republican influence in California, the rules governing searches and seizures had been greatly liberalized to make the cop's job easier and enhance the already prodigious arsenal of prosecutors in court.

"There he is."

Ben looked up, following Frank's eyes. A short, stocky man in a crumpled beige suit was getting out of a car a few spaces ahead of where they were parked.

"Hal Bernard," said Frank.

"You know him?"

"Nope. Thought you might."

Ben shook his head. The idea was that these attorneys, the special masters, were supposed to be objective and independent. No relationship to the subject of the search, or the cops.

Ben and Frank caught up with Hal Bernard in the lobby of the building. Bernard was standing on one foot, shining a pair of worn cordovan wing tips on the back of his pants as he waited for the elevator.

"Mr. Bernard." Ben extended his hand as the beige suit turned. "I'm Ben Green and this is Frank Chen."

"Ah, Mr. Green." Bernard grabbed Ben's hand, then Frank's. "You'll be handling this investigation?"

Ben nodded.

Hal Bernard pulled a copy of the warrant from his coat pocket. "Now, let's see here." He was rifling through the attachments to the warrant, making sure everything was in order. "Dr. Samuel Hirsch, Suite 801. Documentary evidence relating to his treatment of Ezekiel Thibodoux." Bernard looked up. From his flat expression, Ben figured that Hal Bernard had no idea who Ezekiel Thibodoux was. That was good.

"A child-molesting investigation," murmured Bernard, reading further. "It all seems in order." He placed the warrant back in his pocket. From his other pocket he removed a blue-backed copy of the same warrant, with which he would formally serve Samuel Hirsch.

Ben looked at Frank Chen, wondering if Frank was thinking the same thing. While waiting in the car, an idea had occurred to Ben. If he could get Hirsch to consent to the search of his office, it might render the validity of the actual search warrant moot. At least, should the warrant prove insufficient upon later court challenge, a judge, wanting to allow the evidence into court, could still rule the evidence admissible based on Hirsch's consent to the search. It was a long shot, but if Hal Bernard went along with it, it would give them one more avenue to go down in court, something for the judge to hang his hat on in ruling that the documents were admissible.

"Uh, Mr. Bernard. You mind if we talk with the doctor a few minutes beforehand?"

Hal Bernard's flat disinterested look disappeared. Ben couldn't tell whether Bernard was offended by his inquiry or just curious. Either way, he obviously figured that he didn't have anything to lose by asking.

"What did you have in mind, Mr. Green?"

Just curious, Ben thought, feeling relieved. "This is a very touchy case, Mr. Bernard."

"They're all touchy, Mr. Green. When you start dealing with professionals, doctors, lawyers and the like, they're all touchy."

"What I mean is, there are small children involved here." Ben didn't want to have to tell Hal Bernard that Ezekiel Thibodoux was an L.A.P.D. detective. The warrant said nothing about that. If Bernard sensed that there were extraordinary political consequences to his actions, with the attendant publicity down the road, he'd be more apt to go strictly by the book.

"Just a few moments," added Ben. He could see that Hal Bernard wanted to help them. Bernard was not a criminal specialist, though he, by virture of his position, was not a novice to the workings of the criminal courts. Bernard's job was to follow the directives of the statute. In reality, though, if the cops or the D.A.'s put him on their shit list, he could kiss his job as special master good-bye.

"The procedure," said Bernard, "is that the special master make the contact with the subject whose premises are to be searched. That a copy of the warrant be personally served by the special master on said subject." Bernard paused. Ben couldn't tell whether he was trying to remember the remaining statutorily defined procedures, or whether he was figuring the risks of acceding to Ben's request. Bernard looked tired, with the beginnings of grayish-blue bags under each eye.

"I'm going to get a cup of coffee," he said. His eyes wandered to a small snack shop in the lobby. "As far as I'm concerned, Mr. Green, we'll meet for the first time in Dr. Hirsch's office."

Ben smiled, nodding his silent appreciation. He and Frank watched Bernard amble over to the snack counter where he bought a Styrofoam cup of coffee and a doughnut wrapped in plastic wrap. He sat at one of two tiny Formica tables just outside the snack counter and carefully sipped at the steaming coffee. Ben and Frank took the next elevator up to Samuel Hirsch's office.

The ride to the eighth floor seemed slow. Ben wondered

if the second thoughts he was having about the propriety of his conduct were making time pass so slowly. He knew that Francis Powell would approve of how he had handled Hal Bernard *if* his efforts proved successful. If his tinkering with established legal procedures screwed up the case, then it would be Francis who would take the heat in the press and from his political enemies. Ben didn't want to let his friend down. Powell was one of the few who had been there for him during his worst times, after Julie had been murdered. His old friend had gone out on a limb, taking him on in Internal Affairs when nobody else was willing to take the chance on a psychiatric basket case and burned-out attorney, friend or no friend.

They followed the signs to Suite 801. Mostly other doctors on this floor. No pediatricians, Ben figured, since it was deathly quiet. Recessed lighting, thick carpets. Discreet nameplates in brass on the wall near the doors.

Samuel Hirsch's waiting room was tastefully decorated in shades of gray and cream. A Delacroix reproduction of a nighttime snow scene adorned the far wall. An Escher drawing, elegantly framed, hung over one of the sofas. The only vibrant color in the room was from an arrangement of fresh flowers in a Chinese-style vase. The vase sat atop a marble corner table that separated two love seats, each covered in a soft, textured, cream-colored fabric. Issues of *Psychology Today, Los Angeles* magazine, and *Town and Country* were neatly sorted atop the glass-and-marble coffee table.

"Hello, we're here to see Dr. Hirsch." Ben showed his identification to the young receptionist who sat on the other side of a sliding-glass window. She actually read the words on the I.D. and seemed to be looking back and forth, matching the picture with the face. Careful, Ben thought. Not a good sign. But then again, this was a place where people spilled forth their deepest darkest secrets. Confidentiality was the cornerstone of the physician-patient relationship, especially here. Instantaneously, the rationale for all he had read about the legislative statute and the special procedures for serving search warrants became clear. There was a good reason for all this. Something he could readily identify with, given his own experience as a lawyer and as a former psychiatric patient.

"Gentlemen, if you will follow me." The girl at the window had disappeared for a moment, only to return, standing at the door and beckoning them inside. Dr. Hirsch's office was at the end of a corridor lined with interview rooms, a small lunchroom with a refrigerator, coffee service, and microwave, another office for secretaries, and a computer room where printers clattered mutely beneath soundproof plastic covers. Samuel Hirsch was seated behind a modern oversized mahogany desk. He stood and extended his handshake to the two officers as they entered.

"How can I help you, Officers?" Hirsch motioned for the two men to take seats opposite his.

Ben and Frank had previously agreed that Ben would do all the talking. Frank Chen was seated next to Ben, his eyes wandering around the room, taking in the man via his books, photographs, awards, and magazines, each neatly occupying their individual spaces within the small office. When Frank twisted his upper torso, the butt of his gun was clearly visible. Ben saw that Hirsch noticed it right away, his eyes, for a moment, stuck on the weapon, unable to pull away. It was that way with most civilians. The sight of a gun in real life was a lot different than seeing TV cops shooting it out on the screen. It made you stop, especially a cannon the size of Frank's, the inevitable thought coming to mind: *Is that thing real?*

"We're investigating a child molestation–murder, Dr. Hirsch. You've probably heard of it. The Erin Dailey girl?" Ben waited, seeing the knowledge register on Hirsch's face. The newspapers had been running stories regularly. Parents were writing to their congressman, police chiefs across the state were using the girl's disappearance as a reason to bulk up the size of their police force, and there had been a marked increase in the number of parents driving their children to and from school.

"Our investigation has led us to believe that one of your patients may be involved. We have taken the precaution of securing a search warrant for your records regarding this particular patient." Ben pulled out a copy of the warrant and handed it to him over the desk.

Hirsch started reading, flipping the pages, but Ben could tell that the doctor was thinking what his next move should be, rather than concentrating on the legal mumbo jumbo. Most people never had the experience of being served with a search warrant. It could be understandably very rattling to see a group of officers on your doorstep armed with a piece of paper that authorized them to enter your house and conduct a room-by-room intrusion into your personal affairs. Samuel Hirsch was no exception. Now was the time to strike, when Hirsch was shook up, unsure of what next to do, when the intimidation factor of having two police detectives, *armed* police detectives, sitting opposite him would be too much for him to handle.

"As no doubt you are aware, Doctor, there are procedures specifying and controlling such searches." Tread carefully here, Ben told himself. The last thing he wanted to do was to alert Samuel Hirsch to the panoply of constitutional and statutory rights he had to assert in resisting this governmental intrusion into his own, and his patient's confidential communications.

"We are awaiting the arrival of the special master who has been assigned to formally serve the warrant in your matter." *Your matter,* that sounded good. Ben could see the added concern cross Samuel Hirsch's face in the form of deepening wrinkles over both eyes. Hirsch stuck a finger into the collar of his shirt, attempting to loosen his tie.

"What I thought," said Ben, in his best soft-spoken, good-cop routine, "was that we might, should you agree, dispense with some of the formalities. That is, from our information, this patient has already been identified as the perpetrator in the Dailey girl's murder." That wasn't entirely true, Ben thought, but close enough. He had interviewed Josh Gordon and found the young boy not at all hesitant to positively say that Thibodoux was the same man he had seen with Erin Dailey the day she was abducted. Still, Josh Gordon was only ten, and had been more interested in Ben's not bringing to his parents' attention the fact that he was riding his bike where he wasn't allowed to be. All witnesses, especially child witnesses, were subject to loss of recollection over a period of time. If in fact Thibodoux was the killer, and was charged with the crime, it could be months if not years before the young boy would be called to testify as to his observations. Ben had seen cases deteriorate right before his eyes, in open court, due to the effects the passage of time had on a witness' recollection.

"May I ask the patient's name?" Hirsch seemed impressed with the show of authority. That was a good sign. As long as Hirsch realized the gravity of the investigation, there was a good chance of the doctor's going along with their plan.

"Ezekiel Thibodoux," said Ben, watching for a change in the doctor's expression that might give something away. What he saw was far from subtle. Hirsch sat ramrod-straight in his chair for a moment, eyes practically bugging out. Then, as if he realized what he was doing, he clasped his hands behind his head, leaned back in the chair, and made a great show out of trying to appear relaxed.

Samuel Hirsch's mind flashed back to his last session with Zeke Thibodoux. All the questions Thibodoux had asked about confidentiality. So this was the reason. And if in fact it was Thibodoux's fear of disclosure that had prompted him to secure assurances of continued confidentiality, then what did that indicate? What did he have to hide?

Hirsch was confused. His practical side told him that Thibodoux was fearful of disclosure for one reason: he was guilty. But guilty was a legal term, and Samuel Hirsch had little use for the nit-picking of lawyers. The few times he had had to testify in court, the lawyers treated the proceedings like a circus, with him, Dr. Samuel Hirsch, as the act in the center ring, making a mockery of his concern, his life's work. Lawyers! All they were interested in was making a buck. It didn't matter which side they took, as long as the money was there. Hired guns. Prostitutes was more like it, he thought.

Still, this was murder. The murder of a small child. He had read the newspaper accounts of how the body was found, beheaded. It would take a strong man to do something like that. A psychopath so twisted and demented by what life had inflicted upon him that performing such an act had become a release, an attainment of a higher mental state. In his mind, Hirsch ran through his previous sessions with Thibodoux, his extensive notes, his observations of the man. The grisly tales of mayhem, spoken with an almost religious fervor, were beginning to fall into place, take on new meaning. What he had thought were merely the psychological ramblings of a stressed-out cop having to deal with the nightmarish reality of his day-to-day life, seemed now to be something quite different. Something frightening in its ramifications. Hirsch thought, It could very well be Ezekiel Thibodoux. The person that had committed this horrendous act.

Samuel Hirsch was beginning to feel that a little legal help, professional advice, was what he needed. He'd had a lawyer incorporate him when he first started out, and another to handle the lease for his office. And over the years, he'd made the acquaintance of a few attorneys, though cocktail-party chatter was about the extent of his involvement. He didn't care for lawyers, with their huckster mentality. They saw him as a huge dollar sign, someplace to send their hourly billings and retainers. A rich doctor, with bottomless pockets. No, he didn't care much for lawyers.

But now he wished he had one. Sitting right there next to him. Whispering in his ear, telling him what to say and what not to say, just like they did on the television during those congressional hearings.

"What sort of information would you be looking for, Mr. Green?"

"Thibodoux's file. Any records you have kept concerning your observations. But more specifically, any statements he might have made to you that would bear on this case."

Hirsch thought of the tape recordings he had made of Zeke Thibodoux under hypnosis. This Mr. Green and his friend would be very interested in those.

"And if I refuse?"

"You have that right, Doctor. As I mentioned, a special

master will be arriving here shortly. Should you claim that any of the documents relating to Mr. Thibodoux is privileged, then the special master is obligated to seal those documents and bring them to court where a judge will make the decision as to their disclosure and use in any future courtroom proceedings involving Mr. Thibodoux. Of course," Ben added, realizing that he was reaching, "that could possibly create a situation where you would be called to court to testify at an *in camera* hearing in the judge's chambers."

Ben watched Hirsch's eyes. The doctor seemed to be fixed on Frank Chen's gun, though he didn't have the same impressed look as before. Daydreaming now. Perhaps figuring the odds, trying to make his choice.

"And if I consent to let you take what you want? Then what?"

"Then the documents will be seized, subject, of course, to their future return to you. We'll fill out a complete inventory of all items. The D.A. will review the inventory and determine the admissibility of the various documents. If the D.A. determines the documents to be legally admissible, and if they bear on the issue of Mr. Thibodoux's guilt, then a case will be filed against Mr. Thibodoux for the crime or crimes that the D.A. feels can be proven, and the documents will be introduced as evidence at the time of trial." Ben watched Hirsch carefully. They'd gone beyond the point of no return. Hirsch would either succumb to their subtle intimidation, wanting to do the right thing, or he'd stand firm, deciding that he personally had little to gain by violating a patient's confidence. Ben heard some discussion outside the closed door of the office. He figured that it was Hal Bernard speaking with Hirsch's receptionist, and that his time alone with the doctor was quickly coming to an end.

"I can appreciate the seriousness of this investigation," said Hirsch.

"I know you can, Dr. Hirsch. The lives of young children . . . *innocent* young children are at stake. The longer we wait, the more likely it is that additional lives will be wasted."

Hirsch righted himself in his chair and tentatively reached for the telephone. "You feel that Thibodoux is the one? You're sure of that?"

Ben nodded, as if not actually verbalizing his answer was in some way less deceiving. He caught Frank Chen covering a smile with the thumb and two fingers of his right hand.

Samuel Hirsch smiled quickly. Nervously. He'd made up his mind. "Karen," he said into the receiver, "please bring me the complete file on Ezekiel Thibodoux." Hirsch paused a moment, listening, then said, "Send Mr. Bernard in, and please hold all of my calls." When he replaced the receiver on the hook it was with a noticeable sense of decision.

"Mr. Green," Hirsch said, "you'll have your records in a moment. Can I interest either of you gentlemen in a cup of coffee?"

CHAPTER 9

It always came back to the lips. Always the lips. *Her* lips. The image was never far beneath the surface, roiling and struggling to assert itself. He supposed any further effort to suppress the image would, as before, be doomed to failure. So he got back at the image, his memories of her, in his own way. With the children.

Ezekiel Thibodoux sat on the stone inside the cave, his eyes barely open, his mind flashing pictures from the past, mixed with the silent-movie flickering of the lantern on the rocky walls. His children were all there, their tiny child heads opaque, colorless, devoid of what other people would consider life. But other people's reality was not his. For Ezekiel Thibodoux, his children were filled with His spirit, the spirit of the Lord. They had been delivered into a state of unequaled grace. The Lord had spoken to him, telling him which to choose, and then, filling him with His life force as he delivered each child into Eternal Life.

Ezekiel Thibodoux removed his knife and held it up to the light, examining the smooth, shiny contours of the upturned blade. A Buck knife, with the molded ebony-colored phenolic handle. Practically indestructible. The high-carbon steel blade holding an edge so fine that at times he'd been tempted to forgo use of his SawBuck to go through the bone and tough fiber portions of the neck. Both knives had served him well. And now he had his family, the beautifully shaped heads, childlike in their innocence, to remind him of his achievement.

But still there were the lips.

He'd tried removing the lips, slicing them carefully from the face. And, for a time, that had worked. For a while, without the soft crimson tissue below the nose, all that was visible was a razored hole. But soon his eyes began to deceive him, replacing the lips back in their position. As if by their very absence, their existence was strengthened. Even worse, his eyes had turned the lips from horizontal to vertical, mocking him with the obscene memories, the nightmares, that his little trick had created. Those lips, their position transposed, thrust him back to her bed, his mother's arms, and what she had made him do.

Come, my beautiful little boy, my son. Play the game with your momma. Spread Momma's soft lips. That's it . . . that's what makes Momma feel good. My little man. My beautiful little man. Make Momma feel good. Make Momma love you . . .

A feeling came over him, as it always did when he thought of her and what she made him do. An anger that took him away from himself, out of control. He held the knife like a dagger, watching his hand shake ever so slightly, imagining what he would do to her now, if he only had the chance. And, at the same time, against his wishes, he realized that he was getting harder, that in some way completely outside of his understanding, these repulsive memories of her excited him.

Thibodoux rocked himself off the stone and over to the corner of the cave where he kept his Polaroids, his tapes, and the small plastic vials of semen. He inspected the vials, each bearing the name of one of his children, each dated to match the name and date on the back of his Polaroids. He was still hard, but not, he thought, for the right reasons.

He began shuffling through the photos, handling them carefully, his mind racing back and forth between images. He was throbbing now, lost inside his memories. He placed a cassette in the machine and listened to the initial crackle of the tape. Then his own voice, speaking so nicely to the child. He sounded good. Sweet.

Then the crying. Their music of deliverance. They didn't understand, the children. They were incapable of knowing that he was delivering them to a far better existence. That the pain was only temporary. Short-lived. That soon they would be His children. He was getting incredibly hard.

When it was over he capped the vial of semen and placed it with the others. His life force was special, and should not be polluted. Women were evil, not to be understood except to know that they were evil. God had told him this. God had explained about his mother, and what she had made him do to her. He had not understood until then, until God had lifted his guilt and taken it onto His shoulders, requiring in return only that he become His servant, delivering the children unto Him.

But now there was the boy. The boy would say things to make it end. God had spoken to him about the boy. The boy had to be delivered unto the Lord. God had told Ezekiel Thibodoux that this was required of him.

Thibodoux took the stringer on which hung the members of his family and held it in front of the lantern, watching them twist gently, alive with the fluttering light from the lantern. His momma was no longer there. With his children and their voices, she was, for the moment, buried deep within, unable to touch him. Ezekiel Thibodoux was at peace with himself.

CHAPTER 10

"Has Powell made up his mind?"

"Not yet."

"What's he waiting for? Ya know, Ben, if we pop Zeke now, he'll have his lawyer down there within the hour. It's not like we're dealing with some cherry. No way a judge is going to view this as anything but an arrest. That means forty-eight hours and we gotta either charge him with something and arraign him, or cut him loose."

Ben and Frank Chen were parked a few houses down from Ezekiel Thibodoux's neat little ranch-style bungalow in Canoga Park, a middle-income neighborhood in the west San Fernando Valley. Ben had convinced Hal Bernard that the records and tapes they'd seized at Samuel Hirsch's office were the result of a consensual search, and thus did not require sealing and review by a judge. What it had boiled down to was Sam Hirsch telling Hal Bernard, go ahead, here are the records, I don't want to interfere with your investigation.

Ben hoped that Hirsch's intent would be clear enough for a judge to later rule that the documents were not the result of a search pursuant to warrant. Ben was sure that Thibodoux's lawyer would claim that Hirsch was intimidated, and had handed over the documents because he'd been shown the warrant, and not because he desired to disclose a patient's confidential communications. Hirsch would end up testifying, along with Hal Bernard, and a judge would make the ultimate decision on the issue of consent.

But the consent issue would be merely the first hurdle. Even if the warrant was not knocked out, even if the judge ruled that the search was consensual, there was still the issue of doctor-patient privilege. Thibodoux would allege that confidential communications between himself and Hirsch were privileged under the law and thus were inadmissible against him in court. That, Ben figured, would be the tougher issue.

"Is the stuff on those tapes any good?"

Ben looked at Chen, then down the street at the front of Ezekiel Thibodoux's home. They'd been waiting for nearly two hours, and it was starting to get dark. Powell had told them to bring Thibodoux in for questioning after receiving Ben's report on Josh Gordon and a preliminary review of the documents seized from Thibodoux's psychiatrist. Ben was following orders, but wasn't at all sure whether they weren't jumping the gun.

"A mixed bag," answered Ben. "Hirsch seems to think that most of the hallucinatory stuff under hypnosis goes back to Thibodoux's childhood. Apparently there was a thing going on between him and his mom. His father was a big authoritarian type. Used to beat him and the rest of the family, or so Hirsch's notes reflect.

"What's hard to understand," said Ben, "is how much of this stuff is just in Thibodoux's head, and how much of it, if any, is real."

Frank Chen turned and looked inquisitively at Ben, waiting for an explanation.

"Thibodoux talks about 'the children' during these sessions. And 'delivering the children to God.' There's a lot of religious, biblical-type stuff in what he says. He keeps talking about 'his children,' but never comes out and actually admits to kidnapping or murder, or any sort of molestation for that matter. There's nothing solid to tie him to the Erin Dailey case."

"What about Hirsch?"

"Hirsch's notes reflect that he feels Thibodoux is under a lot of stress from his job. That given his history with his mother, and they don't really go into much detail there, that Thibodoux is a walking time bomb. Hirsch says that perhaps some time off from the job would be a good thing."

"For us all," said Chen, smiling.

"Hirsch also wrote something else, more of a note to himself, about a possible dual personality. Two forces within Thibodoux fighting for control."

"What did Powell say about all that?"

"Not much. I showed him what we had. It was his idea to pick up Thibodoux for questioning. I guess he feels there's enough to get a filing."

Frank Chen pulled a thermos from between his legs. He twisted open the top, using it as a cup. He then poured the contents of the thermos, chicken soup, into the cup and resealed the thermos. From a brown paper bag on the floorboard he removed a package covered in aluminum foil wrapped in a ball shape. After peeling away the foil, and another layer of plastic wrap, Chen gingerly dropped a small matzo ball into the thermos cup.

"You wanna bowl of soup?" Chen extended the cup toward Ben. The aroma was out of this world.

"Is that what I think it is?"

"Matzo-ball soup," said Chen, grinning. "Rhoda makes the best. Go ahead, take it. I got another cup in the bag. Go ahead."

Ben took the soup and slowly sipped from the cup. Chen was right, it was marvelous.

"I never figured you for a matzo-ball sort of guy," said Ben. He watched as Frank Chen prepared a cup of soup for himself, plopping the doughy yellow ball very carefully into the steaming chicken broth.

"Yeah, most of Rhoda's family gets a real kick outta seeing me scarf the stuff down. I love it. And you should taste her chopped liver! To die for . . ." Chen laughed, and Ben joined in. "I get chow mein, wonton, sweet and sour, the whole magilla when we go to my side. Don't get me wrong, I could live on that stuff. Rhoda too."

Ben had just brought the cup of steaming liquid to his lips when he spotted the pair of headlights slowly moving up the street. The headlights stopped at Thibodoux's driveway, then turned in.

"There's our man," said Ben, looking for somewhere to put the matzo-ball soup. Chen had already disposed of his and was partially out the door, his hand automatically patting the side of his chest where his gun rested. Both men strode quickly across the street, intercepting Ezekiel Thibodoux midway between his car door and the front porch.

Rebecca Thibodoux listened carefully for the sound of her husband's car in the driveway. She had her barbecue-flavored Fritos corn chips, the giant economy bag, perched on her lap, and was watching one of her favorite TV shows, "Lifestyles of the Rich and Famous." Ezekiel told her such shows were trash, the work of the devil. Ezekiel said that all TV was evil, except for Pat Robertson and Jerry Falwell, and lately, he said, he wasn't too sure about them. Jimmy Swaggart's fall from grace had hit Ezekiel hard, testing his spiritual commitment.

But she liked "Lifestyles," with that pudgy little English guy getting all excited. There he was now, talking to that Arab fella on his boat, the richest man on earth. Imagine!

She reached for the controls to her Contour Bed, the one she had bought from Jack Linkletter on the TV. She'd begged Ezekiel, telling him that it would be good for his back. And good for her, too, since she so often felt poorly and spent so much time in bed. With the hand that wasn't inside the Fritos bag she found the controls and pressed the switch operating the head of the bed, moving it upward. There, that was perfect.

Jeremiah and Josiah, her two cats, softly purred at the vibration from the bed's motor. "Whatsa matter, babies? You know Momma's just movin' this little ol' bed a little. Come to Momma, babies." She extended her hand, the one that had been inside the Fritos bag. Both cats jumped toward her, eagerly licking her fingers.

"That's right," she said, watching the cats' tongues darting in and out, licking her fingers clean. She pulled her hand away and the cats paused momentarily, then returned to the foot of the bed where they lay partially on top of one another. Rebecca stuck her hand back inside the Fritos bag and continued to eat.

"Momma?"

Rebecca hadn't noticed her youngest, Mary Esther, enter the bedroom. "What is it, child?"

"Daddy's home."

Rebecca quickly turned off the television and rolled the top of the Fritos bag closed. "I didn't hear the car," she said, slowly swinging her legs over the side. "Give Momma a hand, child." Rebecca waited as her thirteen-year-old daughter came near, wrapped both arms around her waist, and provided support. The two of them, in embrace together, shuffled to a metal walker that stood just to the side of the bed. Rebecca wedged herself inside the walker, breathing heavily, and wiped her brow.

"Momma?"

"Yes, child," she snapped. The girl asked so many questions!

"There're two men talking to Daddy in the driveway, Momma."

Rebecca looked at her daughter, wondering if she was making up stories again. They'd called her from school last month about these stories. The teacher was worried that maybe something was wrong at home. The principal wanted to give Mary Esther some sort of counseling. Boy, when Ezekiel heard of that he just about went through the roof. There'd be no counseling for any of his daughters. No sirree. It was bad enough, he'd said, that the government forced him to send them to their schools. Now this!

"What sorta men?" she asked.

"In suits," said Mary Esther. "Like Daddy."

"Police?"

Mary Esther just shook her head.

"You go to the front and see if the men are still here, child. I'm gettin' tired. I gotta sit down for a spell. You be sure and tell your momma what's goin' on outside." Rebecca Thibodoux maneuvered the walker to a chair beside the bed. She'd wait here for Ezekiel with the TV off so that he didn't come in and get mad right away.

"Make sure your daddy's dinner is warm," she yelled as Mary Esther started for the front of the house. "You know how he gets if his dinner ain't heated up proper." She reached for the remote control and was about to turn the TV back on when she thought better of it. Robin Leach was with a bunch of soap stars, her favorites, someplace in some foreign country, drinking champagne and eating those little black fish eggs. Rebecca would have liked to have seen that. But Ezekiel was just outside, and if he came in and caught her watching, he'd start to yell, maybe worse.

"Come on, you lazy cats," she said. The cats didn't move. She reached for the Fritos and finished the bag, waiting for her husband to come in the door.

The men were policemen. Mary Esther Thibodoux knew that. One of the men, the small one, had a big gun that flashed when he turned his coat open. Her father stood near the headlights of the car, talking to the men. He didn't look very happy, like maybe they were having an argument. The smaller man kept patting his side where she knew he kept his gun. Just like her father did.

They weren't exactly yelling at each other, but she could tell that her father was upset. He had that look, eyes unmoving, lips pressed together, that she knew meant he was mad.

Then the three of them walked down the driveway and up the street. Mary Esther moved to the front door, cracking it open slightly so that she could see them. The two men and her father walked to a car parked across the street. The small man opened the door for her father and her father entered. The small man got into the backseat with her father. Mary Esther thought that was strange, since, when she had seen her father with his partners, they always shared the front seat.

She heard the engine rev, then the lights flash. The car then turned and started back toward the house. Mary Esther closed the door just a hair, watching the car pass the house. Her father was looking straight ahead. He still had that look, his mean look.

Mary Esther closed the door.

"Mary Esther? Mary Esther?" Her mother was yelling for her. "Child, what's goin' on out there?"

Mary Esther thought they were police. Yes, she was pretty sure of that. The way her father had acted with them made her sure.

"Mary Esther, you hear me, child?"

She'd wait and see. There was much she had to tell them. But not with her father around. She would have to be sure that he didn't find out. Maybe they were just his friends, and they needed him at work for something. That could be all that it was. And if she went down there now, and told them about it, then she'd be in real trouble. Her father would whip her until she bled, like he had her older sister.

"I swear, child, if you don't come down here and tell me what's goin' on out there, I'm gonna tell your father! You hear me?"

"Yes, Momma," she said, though not loud enough to carry. She would wait and see what happened. Time would pass. If he didn't come back home, she knew exactly what she would do.

"Yes, Momma," she said, heading for the bedroom. "Daddy's gone with the men. You can turn on your show, Momma. I'll help you into bed."

CHAPTER 11

He had never been fat, but the love handles were steadily enlarging and he feared that pretty soon he'd look like one of those couch potatoes, office types, taking lunch in their shirtsleeves down at the mall, tossing down pizza and beer. Claire said that he needed some regular exercise, and when he'd displayed a total lack of interest in that suggestion, she came home one evening with a large box strapped to the top of her car. A Motobecane tandem, a bicycle built for two. "If you're not going to get the exercise by yourself," she'd said, "then I'll make you feel guilty until you do."

He admired Claire for that. Buying the bike, given his history, was a chancy thing. He could have reacted unexpectedly, considering the memories that the bike was likely to stir up. But she knew him well. In certain ways better than he knew himself. It was time. Over the years since Julie's death he'd seen people riding. He'd even considered taking the sport back up. He missed the exercise, and it was one of the few things he had been able to do that cleared his mind.

Still, the bike and his morning rides, along with Claire and the courtroom, reminded him of the Rashid James trial and its aftermath. And, more importantly, the rape and murder of his daughter. He'd overcome the hurdle with Claire. Maybe Claire was right. He should confront his demons head-on at this point. He was stronger now, and the only way he'd ever get a handle on his emotional baggage was to face facts.

They rode down Ventura Boulevard in the early-morning hours. At six in the morning, on a weekday, traffic was just starting to bunch up in the bumper-to-bumper condition, where it would remain for the rest of the day. Studio City was beginning to come to life, the early risers arguing with the waitresses over breakfast at Art's Deli, and store owners carrying cups of steaming coffee from Dupar's. Ben and Claire headed down Ventura toward Vineland, past the sleazy motels awaiting the wrecking ball of the mini-mall captains of industry. Claire was in the back, constantly urging Ben to pedal faster, giggling and poking him, pinching his love handles as if to increase his incentive. "Come on, Green," she yelled on one short uphill stretch. "You can do better than that!" Ben tried to smile, but found it hard to do anything that interfered with his efforts to catch his breath.

A few blocks further down, Ben maneuvered the bike into the left-turn lane and headed toward Universal City. They weren't quite in good enough shape to manage the climb up toward Universal Studios, so they continued past the amusement park, pedaling north toward Riverside Drive. From Riverside, they started back, past the film studio buildings, then up to Ventura again. The last push was up three blocks on Coldwater Canyon to the place where they had parked. Ben had carried the bike on the car, the upper canyon roads being too steep and too dangerous for them to handle on the tandem.

When they pulled into the driveway back at Ben's house, Francis Powell's black Cadillac was parked to the side, engine running. The rear windows of the Cad were darkly smoked, but Ben recognized Roy, Powell's driver, seated behind the wheel. The left rear window of the Cad lowered, its tinted gray glass smoothly humming.

"Ya know," said Powell, seated in the backseat, "it's a lot better for you if you actually ride the bike instead of carrying it on top of your car. You'd be surprised."

Claire laughed, then said, "You look like you could stand to lose a few pounds yourself, Francis."

Francis Powell frowned, patted his stomach and nodded.

"To what do I owe the honor of this visit?" Ben stood at the open car window. He could feel the cold wisp of air conditioning coming from inside.

Powell, with the crook of his finger, motioned for Ben to join him. Reports and folders littered the backseat, and Powell had a small stack of the same on his lap.

"We've got until tomorrow morning to either fish or cut bait with Thibodoux." Powell was speaking while thumbing through a brochure on an upcoming law-enforcement conference in Monterey. The Technicolor cover of the brochure depicted the rocky Pacific coastline at sunset, a solitary bird silhouetted against a fiery orange sky.

"You've got everything, Francis. Will the D.A. file it?"

Powell shook his head, his curled upper lip registering disgust, like he had just regurgitated something unpleasant.

"Fuckers are backing out," said Powell. "Lanier and his lapdogs say they're thinking about recusing themselves on this one."

"What?"

"Lanier says that his office is too close to Thibodoux. That they'd have a conflict of interest in prosecuting him given their longstanding relationship."

"That's bullshit."

"You're damn right it's bullshit. Eli Lanier's got his sights set on the attorney general's office. He wants to make the move from D.A. to A.G. as painless as possible. He figures this thing with Thibodoux is a bomb ready to explode. That he's got little to gain and a whole lot to lose by prosecuting Thibodoux. So he's taking the easy way out."

"That means the attorney general's office will take over."

"Yeah, and that works out just great for Lanier." Powell got that curled-lip look again. "If the A.G. blows the case and Thibodoux walks, then Lanier comes out smelling like a damn bouquet of roses. If the A.G. gets a conviction, it doesn't hurt Lanier since Jim Craig's going to retire from the A.G.'s office this year anyway."

"You talked to Craig?"

"Not yet," said Powell. "I will though. Soon as we decide where we're going with all this. One thing, though, Benny. With Lanier and his merry band no longer in the picture, I want you to handle the actual prosecution of Thibodoux, if we ever get to that point."

"What about the A.G.? I'm sure they've got lots of young turks chomping at the bit to get their teeth into a juicy media circus like this."

"That's what I'm afraid of, Benny. I don't want some young stud straight outta law school trying to make a reputation for himself on this case. I've seen that shit backfire on more than one occasion. We'll have the A.G.'s help on this, but they'll assist you. I want you to work lead on this one."

Ben nodded, thinking back to his discussion with Francis Powell at Kenny Chen's bar-mitzvah, and how Powell had said this would probably be no big deal. Yeah, right.

"Okay," said Powell, reaching for the Ezekiel Thibodoux case file. "That's decided, now let's figure out whether we have enough evidence to charge the son of a bitch in the first place."

The two men went through the file, page by page, discussing the strengths and weakness of the prosecution's case.

"What it comes down to," said Ben, "is that we've got Josh Gordon's identification, which, the last time I spoke to the kid, was pretty decent. And we have the tapes and records of Dr. Hirsch, which, as we've discussed, are going to be challenged, and challenged hard, by Thibodoux."

"You think the warrant will hold up?"

"Probably," said Ben. "Depends on the judge. Hirsch went along with the program, and most judges would probably view his statements as constituting legitimate consent to search. Of course, he had already been shown the search warrant, so a judge, if he were so inclined, could rule that the consent was not voluntarily given. Depends."

"On what Hirsch says, right?"

"That, and our testimony. Frank's and mine."

Powell nodded.

"Then there's the problem of Thibodoux claiming that the tapes and shrink records are all privileged, even if the search is ruled legal."

"Doctor-patient."

"Yep, and I'll tell you up front, Francis, that's one helluva good argument for the defense." Ben paused. Powell's face had taken on a pained expression. "Is there something else I should know about, Francis?"

"The Gordon kid," said Powell. He moved around uncomfortably in the backseat. "I just got a call from Parker. The press is calling about a report that the Gordon kid has reneged on his previous statement. Supposedly, one of the deacons at Thibodoux's church went out to talk to the kid, accompanied by a contingent of Thibodoux's fellow churchgoers and friends. They say the kid admitted that he'd made the whole thing up about seeing Thibodoux with the Dailey girl."

"What?"

"Now calm down, Benny. I gotta unit out at the Gordon place right now. You know these religious kooks. I'm sure they went out there and confronted the kid and the kid got scared and just said anything they wanted to hear."

"But Jesus, Francis! That kid is the whole case. Shit! I can just see it now. Thibodoux's lawyer will have a field day with this. By the time this thing gets to trial, that kid'll be scared shitless. He won't know what to testify to."

Powell contemplated Ben's statement for a moment. "It's my call, Benny. And I gotta make it before the forty-eight hours is up. Once we cut Thibodoux loose he'll be able to cover his tracks. Our job will be just that much harder."

"Listen, Francis. With Josh Gordon recanting his story, we don't have much of anything on the guy. Even if all the shrink stuff comes floating into court, that stuff is pretty ambiguous. Even Hirsch's notes reflect his opinion that Thibodoux is just a stressed-out cop, and that all the hypnosis mumbo jumbo is because of his job. Hirsch feels Thibodoux is not talking about himself in those tapes, but about his cases. It would be very easy for a defense attorney to put Thibodoux on the stand and have him explain that he'd gone to see a shrink due to the pressures of the job, having to face those sleazebag molesters day in and day out, having to see the childrens' ruined lives. That the ramblings on the tape are merely the reflection of that stress. That he can't stop thinking about his cases, about the children that are suffering. Hell, he'll have the jurors wiping the tears from their eyes."

"Go shower and get dressed," said Powell. He motioned for his driver, who had been standing outside of the car smoking a cigarette, to come back. "I'll meet you downtown at two. We'll go over all this one more time. Maybe it'll look better."

Ben shrugged a laugh, shaking his head. "Yeah," he muttered, "and maybe we'll come across the videotape of Thibodoux committing the crime."

Francis Powell didn't smile.

They were seated in a small interview room on the seventh floor of Parker Center. From the square of window, Ben watched the cars snake their way, bumper to bumper, down Temple Street. The old Hall of Justice stood like a weathered gray outcropping of stone, dwarfed in the shadow of its successor, the glass-and-steel high rise of the Criminal Courts Building. The Hall was now relegated to secondary functions in the criminal justice system: coroner hearings and the housing of the overflow from the Central Men's Jail.

The searing heat had continued without relief for over a week. Ben placed his hand against the glass, feeling the warmth of the air outside. Today, like the previous day, the AQMD had announced a smog alert, warning young and old to stay at home, not to exert themselves. The cloverleaf freeway interchange was covered by the same white haze that enveloped the skyscraper buildings, obscuring all but the faintest traces of foothills, choking the lungs, and burning the eyes. It didn't pay to go outside.

"So what you're telling me," said Powell, "is that we don't have enough to hold Thibodoux."

"As much as I hate to admit it, that's right."

Powell had his feet up on the city's standard-issue steel desk. It was a far cry from his oversized penthouse office decorated in soft hues of blue and gray, with the huge lacquered rosewood desk and matching hutch. Ben noticed the beginnings of a hole in the sole of Powell's shoe and wondered if the chief was having financial problems, or was, instead, just too busy to go shopping.

"Mmm." Powell continued leafing through the reports, hoping to spot something he'd missed the first five times he'd read them through. Finally, he tossed the paperwork on the desk and said, "You're right. If I didn't want this guy so badly, I would've told you that this morning. There isn't enough, especially with the kid starting to change his story."

"So we cut him loose?"

"Yeah. At least until we get more on him, or we're sure that Josh Gordon's I.D. will hold up. No use trying to push this thing through, then get to court with our guns empty." Powell shook his head. "Jesus, I just hate to do that. No telling what Thibodoux will do now that he knows we're on to him."

"No choice, Francis. I'll call down."

Both men stood, and Ben followed Powell out into the hallway. They walked together to the reception area just opposite the elevator.

"I want daily briefings," said Powell, moving toward the closed elevator doors. Ben was about to respond when the receptionist called his name.

"There's someone here to see you, Mr. Green." Ben followed her eyes to the row of chairs just to the left of her desk. Seated on the chair furthest from the desk was a young girl, not more than twelve or thirteen, Ben guessed. Her mousy brown hair fell plainly on her shoulders. She wore a simple navy cotton dress with white cuffs and a white collar. The cuffs were worn and frayed, as was the hem of the dress. The shoes were the type Ben remembered as Mary Janes. Ben hadn't seen a pair of those since Julie had been a toddler. The kids nowadays all sported Nikes or Reeboks in fluorescent colors at seventy-five dollars a pop. Ben glanced at the receptionist, who merely raised her eyebrows and shrugged her shoulders, then went back to answering the phone.

"Can I help you?" Ben approached the girl. He was aware of Francis Powell's presence behind him. The girl remained seated. On the floor between her legs was a small red toolbox. The girl opened the toolbox and removed a pair of Vise-Grips, handing them to Ben.

"My momma brought me," said the girl. "She's downstairs in the car. I'm Mary Esther Thibodoux. I think you know my daddy."

CHAPTER 12

"I received a very interesting call last night." Antoine LeDoux was stuffing his Italian leather briefcase with his file on the Asian Crazy Boys case. Judge Boynton had just sustained the petition against all the minors, found them all guilty. A date had been set for sentencing, called disposition in juvenile court. LeDoux, like Ben and the other attorneys on the case, was readying to leave.

"All your calls are interesting, Lucky." Ben was anxious to get back downtown and find out what the crime lab had been able to make of the Vise-Grips and toolbox brought in by Mary Esther Thibodoux.

"Benny, my man, I think you'll be very interested in this one." LeDoux had an aggressive feline look, like he'd just swallowed the canary and didn't much care what you thought about it. "Does the name Ezekiel Thibodoux ring any bells?" Ben saw all teeth, perfectly matched and pearl-white. LeDoux's dentist was a real craftsman.

Ben shrugged, trying not to let on that he was curious as hell about Zeke Thibodoux's relationship to Lucky LeDoux.

"Suit yourself," said LeDoux. He removed his Porsche Carrera sunglasses from his suit pocket. "I just heard that you were the Man on this one. Thought we might have a little talk-around, ya know."

"Whadya mean, 'talk-around'? Has he retained you, Lucky?"

LeDoux smiled. "Not yet. We're working on the financial arrangements. Though it would appear that that won't be a major problem."

"He can afford you on a cop's salary?"

"Benny, Benny . . . You know how that works. The man's got relatives, friends . . . People in the community who believe strongly in his innocence." LeDoux was standing at the doorway to the courtroom, blocking Ben's exit. "And from what I've seen so far, I don't blame them. Pretty weak case, Benny. Pretty damn weak."

Ben wondered whether he should mention anything to LeDoux about the toolbox that Mary Esther Thibodoux had brought downtown, along with her explanation of what her father did with that toolbox. If Lucky LeDoux knew what Ezekiel Thibodoux's daughter had said, he might not have been so cocky.

"Yeah," said Ben, moving toward the door, "we try and make 'em that way so guys like you can experience the thrill of victory every once in a while. That agony-of-defeat stuff gets a little old, doesn't it, ol' buddy?"

LeDoux laughed, hurriedly following Ben out the door and down the corridor toward the parking lot.

"I hear Eli Lanier's chickened out on this one." LeDoux was walking alongside Ben, trying to keep up. "That it's just you and the A.G. Jesus, the A.G. couldn't try his way out of a paper bag. This ain't no Medicare fraud case, man. If Lanier doesn't want any part of it, then it's gotta be hinky, right? Eli Lanier may be slimy, but he's not stupid."

"I wouldn't know, Lucky. You know Lanier, if it isn't going to help him, he'd just as soon dump it. He's looking down the road toward the election. And don't go selling the A.G. short, Lucky. Talk to Angelo Buono and Ken Bianchi, see what they say about the A.G."

"Yeah, yeah. So when's the prelim supposed to be?"

"Don't know. The P.D. represented him at the arraignment. It was put over for a week to allow Thibodoux to retain counsel. No bail was set. But I suppose you know all that."

They had reached Ben's car. LeDoux's big black Mercedes sedan was parked a few spaces down. Ben heard the chirp from LeDoux's car alarm and was momentarily startled.

"I'll call you," said LeDoux, watching Ben get behind the wheel. "When he comes across with the retainer. Informal discovery, right?"

"No problem, Lucky." The inside of Ben's car was like an oven. He started the engine and turned the air-conditioning to high. He watched LeDoux in his rearview mirror as he entered his car, then backed out of the space, waving as he passed. Retaining Antoine LeDoux was a smart move on Thibodoux's part. LeDoux was well-known among the downtown judges, aside from being one of the best criminal defense attorneys in the city. Ben also figured that his friendship with Lucky LeDoux was known to Ezekiel Thibodoux. Maybe, by hiring LeDoux, Thibodoux was seeking some sort of leverage, playing on their friendship. It made Ben only slightly uncomfortable, and that was primarily due to the fact that LeDoux was a formidable adversary. Any hopes Ben had of waltzing this case through court without much trouble began to fizzle with the prospect of having Antoine LeDoux on the other end of the counsel table. Their friendship, Ben knew, would not get in either man's way. They would both fight tooth and nail in court and then be able to buy each other drinks afterward. It was the sort of relationship they'd built up over the years.

The crime lab report was on Ben's desk when he got downtown. Two pages, mostly fill-in-the-blank style. The prints on the toolbox and the Vise-Grips were Thibodoux's. No big surprise there. There were traces of blood on the Vise-Grips, which matched that of Erin Dailey. This raised Ben's hopes, until he read further and saw that both Thibodoux and the Dailey girl had the same blood type. Incredibly bad luck. Thibodoux could, and undoubtedly would, claim that the blood on the pliers was his, and that he cut himself working with the tools.

The boys in the lab also found traces of steel wool in the grooves of the pliers, along with remnants of detergent or soap. One didn't have to be an experienced forensic pathologist or criminalist to draw the conclusion that

Thibodoux had scrubbed the pliers clean, or at least he believed that he had. The steel wool and cleanser were the likely result of a Brillo pad or S.O.S., or something of the kind, according to the lab report. That might be something to talk about at trial, the fact that the man scrubbed his tools, though an excuse would be easy for Thibodoux to fabricate. Without something to connect Erin Dailey to those tools, their existence would be of minimal importance in court.

The lab, according to the note paper-clipped to the formal report, was still in the process of matching the groove marks on the pliers with those found on Erin Dailey's body. It was close, painstaking work, and might prove to be fruitless, but it had to be done.

The scientific evidence to date appeared not to be the key to convicting Ezekiel Thibodoux. Ben tossed the reports inside his case folder. He was still thinking about his discussion with Lucky LeDoux, about what he hadn't told LeDoux. What only he, Powell, and the A.G. were aware of. He wrote a note to himself, to remind him to put Mary Esther Thibodoux on tape.

The young girl had been hesitant to say anything when she brought in the tools. Slender, plain, with eyes set deep in an otherwise nondescript face, Mary Esther had, at first, refused to answer any of his questions. Yet Ben knew there was a reason for her presence, some rationale behind her bringing her father's tools with her. She was unwilling to take the next step by herself. Ben had seen kids like that before. Traumatized, molested, violated beyond understanding. They disassociated from reality. The person or persons who preyed upon them became their only anchor to the world. Losing that person, or violating that person's trust, was like cutting the lifeline and free-falling in space. It was a tremendously difficult step to take, even though, looking in from the outside, it was the only step.

And there was always the element of guilt. The victims of child molestation and abuse, unable to rationally think it through, inevitably felt that their plight was in some way their own fault. There was no other rational way to explain the horrors that had befallen them, other than to accept the degradation, the loss of self-esteem, as somehow being their due.

Ben knew there was something behind those deep, dark eyes. He had seen enough children in similar positions to know that once the box was opened, once he discovered the key, the horrors of Mary Esther Thibodoux's childhood would spill forth like raw sewage. But he needed to handle her properly. If he pushed too hard, too quick, she'd clam shut even harder.

Ben looked at his notes of their initial conversation. Mary Esther's admission that her father had molested both her older sister and herself came as merely a mild surprise. Incest was not uncommon among pedophiles. They took their pleasures wherever they could find them. And moving from one child to the next, down the line, was also common. Eventually, the victims grew old enough to move away, distance themselves at least from the daily physical torment. The psychological scar tissue, though, never disappeared.

The fact that Ezekiel Thibodoux had molested his own daughters might be relevant at the time of trial. The law allowed such evidence of uncharged sex offenses to show a pattern of behavior, or what the law termed modus operandi. Yet it was a far cry from showing that Thibodoux had sex with his own children to proving beyond a reasonable doubt that he molested, mutilated, and murdered Erin Dailey. The incidents with his own children were helpful only if one or both of the daughters were willing to testify, and, more important, if Ben could establish a solid link between Ezekiel Thibodoux and the victim of the murder.

This last part was what interested Ben. Something Mary Esther Thibodoux had touched on in their interview. Something she had said about her father yelling at her and striking her across the face one evening in their garage. She had merely gone out to tell him that her mother's medication was running low. Her father was at his workbench, his back to her. She had gotten close enough to see that he was looking at something. Pictures, photographs, she thought. The tool chest was nearby.

When she spoke, she caught him completely unawares. He turned quickly, then, swung with his right hand, catching her on the cheek and knocking her off her feet. Sprawled on the hard concrete floor, her hand immediately went to the cheek where she had felt the sting. She was more surprised and frightened than hurt. In that instant, with her father standing over her, she saw one of the pictures. It had been knocked to the garage floor and lay between them, askew. Upside down, she thought. Her father quickly grabbed the picture and told her to leave. He took one step toward her and she curled up in a ball. Then, seeing that he was waiting, she quickly got to her feet and ran back inside the house.

She told Ben that she remembered being hit, and feeling the sting. She remembered seeing her father, angry, like a wild animal, breathing its warm stale breath over her, trying to determine its next course of attack. She remembered being frightened.

But not so frightened, Ben thought, that she didn't get a good look at the face in the photograph.

CHAPTER 13

This part of practicing law he could do without. So demeaning, so . . . *lower-class.* But for Antoine LeDoux, this was a necessary evil, visiting clients who were guests of the county of Los Angeles, and having to strip clean of all metal objects: his fourteen-karat gold money clip, sunglasses, belt buckle, loose change, his Montblanc fountain pen with the gold nib . . . So *demeaning.*

Ezekiel Thibodoux was being housed in the keep-away unit, along with the other child molesters and certain other sex offenders. That made it take longer for the sheriffs to get to Thibodoux's level, order him out of his cell, and accompany him downstairs to the attorney interview room. It was worth it, though. Especially for a guy like Thibodoux. If he were merely the standard-issue child molester, he'd find his time in custody extremely unpleasant, at best. And if he ever made it to the joint, Thibodoux's days in prison would not only be unpleasant, but, if placed among the general inmate population, he'd find his remaining time on earth to be severely limited. Regardless of the horrendous crimes of violence, greed, and unfathomable callousness represented in the jail population, the average jailbird viewed himself as perfectly suited to stand in judgment and mete out punishment when it came to child molesters. Most prisons segregated child molesters for this reason, to keep them alive long enough for them to serve their sentence.

Ezekiel Thibodoux not only had this cross to bear during his incarceration, but he was also a cop, or an ex-cop. The few law-enforcement officials who chose the wrong fork in the road and ended up behind bars were always segregated from the rest of the custody inmates. Just from a liability point of view, it wouldn't do to have a former police officer sodomized or beaten to death because the county of Los Angeles was negligent in placing him within the easy reach of those convicted felons whom the cop had previously arrested.

Antoine LeDoux passed through the metal detector without setting off the buzzer, grabbed his pen, money clip, belt, and the rest of the items he had neatly stacked on the small counter, and headed for the sally port that separated the attorney conference area from the lobby of the Men's Central Jail. He'd brought a catalog from Barneys, to give him something to do while he waited for Thibodoux to be brought down. On his last trip to New York, he couldn't resist purchasing a couple of suits to add to his collection, one of which—the Gieves & Hawkes charcoal chalk-stripe three-piece cashmere-and-lamb's-wool with side vents and pleated trousers, which had set him back about fourteen hundred—he was wearing today, along with his pale blue cotton broadcloth Burberry shirt with the spread collar, and a Gianni Versace silk tie.

"Visitor for Thibodoux." The young deputy sheriff manning the intake desk looked up, spotted LeDoux waving his hand, and gestured in his direction. LeDoux was aware that a few heads turned at the name, mostly other attorneys who had undoubtedly followed the newspaper and television reports and were familiar with the facts surrounding Ezekiel Thibodoux's arrest. The crying, forlorn faces of Erin Dailey's parents had been plastered across the television during the first few days after her headless body was discovered.

A fund had been set up in the dead girl's honor, along with a reward for information leading to the capture and conviction of her killer. Until recently, the story had been relegated to the back sections of the *Times*, and had all but disappeared from the TV. With the arrest of Ezekiel Thibodoux, it was all being stirred up once more, and each network allotted time on the local news for coverage of the story. It was the perfect setup for Antoine LeDoux: a high-publicity, gruesome murder, with an ex-cop as the primary suspect. Lots of daily media coverage, and a client with an apparently unlimited source of funds to pay his fees.

The pressure was on the prosecution to get a conviction, what with the grieving parents in court every day, and the angelic, innocent face of Erin Dailey on the television every evening. The specifics as to the manner of her torture, the graphic details, were left for the print media to exploit, a task they seemed to relish, sparing no anatomical detail they'd been able to glean from the coroner's report.

For a split second, gazing across the conference room, Antoine LeDoux thought of his friend Ben, his mind taking him back to their last adversarial courtroom encounter a few years ago. They'd both represented defendants in the Rashid James trial, though LeDoux had been able to strike a deal for his client to testify against Ben's, leaving Ben to go the trial alone. The ultimate result of that case was well-known, not so much for the verdict that was returned as for the reverberating shock waves it had sent out.

Thibodoux was making his way to the small interview cubicle. LeDoux smoothed his tie along the contours of his stomach, then made sure the knot at the collar was tight and snugged up as it should be. He put on his smile, stood, and motioned across the table for Thibodoux to have a seat. Neither man extended a handshake, both well aware that physical contact between inmates and visitors was not allowed. Warnings to this effect were printed in large red letters on the walls of the room. Under those warnings, in smaller lettering, was the admonition that inmates were not allowed to smoke. LeDoux didn't smoke, and always considered it to be the height of inconsideration, and very bad for business, to light up in front of his custody clients. A good number of his former clients would not think twice about beating another inmate senseless just for his cigarettes. Why tempt fate?

Thibodoux asked, "Did you get the check?"

LeDoux thought Thibodoux was beginning to exhibit

the signs of his incarceration. Most people, even cops who'd spent their lives around inmates and jails, eventually showed the telltale signs of incarceration. Two- and three-day growths of beard, and hair only partially combed, usually a quick hand-through in the morning. Breath that soured from cigarettes, candy bars, and Cokes without brushing. Papers, wrapped in a rubber band (paper clips were taboo) and stuffed neatly in the front flap pocket of the denim-blue county jail shirt, removed deftly, after hours of practice, and unfolded with great care. The documents—bail information, property receipts, perhaps a copy of the criminal complaint—looking like the Dead Sea scrolls, having been folded and unfolded so many times. After a longer period of time, the inmates who had more completely begun to adapt to life behind bars took on additional traits noticeable to the trained eye. These were the prisoners carrying the large cardboard accordion files containing copies of their court documents. Some wore the cheap beige plastic county-issue thongs, their tennis shoes having been stolen by other inmates. Often times a crucifix, made of twisted string, hung neatly tucked beneath the Adam's apple, to go along with the paperback copy of the New Testament that they'd received from the jail priest. Demand for the Bibles was always greatest just before sentencing.

"The money, for now," said LeDoux, "is taken care of. Don't worry about that." He put aside the Barneys catalog and pulled a file folder from his briefcase.

"I just want to make absolutely sure," said Thibodoux, "that there's no problem with the money." He forced a smile. "I know how you guys are about that."

LeDoux wanted to ask him what he meant by that, if perhaps he, Thibodoux, was willing to perform *his* job for free, just for the fun of it. LeDoux decided to remain silent. Now was not the time to hammer a spike into the attorney-client relationship.

"Let me tell you what they have on you." LeDoux referred to a page of notes he had earlier prepared. The notes were in his very careful and precise hand, and took up the better part of a page of a yellow legal pad. "First, they've got this kid. You know about that. Josh Gordon. Says he saw you and the Dailey girl in the street, near her house. That you placed her inside your camper, then drove off." Thibodoux looked as if he were about to speak, LeDoux thought, perhaps to correct something he'd said. Instead, he placed his hand over his mouth, and with his thumb and forefinger pinched at his nostrils waiting for LeDoux to continue.

"The kid is only ten. There's some indication that he may have recanted his first identification of you. That business with those people from your church. I haven't had a chance to talk to them yet."

"They'll help," said Thibodoux, taking a deep breath and puffing out his chest. "They're God-fearing people. If they say the boy's lying, then he's lying."

Thibodoux had the upright, spacey look of the true believer whose beliefs had been unjustly challenged. LeDoux wondered if the rest of the church members would come across as rigid. "I'll check them out," he said. "It'll be some time before the kid has to testify. A lot can happen in that time. You know that." Thibodoux deflated slightly and nodded. "Meanwhile, I don't expect that the D.A., I mean Green and the attorney general's office, will go along with any sort of bail."

Thibodoux shook his head slowly back and forth, appearing only mildly upset, reconciled to the fact that the prosecution thought him too much of a risk to agree to bail.

"As you know, on special-circumstance murders, the law provides for no-bail, if the judge feels it's appropriate." LeDoux paused momentarily, smiling to himself, thinking about all the cops he'd come to know over the years, and how, to a man, they favored the practice of refusing bail in serious cases. In general they were in favor of fewer rights for the accused, and substantially stiffer penalties upon conviction. Looking at the flat expression of disappointment on Ezekiel Thibodoux's face, LeDoux reflected that you had to actually be charged with a crime, dropped into the giant gear-wrenching machinery of the criminal justice system, before you truly appreciated the fact that constitutional protections served some useful purpose.

"In most cases," said LeDoux, "the judge goes along with the prosecution's request. Given the nature of this crime, your status, and the high publicity surrounding the trial, we'll make a request for bail, even a high bail, but don't be surprised if the judge doesn't go along with it."

Thibodoux waited for LeDoux to finish, then asked, "Why isn't the D.A. handling this case? What's the story with this Green?"

"Conflict of interest," said LeDoux. "That's why Green was there when you were picked up. Eli Lanier didn't want to handle it. Said his office has too many contacts with you, previous cases, deputies who know you too well."

"That's bullshit."

LeDoux was somewhat surprised at Thibodoux's choice of words. It didn't go with his deacon-like demeanor. "Yeah, you're right," said LeDoux. "It's political. But I don't see how it harms you. Green's a good lawyer, but he's not a dyed-in-the-wool prosecutor. Some of those guys, all they think about is getting a conviction. Cooperation with the defense is a concept they want nothing to do with. We shouldn't have that problem with Green."

"He's a friend of yours, isn't he?"

LeDoux tried not to smile. Thibodoux was asking a question, the answer to which, LeDoux was sure, he already knew. "We've handled some cases together," he said. "But don't expect any favors. This case is too high-profile for Green or anyone else to go out on a limb. He'll be fair, but I doubt whether he'll do you or me any favors."

Thibodoux nodded. LeDoux sensed that his client's mind was elsewhere, thinking down the line, perhaps, toward the trial. LeDoux removed the lab report from his file. "Maybe you could shed some light on this. They've analyzed a tool chest and some tools of yours." LeDoux kept a subtle eye on Thibodoux's reaction. The subtlety was unnecessary. Thibodoux suddenly jerked upright in his chair and slammed his palm on the table, drawing the attention of the deputy on the other side of the room. LeDoux motioned to the deputy that it was all right.

"What is it?" LeDoux waited for an answer. Thibodoux was staring at a spot somewhere on the wall over LeDoux's right shoulder, his eyes fixed, his teeth grinding in anger.

"You better tell me now," said LeDoux, leaning forward and lowering his voice, hoping that Thibodoux would take the hint. "I don't want any surprises in court, and neither do you."

"Is that the lab report?" asked Thibodoux. He was reaching for the copy of the report that rested on the desk between them. He picked it up and began reading, oblivious to everything except the words on the page. When he finished, he seemed to breathe more slowly. He tossed the report onto the table and grinned nervously. "They've got nothing," he said. "Absolutely nothing."

"I agree," said LeDoux, but he was concerned about his client's initial reaction to the existence of the report. "Can you tell me why the cops might think that these tools are important?"

Thibodoux shook his head. "Nope."

The answer had come too quickly. LeDoux had seen it before, and knew that his client was holding back, lying. LeDoux cleared his throat, preparing for another violent reaction. He continued, "The tools were brought to the cops by your daughter, Mary Esther."

Thibodoux remained calm, at least on the outside. He pursed his lips looking downward, then back at LeDoux. "Stupid girl," he muttered. "Both she and her mother . . ." Thibodoux cut himself short, clearly deciding, for the moment at least, not to take LeDoux any further into his confidence.

LeDoux noticed the shift in gears. It was common with defendants to fill their attorneys in on the actual truth in drips and drabs, as the defendants saw fit. The problem with this practice was that it often led to the lawyer's being surprised at the time of trial because of information not disclosed to them by the client. The inevitable bottom line of this practice was that the client suffered.

"Listen," said LeDoux, easing back in his chair. He could feel the perspiration on his back begin to trickle uncomfortably down toward the waistband of his pants. The room had the fruity-stale odor of too many unwashed human bodies. "I know you probably know all this, but I'm going to say it anyway. If you want me to represent you, you've got to be totally truthful with me. Not just what *you* want me to know, but everything. I'll decide what is and is not important." He leaned back, giving Thibodoux his I-don't-give-a-shit nonchalant routine. "Now I can go into this thing only knowing part of the story, if that's what you want. It's fine with me if you don't want to tell me the whole thing. I can't crawl into your brain and pull out the facts. There's no way I can force you to tell me the truth. But what you have to understand, Mr. Thibodoux—Zeke—is that it's only going to hurt you. I won't be the one going to jail if I screw up at trial because you failed to tell me something that *you* didn't feel I should know. Do we understand each other?"

Thibodoux nodded. He still seemed focused on something other than their conversation.

"Now," said LeDoux, wanting to say something that would get, and keep, his client's attention, "since we're getting all the bad news out in the open, you should know that they've executed a search warrant for your psychiatrist's office." LeDoux looked Thibodoux straight on, glad to see that wherever Thibodoux had been previously, this last bit of information had jerked him to attention.

LeDoux continued, "I haven't seen all the information they obtained from . . . Dr. Hirsch, is it?" Thibodoux was silent, an angry red color visibly rising into his face from his neck. "But, just on the basis that Hirsch is a psychiatrist and you had a physician-patient privilege with the man, we're going to challenge the sufficiency of the warrant, and the ultimate admissibility of the records at the time of trial." LeDoux waited, hoping that Thibodoux would fill in the blanks. He didn't. "What are they likely to come up with from your psychiatrist's office?"

Thibodoux thought of his last conversation with Samuel Hirsch. This was what he had been concerned about. Stupid. Now he had been stupid and careless on more than one occasion. It was beginning to look like a pattern. He wondered to himself why it was happening. He had always been so precise in the past, so careful.

"I had some problems with my job," said Thibodoux. "Hirsch thought it was stress. Job-related stress."

"Well," said LeDoux, "that, if anything, will help you in front of a jury. The sympathy factor. If that's all they come up with, the psychiatrist's stuff will be no big deal." LeDoux paused. He could see that Thibodoux had drifted off again. There was much, he thought, that Ezekiel Thibodoux was choosing to hold back. LeDoux hoped, for his client's sake, that Thibodoux didn't hold back for too long.

"From the looks of it," said LeDoux, readying to leave, "the Gordon kid is the strength of the prosecution's case. If his I.D. is tainted, even in the slightest, you have a good chance of beating this thing at the preliminary hearing. I want you to start thinking about what you were doing on the date the girl was kidnapped. Be specific. I want a list of anyone who could corroborate your alibi for that date and time."

Thibodoux nodded in agreement. "No problem," he said. "I'm innocent. Francis Powell and his friends will regret their decision to do this to me. I've spent my entire career in the department helping to put child molesters behind bars. It's an outrage that this should be happening to me." He paused, looking to LeDoux for confirmation. "You believe that, don't you?"

"Of course," said LeDoux. He had heard similar strenuous and apparently heartfelt protestations of innocence before. His response was automatic. "Meanwhile," he said, "I'll get in touch with Green. I've got an understanding with him about informal discovery. Still, it doesn't hurt to remind him every so often. If he's got something more, I want to find out about it as soon as possible. We'll get you arraigned next week, and set a prelim date." LeDoux stood, bringing his briefcase up from the floor and placing it on the table between them.

Thibodoux remained seated. "Let me ask you something," he said. He was stroking at his upper lip with his finger, looking at the cigarette-scarred surface of the wood desk. "This Green . . . He's the one that lost his daughter a few years back, isn't he?"

LeDoux hesitated. His mind quickly flashed on the Rashid James trial. Not only had he represented the codefendant, but he had also ultimately been involved in the arrest and conviction of the presiding judge Walter Sconce. LeDoux had gone to visit Ben afterward at the convalescent home, after Ben's breakdown, but had found his friend's drug-induced indifference too difficult to handle. LeDoux wondered why Thibodoux had chosen to bring up the incident at this particular moment.

"Yes," answered LeDoux. "Three years ago. His teenage daughter was on her way out to see him. She was found raped and murdered near Barstow."

"They never caught the guy, as I remember," said Thibodoux.

"That's right."

"And Green, he was hospitalized, flipped out. Put out of commission for quite a while afterward."

LeDoux didn't answer. "Why do you ask?"

"Oh, nothing," said Thibodoux. A small smile turned the corners of his mouth, then was gone. "Just curious."

Ben had heard of the place, but it was Claire that insisted they try it. She kept track of interesting restaurants like some people calendared their monthly car and insurance payments. Tonight it was the Bistro Gardens at Coldwater. The place had just opened to rave reviews in the newspapers, and reservations were already nearly two weeks in the waiting. Ben hoped Claire's choice would be a good one since the restaurant was conveniently located, on the south side of Ventura Boulevard, just a stone's throw down Coldwater Canyon from the house.

They entered to a wide foyer furnished with flower-laden antique sideboards. On one of the sideboards was a huge cornucopia of fresh vegetables centered between two large porcelain bowls, one filled with a mound of artichokes, the other filled with fresh fruit. Further down the foyer, on the right, was the bar, done in conservative wood tones that matched the trim throughout the spacious interior. Opposite the bar, and occupying the entire left side of the restaurant, were two large dining rooms. The far room had an atrium ceiling, giving the effect of an oversized conservatory. Around the perimeter of the room were French doors and windows open to the cool early-evening air, adding to the pleasant garden effect. In the other, slightly smaller room, the soffitted ceiling had been painted with a mural of intertwining pastel vines and flowers. The twilight breeze whispered through an open French window, rustling the corners of the nearby tablecloths. Ben got a good feeling from the place, and hoped that the food and service were up to par with the ambience.

"Order a drink," said Claire, after the maitre d' had shown them to a table in the far corner of the smaller dining room.

"That bad, huh?"

"Worse. But nothing out of the ordinary."

"It's the Thibodoux case," he said, opening his menu and quickly glancing over the numerous entrées. He thought he'd been doing a pretty good job of hiding his concern. But Claire seemed to notice even the slightest shift in his moods. He spotted the waiter and motioned toward him.

"Some white wine?" Ben asked over the top of the menu.

Claire nodded. She was busy reading.

"An Absolut, straight up with a twist," he said. The waiter just listened, not writing down the order. "And a bottle of Johannisberg Reisling. Château St. Michelle, if you have it."

"We do, sir." The waiter bowed slightly at the waist and moved quickly toward the bar. They waited in silence for a few moments, each reading over the extensive menu. After a few minutes, the waiter arrived with Ben's Absolut, along with the wine. They both watched as the waiter, a young man with long sandy-blond hair pulled neatly back in a ponytail, deftly opened the bottle of wine and offered it to Ben to taste. Ben motioned that Claire would do the tasting, which she did. The usual ritual finally finished, the young man with the ponytail placed the bottle in an ice bucket, smiled, and left them to their drinks.

"Ezekiel Thibodoux come up with any surprises at his arraignment today?" Claire sipped at her wine.

Ben thought how utterly perfect she looked. She'd recently changed the color of her hair, adding highlights that seemed to enhance the softness of her complexion, its fragility. She still wore her golden-flecked auburn hair just below shoulder-length. It had a natural-looking wave as it caressed the area between shoulder and cheek. He couldn't remember whether that had been added by her hairdresser or not. Either way, it looked good. With warm, welcoming eyes, she smiled and placed her hand atop his. It was her way of relaxing him, getting him to relax. Her fingers felt smooth. Cool and delicate. She played on the web of his hand with the tip of a polished nail, gently stroking back and forth. He found it surprisingly exciting.

"He's got Lucky LeDoux. Did I already mention that?"

She nodded, taking another sip of wine.

"Yeah, well, LeDoux tried to get bail set on the guy, but the judge would have none of it. I don't think Lucky actually expected he'd win that one. One of those deals where you have to ask anyway in the hope that it'll help the next time around."

Claire said, "Like they say on TV, in the basketball games, where the coach argues with the referee every call, even though he knows he's going to lose the argument, so that he might get the next call, right?"

"Something like that." Ben smiled, surprised that she'd remembered that. "We've got a prelim date in two weeks. I need to talk to Josh Gordon again, make sure he knows what he's supposed to say."

"What about those church people? I thought they got the boy to renege on his statement."

"Not as far as I can tell. Of course, they won't talk to me. But the kid and his parents say Josh told them no such thing. Maybe Thibodoux's church cronies just heard what they wanted to hear."

"And the girl, Thibodoux's daughter? What about her?"

Ben saw the waiter moving their way. "That's what I've been thinking about. I think she's the key to the whole case. I'm convinced there's a lot she hasn't told me. She's petrified at the thought of going up against her father."

They interrupted their conversation to place their orders. When the waiter left, Ben said, "I think Mary Esther—that's Thibodoux's youngest, the one that brought in the tool chest—recognized the face in the pictures."

Claire was buttering a roll. "The ones she said she saw her father with in the garage?"

"That's right. We got a warrant and tore the place apart, but he must have already gotten rid of them. I think she knew the face, though. I think, from her expression, that she recognized Erin Dailey as the little girl in the photograph."

"But she's afraid to say."

Ben nodded. "Uh huh. Apparently Thibodoux's been molesting Mary Esther, along with her older sister. I haven't had a chance to talk to the older sister. We're still trying to locate her. There's supposedly a son, Thibodoux's firstborn. Nobody in the family knows his whereabouts. He left home about a year ago after a knock-down-drag-out fight with his father. According to Mary Esther and her mother, Thibodoux had his way with both daughters, maybe even the son."

Claire's face took on an expression of shocked disbelief. She put the buttered piece of roll back on her bread plate, and asked, incredulously, "And the mother knew all this was going on and did nothing to stop it?"

"Probably. It's typical, though. She figured she needed him too much to turn him in. The family breadwinner, father figure, her lover. And even if she had tried to tell someone, who'd believe her? I mean, Zeke Thibodoux is an experienced, respected detective for the Los Angeles Police Department. He ruled that family with an iron fist. She probably thought that in addition to losing her husband, if she had said anything about what he'd done to the children, he would have beaten both her and the kids senseless. Mary Esther said he'd done it before."

"So she just closed her eyes to the whole thing."

"Unfortunately, that happens all too often in incest cases. We're lucky in this one, though. If it weren't for Mary Esther Thibodoux, we wouldn't have the toolbox, or the information about Thibodoux's Polaroids. The toolbox, so far, has not proven too useful. But the lab boys are still working on it." Ben finished the rest of his vodka and raised his glass, motioning to the waiter for another.

"Are you going to call the daughter to testify at the prelim?"

"I'd like to," said Ben. "Except right now she's too scared of her father to testify. And believe me, Ezekiel Thibodoux is well aware of that. He figures all we got is the testimony of Josh Gordon, which LeDoux can attack at the time of trial. Without something concrete to tie him to the Dailey girl, Thibodoux knows he's got a good chance of skating. He figures there's no way that his daughters or his wife will come forward to testify against him."

"Controls them even from behind bars, huh?"

"I'm working on that part," said Ben, then thanked the waiter for the new drink. He sipped the icy-cold liquid from the rim. "I don't want to push the girl too hard. If I work with her, stay patient, I'm convinced she'll tell me more. She's got it all in her head, all I have to do is figure a way to get inside. That means getting her over her fear of her father." Ben took another sip of his vodka, gazing out the window toward the street. "If I could just get her to identify the face in the Polaroids, then maybe the whole thing with the toolbox and the psychiatrist's records would fall into place."

The waiter was once again moving toward their table, this time laden with plates on one of his outstretched arms. He carefully placed the food in front of them, turning the plates for a precise presentation. Claire had ordered escargot in puff pastry that looked scrumptious. Ben, as usual, had smoked salmon, which arrived with capers, onions, chopped egg, and small toasted triangles of bread. They both dove into the food.

After a few minutes of silence in which they were too busy devouring their appetizers to speak, Claire leaned back in her chair, dabbed at the corners of her mouth with her napkin, and took a sip of wine. "Sara left a message on the machine today," she said, acting as if the call were of no particular consequence, but, at the same time, closely observing Ben's response.

Ben stopped eating, but only momentarily, then took a large bite of the open-faced lox sandwich he'd constructed. "Oh?" He was chewing, seemingly not intent on what Claire had said.

"You sent her a check, didn't you?"

He nodded, scooping up some errant capers with the corner of his toast. He maneuvered them atop the bread, only to have them roll off.

"She said you needn't have done it. That she'd already paid for the repairs to the grave site."

"I know," said Ben, giving up on the capers and placing the toast on his plate. He wiped at his mouth. "I just thought it was the right thing to do. There's no reason why Sara should have to face this thing alone. It's only money. That's the least I could do, since she was the one who had to make the actual arrangements. It's nothing, really." He went back to his smoked salmon.

Claire said, choosing her words carefully, "You know what this week is, don't you?"

"I do," he answered, still eating, not looking at her.

She knew it would be better out in the open. They had an unstated pact about such things since Ben's confinement in the convalescent home and his shutting her out of his life in the months thereafter. No more secrets. No more allowing worries and concerns to stew inside until they tainted and soured the way they looked at life, and each other.

"She'd be eighteen this week," said Claire. "Sara mentioned it in her message." Now it was Claire's turn to avoid his eyes. She busied herself with the rest of her escargot. Ben reached for her free hand, waiting for her to bring it up from her lap. She offered it immediately. He gripped her fingers firmly, surrounding her hand in his. When Claire looked up, she saw that his eyes had become glassy. Ben quickly swiped at the corner of his right eye with his fingertip. But it had missed the mark. A small tear, not yet large enough to drop, had formed and was about to fall.

Ben released her fingers and with both hands brought the napkin to his mouth and nose. Then, with a casualness that betrayed the gravity of his concern, as if it were an afterthought—though Claire knew that it wasn't—he dabbed at his eyes with the napkin.

"I gotta stop drinking these things," he said, lifting his vodka and examining the contents. He motioned to the waiter for another. "It's always worse," he said, "after a few drinks. The defenses drop off, I guess."

In a way, Ben treasured such moments, as painful as they were. He'd managed over the years to erect something akin to the Great Wall when it came to his feelings for his daughter. Self-preservation. He found the existence and maintenance of the wall necessary if he wanted to be able to go about his daily life with any semblance of sanity.

But in these moments when his defenses were down, with Claire, after a few vodkas to relax him, he felt Julie's presence as strongly as he had three years ago on that misty gray-fogged morning when the Highway Patrol officer had given him the shattering news. As strongly as he had felt her loss that November day riding his bicycle down Pacific Coast Highway.

It was as if Julie were still there, inside him. That during such moments she took over his entire being. The doctors had said that such feelings would wane. And it was true, that with the passage of time, such moments, even with the inductive effect of the liquor, had become increasingly rare. Yet still, Julie's face, her presence, remained. At times so close to the surface that Ben was unable to distinguish present from past, reality from memory.

Ben sipped carefully from the new drink. He looked around the room, his eyes resting momentarily on a soft pink rose painted on the ceiling above. "So far," he said, "I like this place." There were some memories, he thought, that were better left unspoken. Claire knew his mind. She followed his every emotion. He could see it in her eyes as she carefully watched him, checking for the signs.

"Good martini?" she offered, gripping his fingers in her fist.

He shrugged an uneasy smile. "Great. Just great."

CHAPTER 14

"All right, gentlemen. I've read the briefs on this issue and I'm ready to rule if there's no further argument." E. Harrison Phipps reclined magisterially against his high-backed leather judge's chair, linking his fingers behind his head, gently rocking back and forth. Phipps had been assigned the Ezekiel Thibodoux preliminary hearing and the prehearing evidence motions. Both Ben and Antoine LeDoux had submitted written briefs on the admissibility of Dr. Samuel Hirsch's psychiatric records dealing with his treatment of Ezekiel Thibodoux. Both attorneys had made their preliminary oral presentations to the court. E. Harrison Phipps, in all of his silvery-haired judicial beneficence, had appeared to patiently and carefully digest each and every word, though both Ben and Lucky knew that Phipps had probably made up his mind after reading the first paragraph of the People's brief. Phipps had spent twenty years as a Los Angeles County sheriff's deputy, reaching the rank of lieutenant before entering law school. After obtaining a law degree, Phipps went straight into the D.A.'s office where he served another ten years prior to being appointed to the municipal court by the then Republican governor. Phipps was the judge to whom the cops and D.A.s took all their weak search warrants for signature. He was a law-enforcement man through and through, and was willing to stretch the law and the rules of evidence past the breaking point if it meant sustaining the prosecution's position on an important issue.

Lucky LeDoux could have filed an affadavit against Phipps under Section 170.6 of the Code of Civil Procedure, disqualifying the judge from hearing the Thibodoux case. He had one to use, and could assert it without having to show that Phipps was actually prejudiced against either his client or himself. The fact that LeDoux had decided against this option was the result of his fear that he could end up with someone even worse presiding over the preliminary hearing, and his gut feeling that maybe Phipps would identify with Ezekiel Thibodoux, a longtime cop wrongly accused.

"I would just point out one more time to the court," said LeDoux, "that under Evidence Code Section 1014, there is a psychotherapist-patient privilege that operates here. The legislature has seen fit to treat this privilege differently than the physician-patient privilege, and has specifically allowed it to apply to criminal proceedings. I would submit to the court that that in itself is evidence of the legislative intent that this privilege be afforded wide latitude, and that any exceptions to its operation be scrutinized very carefully." LeDoux paused, looking down at his notes. He had made the same point twice already, once in his written brief, and then again in his first oral argument. He wanted to be absolutely sure that the record of the defense position was clear on appeal. From the disgruntled look that Phipps had given him during his first oral argument, Lucky had the feeling that if he were to prevail on this issue, it would be on appeal, and not in the courtroom of E. Harrison Phipps.

"As the law specifies," LeDoux continued, "the holder of the privilege is Mr. Thibodoux, the patient. Dr. Hirsch, without approval otherwise by my client, was obligated to assert the privilege and refuse the disclosure of any confidential communications made by my client, his patient, during the course of their sessions together. The nature of the records before the court does not rise to the level of any exception to this privilege. They are ambiguous at best. And, I would respectfully submit, the records are merely indicative of a hardworking, conscientious law-enforcement officer who is feeling the stress of his job and has, quite admirably I must point out, sought professional help to deal with that stress." LeDoux looked over at his client, who was seated quietly next to him. Thibodoux remained head down, gazing at the dark wood of the counsel table, only occasionally glancing upward at his attorney or the judge.

"As for the search warrant," said LeDoux, "it is the defendant's contention that any alleged consent proffered by Dr. Hirsch was done under the pressure of the officers, Mr. Green and Mr. Chen, and the existence of the warrant itself. That is, were it not for Dr. Hirsch's awareness that a search warrant existed, he would not have consented to the search of his office and records. Thus, it is not truly a voluntary consent, and the search of the office should stand or fall on the sufficiency of the warrant, which, as I have amply argued in my written brief, is shockingly deficient under the cases." LeDoux sat down, smoothing his tie and checking the position of the knot under his collar. He then shot his cuffs from his suit coat, one arm at a time, and folded his hands in front of him. For Lucky LeDoux, always fashion-conscious, this argument, like most, was a matter of business, nothing more, nothing less. Ben had rarely seen LeDoux become personally involved or sincerely emotional about any case. The shocked looks, well-timed gasps, even the occasional tear, were all preplanned theatrics to advance the interests of his clients.

"Briefly, Your Honor," said Ben. He waited until E. Harrison Phipps had made the short swivel in his chair and was facing the prosecution side of the table. "I'll not reiterate matters previously argued and briefed by counsel. The court has heard the testimony of Officer Chen and of Dr. Hirsch on the consent issue." Ben paused, checking Phipp's reaction.

Hirsch's moment on the witness stand had been touch and go. The doctor had testified truthfully about the circumstances of the search, but, Ben thought, even Samuel Hirsch was still somewhat confused as to his motives for acceding to the search of his office without asserting the privilege. Ben figured Hirsch was having trouble making up his mind on the issue. The law required that he, as a psychiatrist, disclose to the police or a threatened party information obtained by him in the psychotherapist-patient relationship, if this information posed a reasonable threat to a third party. The law was designed to give to the police and threatened third parties notice of a possible impending attack by mental patients. Psychiatrists walked a thin line in deciding whether their clients' threats were reasonably likely to occur, and thus should be reported, or whether such threats were merely fluff, and thus not worth breaching the psychotherapist-patient rapport, and incurring a possible civil suit by the clients for disclosing confidential communications.

Ben continued, "Under *Tarasoff,* there is the dangerous-patient exception to the psychotherapist-patient privilege. I would submit that the records of Mr. Thibodoux's communications that the court has heard, the references to the children and the killing of the children, along with the rest, is sufficient, under *Tarasoff,* to bring this case within the exception. Under Evidence Code Section 1024, and Welfare and Institutions Code 5328, the confidential communications between the defendant and Dr. Hirsch are excepted from the privilege and are thus admissible against the defendant."

Ben sat down, thinking about the awkwardness of having to prosecute a case that he was personally involved in. He and Francis Powell had discussed this problem in the beginning, and Powell had insisted that Ben wear both hats. Ben had gotten through this hearing by having Frank Chen testify to the search. He made a mental note to make sure that Frank was around in the future to handle any additional investigation so that he wasn't forced into the position of being a witness in the Thibodoux prosecution. As it was, he already was playing fast and loose with the canons of professional ethics prohibiting an attorney from being a witness in his own case.

"Very well, gentlemen. Here's how I see it." Phipps had rocked into an upright position and was peering down at the counsel table. A lock of silvery hair fell out of place and rested in a loose curl in the center of his forehead. His voice rang out with the authority of someone who harbored no doubts as to the certainty of his position. It was a trick Phipps had learned in his early days in law enforcement: sound like you know what you're doing, like you're in control, and the slugs and slimeballs will believe that you are. Phipps had taken this approach with him when he became a judge, often overpowering witnesses and even some attorneys into agreeing with his views by the mere decibel level of his voice.

Judge Phipps went on to state what both Ben and LeDoux had expected. He ruled that the search of Samuel Hirsch's office was the result of the voluntary consent given by the doctor, and that the search warrant was thus rendered moot. Phipps went on to rule that Dr. Hirsch, under the *Tarasoff* case and statutory exceptions, had no obligation to assert the psychotherapist-patient privilege, and that, in fact, the communications between Ezekiel Thibodoux and his psychiatrist were admissible. After rendering his ruling, Phipps announced that the court would take a recess in the Thibodoux case until after lunch, at which time testimony in the preliminary hearing would begin.

"I'll see you in the court of appeals," LeDoux said to Ben, smiling and packing his briefcase. Judge Phipps had left the bench, and most of the spectators had exited the courtroom. Ezekiel Thibodoux was being led into the custody lockup by the court bailiff.

"Perhaps, Lucky. Perhaps." Ben watched as LeDoux pushed through the swinging double doors that led out to the courtroom corridor. Ben was concerned with the fate of this case on appeal. But, like most prosecutors, he had determined to do the best job possible at the trial level of presenting all the evidence he could possibly get introduced, and worry about the appeal when it happened. He knew that you could drive yourself crazy, as a trial lawyer, trying to second-guess what some appeals court might do with the case. Besides, Ben needed the evidence of Samuel Hirsch's conversations with his patient for the preliminary hearing. As it stood, even with that evidence, the case against Ezekiel Thibodoux was not the strongest. Josh Gordon had been showing the strain of being a child subjected to the limelight and public scrutiny that being a star witness in a high-publicity murder trial brought. The media had hounded the young boy and his family for the past few weeks, and Ben was fearful that the boy, under cross-examination, might hedge or change his testimony.

Ben had arranged for Josh, along with Mary Esther Thibodoux, to be kept on ice in separate rooms inside the attorney general's offices, under the supervision of two of the more maternal secretaries. The secretaries had been instructed to keep the children pleasantly occupied until it was the boy's turn to testify.

Ben intended to put Josh Gordon on the stand, though he knew that he'd never be able to convince Mary Esther to testify against her father. At least not yet. Bringing her to court was part of a plan he had to try and get inside the teenage girl's mind, get her to trust him enough to open up. He was still convinced that she held the secret to slamming the door on Ezekiel Thibodoux. The fact that Thibodoux had molested both of his female children would be damning evidence against him, but was also of questionable admissibility. While it wasn't difficult to find a judge to go along with the prosecution's position on close issues at the pre-trial stage, Ben was well aware that such issues could very likely become harder to win at trial. The superior court bench had its share of E. Harrison Phipps types, but there was also a good number of judges whose political and judicial philosophies were not aligned with the prosecution.

Ben was starting to feel the pressure. Erin Dailey's parents occupied their usual position in the front row of the audience section, silently looking on, watching his every move. He felt as if he could sense their expectations rise and fall, every breath they took, as the cumbersome legal process slowly rolled toward its conclusion. Their child was gone. Snatched from them by a killer of unimaginable violence. That she had been killed was crushing in itself. That the small child had been sexually tortured and beheaded was, for all concerned, almost too difficult to even speak of.

When Ben looked back, they were still there, seated in the back section of the courtroom. The husband held his wife's head gently against his shoulder. Her eyes were turned downward, but Ben could see that she had been crying. Ben didn't recall having ever seen her any other way. Her husband was patting her cheek, whispering soothing words. He looked up, glanced for a brief moment at Ben, and tried a smile, which quickly turned into a grimace of resignation. Ben averted his eyes. He headed for the door, hoping that Josh Gordon would come through at the preliminary hearing.

Cobb salads in Francis Powell's office. Powell was on a diet, as usual, but Ben didn't mind since he had the Thibodoux prelim in the afternoon and he didn't want to chow down at lunch and then fight falling asleep at the counsel table.

"So, how goes the battle?" Powell was shifting pieces of lettuce and turkey around, picking out the small pieces of bacon to eat first. Outside the large picture windows of the Chief's office, Ben could barely make out the contour of mountains in the distance. Brownish-gray humps behind smoky clouds. The smog had crept in during the early morning, so that by lunch, with the aid of increasing temperatures and millions of freeway commuters, a gray shroud, like a lethal steambath, was choking the city, its suffocating smoke blanketing downtown Los Angeles.

There was coffee in a ceramic carafe on Francis Powell's desk. On a matching serving platter stood two tall glasses filled with ice, and two cans of Diet Coke. Ben popped the top on one of the cans and poured, waiting for the foamy caramel-colored head to subside before taking a sip.

"It's going okay," he said, smacking his lips. The cola had a sickening-sweet taste when mixed with the salad's bleu cheese dressing. Ben returned the glass to the serving platter. "Phipps ruled in our favor."

"Big surprise," said Powell, chuckling. He sucked at his teeth, then swiped at his mouth with a cloth napkin.

"Once a cop, always a cop." Ben smiled.

"And the kid?"

"We'll find out this afternoon. If he comes through with

any semblance of a reliable I.D., it'll be enough to get us through the prelim."

"No luck with Thibodoux's daughter?"

Ben shook his head. "I have her over at the offices, just in case. Though I don't expect she'll testify. I wanted another chance to talk with her. Maybe bring her to court just to watch. I think she knows a lot she's not telling. She hates her father, but she's also petrified of him. That parental authority runs deep. If I could just get her over that fear, get her to trust me . . ."

"In time," said Powell. "We'll get Thibodoux held-to-answer this afternoon. No way Phipps is going to cut him loose. That'll give us a couple of weeks until the superior court arraignment. By the time LeDoux runs his 995, the lab boys might have come up with something on the toolbox. And maybe Thibodoux's kid'll decide that she wants to testify."

Powell, having eaten all the chunks of bacon and pieces of bleu cheese, threw his napkin on his desk and pushed the remainder of uneaten salad aside. Ben thought there was something tired showing in his friend's face. That old spark, the edge of aggression that had been a Francis Powell trademark, had softened. Perhaps it was the two lost mayoral elections, the inevitable emotional scar tissue of so many political battles won and lost over the years. Or maybe it was Powell's failed marriage, the sacrifice of any sort of meaningful personal life in exchange for his years in the public eye. Not for the first time that week, Ben realized that most of his friends were, like himself, aging, and that the daily battles in the courtrooms and the streets were being left to a younger generation that would soon completely replace them.

"How are things, Francis?"

"Whadya mean, 'things'?"

"You know what I'm talking about, Francis. There's life outside of this office. Neither of us is getting any younger, and I can't believe that my old friend Francis Powell is satisfied with punching a clock and living half a life."

"What do you know about my life?" asked Powell, jokingly. "I got a life. I got plenty of life."

"Yeah, so tell me about it."

"It ain't none of your business, Green."

"Because it doesn't exist."

"Aw, shit, Ben. Whadya expect? A guy like me, my age . . . I can't go out trolling the singles bars. Shit, that'd look real good on the cover of the *Enquirer*, wouldn't it!"

"But there's somebody?"

"There's somebody," said Powell, gazing out the window, lost in thought. "Not real serious. But it could be. Neither of us are in a hurry to tie the knot. Divorce can do that to you."

Ben nodded. He hadn't known that Powell was seeing someone. They had once been intimately acquainted with each other's social life. Over the years that had changed. Francis Powell had moved rapidly up the L.A.P.D. hierarchy and ended up as chief. The passing of time, and Powell's increasing responsibilities, had pulled them apart. Ben was no longer familiar with what Francis Powell did after he left Parker Center. It made Ben think about the Arnie Rosen murder case and his surprise when he'd learned that Powell had been using him, keeping him in the dark at the insistence of the FBI. Ben recalled the resentment he'd felt at finding that out. He had gotten over that eventually, understanding that his boss had had no choice in the matter. Still, it pointed out the void in understanding that had developed over the years between the two.

"You wouldn't be pulling another Jonathan Racine number on me, would you, Francis?"

Powell's brow furrowed. Then he smiled, reaching into his coat pocket for his cigarettes. "There's a blast from the past." He thrust the cigarette between his lips and lit it in what seemed to Ben as one motion. Then, sucking at the cigarette, Powell rolled his head back and blew a plume of smoke at the ceiling. "Jonathan Racine . . ." he said, as if speaking to one of the ceiling tiles. "Your poetry friend. I wonder whatever became of him."

"Probably living in some sleepy little podunk village under an assumed name, wondering if the mob is getting any closer to finding him." Ben thought of his conversations with Racine, and how the bookseller had had to go underground after testifying against the mob. Ben still had the book of Robert Frost poems that Racine had sent him.

Powell smiled. "I hope, for his sake," he said, "that those Federal Witness Protection boys have got their act cleaned up since the Rosen murder. And, to answer your question, no, I'm not holding anything back on this case. I wish I were. I wish I had something important to hold back, 'cause the way this thing looks, unless we get lucky with Thibodoux's kid, or something else develops, we're going to have a hard time convicting the son of a bitch."

"Tell me about it, Francis." Ben thought of the scores of Thibodoux supporters, members of his church, that had lined the perimeter of the corridor outside Judge Phipps' courtroom. Phipps had allowed some of them inside the courtroom, but the great majority, as a show of support for Thibodoux, had kept a vigil while court was in session, standing shoulder to shoulder around the perimeter of the sixth floor of the Criminal Courts Building. It was a media show of the highest order, and Thibodoux's supporters knew it. While Ben and LeDoux battled inside the court, the TV cameras whirred away outside, taking in the entire carnival-like scene for the six o'clock news.

"Don't let those religious fanatics get to you, Benny. They've tried this sorta shit before. It's good for a day or two, then the TV people lose interest. Besides, the prelim'll be over by this afternoon, tomorrow at the latest. Let 'em have their time in the spotlight. It's no big deal. Makes 'em look like the kooks and screwballs that they are."

The disclosure of the Samuel Hirsch information had had little, if any, effect on public support for Ezekiel Thibodoux. The problem was that Thibodoux's tape-recorded ramblings, some under hypnosis, were lacking in specifics. While Thibodoux talked about "all the young children," and the tragedy of their dying, he mentioned no names, no specifics as to how they had died. As Ben realized the first time he heard the tapes and reviewed Hirsch's notes, the ambiguity of the material cut both ways. For his supporters, Thibodoux's plaintive, almost hysterical cries on tape were cries for help from a man who had been traumatized by a life of trying to right a sick society's disgusting and horrendous callousness and cruelty toward the constituent group least able to protect itself, its children.

While most people were adopting a wait-and-see attitude, Thibodoux's church supporters had mounted an aggressive campaign to use the media to bring across their position that a respected member of their flock, a deacon, was being unjustly accused.

So far, the tactics had had little effect on the case. Though Ben knew that as the prosecution wore on, the witnesses, especially Josh Gordon and Mary Esther Thibodoux, couldn't help but be intimidated by all of the public attention. It was the way the system worked. A delicate balance between opposing constitutional rights: the Thibodoux supporters' right to free speech, balanced against society's need to protect itself from killers. The defendant's right to confront and cross-examine the witnesses against him, in counterpoint with the concern that child witness not forever be traumatized and scared by the experience of testifying in court.

The system, Ben mused, usually worked. That is, the result was usually the appropriate one, even if certain parts of the more fragile legal and constitutional framework were less than artistically constructed. The first big test would be that afternoon, when Josh Gordon took the witness stand, hopefully, Ben thought, to identify Ezekiel Thibodoux as Erin Dailey's kidnapper.

CHAPTER 15

Judge Phipps leaned over toward the witness and in his softest voice said, "Now, young man, you realize this is a court of law, don't you?"

Josh Gordon nodded without speaking, and Phipps smiled.

"Josh, you must remember to answer any of my questions, and the questions of the lawyers, out loud. This pretty young lady here—" He pointed to the court reporter seated just in front of the witness. "—has to take down everything that is said. That means, if you shake your head—" Phipps began nodding then shaking his head to demonstrate. "—that the reporter cannot take that down. And she can't take down 'uh huhs' and 'un unhs.' Do you understand?"

Josh Gordon again nodded his head that he understood.

"Now see, you're doing it again." Phipps smiled, but it was evident in his expression that a thin layer of understanding and patience had been peeled off. "Now will you remember to answer all of the questions out loud?"

Josh started to nod his head, then squeaked a yes.

"And you understand, Josh, that you have taken an oath to tell the truth. Do you know the difference between the truth and a lie?"

Josh nodded, then quickly said, "Yes."

"Good," said Phipps. "And have your parents taught you that it's bad to tell a lie, and that you should always tell the truth?"

Josh nodded, and Phipps pointed an admonishing finger in his direction. "Yes," said Josh.

"And what have they told you happens to children who lie?"

"They get into trouble," said Josh.

"And will you always tell the truth here in court?"

"Yes."

Judge Phipps seemed satisfied, if not entirely pleased, that the seriousness of his inquiry had been understood by the young witness. "All right, Mr. Green," he said. "You may proceed with this witness."

Ben started slowly, hoping that Josh Gordon would get the feel for testifying, even come to like the attention. He'd walked the young boy through the empty courtroom the previous day, just to acquaint him with the setting. Ben had seen a number of child witnesses start out petrified, only to later come to enjoy the fact that, for once in their lives, all the adults in the room were listening carefully to what they said, even writing it down word for word.

Ben led Josh through the preliminary testimony, up to his observations of Ezekiel Thibodoux and his camper.

"Now, Josh, I want you to look around the courtroom, and tell me if you see in court the man you saw with the little girl on the day we've been talking about." Ben held his breath for a moment. No matter how sure he'd been that Josh would point to Thibodoux, there was always that split second of uncertainty, especially with a child witness, when you thought, *Oh, shit! He's not going to do it. The case has just gone down the crapper.*

Josh Gordon looked around the room, carefully avoiding making eye contact with Ezekiel Thibodoux. He then nodded his head. They had discussed the fact that Thibodoux would be seated at the counsel table, but Ben had been scrupulously careful not to lead the boy into identifying someone whom he did not recognize. A common trick of young prosecutors was to coach witnesses before coming into court, telling them that the defendant, who had or had not been previously identified, would be sitting at the counsel table. It was a dangerous practice since any experienced defense attorney would, on cross-examination, ask the witness whether he or she had discussed the case with the prosecutor prior to testifying, and whether the prosecutor had said anything to the witness about the defendant being in court and about pointing him out. It could prove very embarrassing in front of a jury, and, more importantly, could taint the witness' identification.

"Can you point him out, then, Josh?"

Josh pointed in Thibodoux's direction, then scooted back in his chair, as if trying to distance himself.

"Can you tell the court what he's wearing today, Josh?"

"He's the one with the beard," said Josh. "He's sitting next to the black guy with the gold watch."

Ben smiled, and Josh returned the smile. Even Antoine LeDoux had to chuckle. Ezekiel Thibodoux, though, remained stone-silent.

"Thank you, Josh. May the record reflect, Your Honor, that the witness has identified the defendant, Ezekiel Thibodoux?"

"The record will so reflect," said Phipps.

Ben went on to elicit from Josh Gordon his observations of Erin Dailey getting into Thibodoux's camper, and seeing the camper drive off. By the time he'd finished with his direct examination of the boy, Ben was convinced that Josh had turned the corner. Josh had acclimated himself to the microphone, pulling it to his mouth with every answer. Ben only hoped that this sense of confidence would continue through Lucky LeDoux's cross-examination.

Try as he might, LeDoux gained little ground trying to impeach the boy's identification. Josh was sure that it was Thibodoux he had seen with Erin Dailey, and that it was Thibodoux who had later sought to question him at his school. He remembered the beard, and the weird way, as Josh put it, the guy's eyes seemed to go in different directions.

"Can you tell us, Josh, what sort of shirt the person you've identified as Mr. Thibodoux was wearing the day you saw him with the little girl?"

"Uh, no. I don't remember."

"Well," said LeDoux, "was it light or dark? Can you tell us that?"

"Uh unh. I mean, no."

Ben would have adopted the same approach had he been Thibodoux's attorney. Few witnesses had photographic memories. Types and color of clothing, approximate weight and height often varied substantially between two witnesses who had identified the same face. In most situations, it was the face that people focused upon.

"And the pants," said LeDoux. "Can you tell us what color pants this man was wearing?"

"Uh, dark, I think."

"You think?"

"Well, yeah. I think they were dark. I'm not sure."

"You didn't get a good look, did you, Josh?"

"Uh, I guess not."

"And how tall would you say this man was that you saw?"

"Uh, I'm not too good at that. Tall though. Real tall."

"How tall would you say that I am, Josh?" LeDoux smiled, standing behind his seated client. LeDoux was about six feet, while Ezekiel Thibodoux, standing, was a good six to eight inches taller.

"I don't know," said Josh. He was looking to Ben for help.

"Well, Josh," said LeDoux, "was the man you saw helping the girl into the camper about my height?"

"Uh, yeah. You're pretty tall. He was about your height." Josh looked around, hoping that somebody would give him a signal that he'd given the right answer.

"No taller than me, though. Right?"

"Yeah."

"Now, Josh, these eyes that you mentioned . . . Can you look at Mr. Thibodoux now and tell me whether his eyes look the same today?"

Ben shot a quick glance at Thibodoux, who remained calmly seated at the counsel table, looking directly at the young witness. His eyes, to Ben, looked perfectly normal.

Josh looked at Thibodoux, then at Ben, then back at Thibodoux. He pursed his lips. Ben could see the discomfort beginning to take hold, the confidence he'd strived so hard to build in the young boy quickly waning.

"I—I'm not sure. Ya know, he looks okay today. I mean, normal, ya know."

"So Mr. Thibodoux, seated to my right, the defendant, does not have the same sort of eyes, the ones you described earlier, as the man you saw with Erin Dailey?"

"They're like it, but different. They don't go off like the other guy's. Maybe you could make him do that thing with his eyes and I could tell you whether it's the same."

Good boy, thought Ben. The fact that Ezekiel Thibodoux had some sort of control over his wayward eye was obvious to Ben. Damn smart kid. Cut through the legal mumbo jumbo and the courtroom tricks right to the core. LeDoux was playing games. Ben knew it. Phipps knew it. It was what defense attorneys and prosecutors did with witnesses: put words in their mouths. Except young Josh Gordon had, totally through his innocence of the system, revealed the guile in LeDoux's tactics.

"Uh, perhaps later," mumbled LeDoux, momentarily thrown off track. He continued on in the same vein, nitpicking with Josh Gordon about specific facial features, the shape of Thibodoux's beard, the manner in which he carried himself, until he'd exhausted the list of minutia pertaining to the young boy's identification. In the end, the identification stood, at least strong enough for Judge Phipps to bind Thibodoux over to the superior court for trial.

LeDoux had succeeded, though, in chipping away at the confidence of the child witness. The theory behind LeDoux's friendly badgering of the young boy was to make the courtroom experience one Josh Gordon would not soon forget. LeDoux's hope was that any uncertainty or intimidation he had created would adversely affect Josh's performance at trial.

Ezekiel Thibodoux seemed pleased with the day's events, and that surprised Ben. Thibodoux, Ben figured, must have considered Josh Gordon's performance less than stellar. A fact that Ben had to face was that Josh's identification was filled with holes that Lucky LeDoux would be quick to point out to a jury. While the boy had stood by his initial identification, he admitted that he'd had some doubts during a conversation with the press shortly after Thibodoux's arrest. Further, all of LeDoux's needling, while not that important to Judge Phipps, would have an effect on a jury. Especially considering the fact that Ezekiel Thibodoux was not the average sleazeball defendant with a record a mile long and a disposition that only a prison queen could love.

And then there was the issue about the admissibility of Samuel Hirsch's records. The fact that Ben had prevailed at this lower level in getting the records admitted would not be controlling at the time of trial. The trial judge in the superior court would not be constrained by the ruling of a lower municipal court judge. Ben could easily lose on that issue at trial, and be without the tapes and records obtained from Thibodoux's psychiatrist. The more Ben considered the pitfalls that lurked down the road, the more he understood why Ezekiel Thibodoux might feel there was a good deal to be hopeful about.

Ben watched as Thibodoux and LeDoux huddled at the end of the counsel table. Thibodoux listened carefully to his attorney's whispered advice. After a few moments, LeDoux packed up his belongings and left the courtroom.

When Thibodoux got up to leave, he smiled, then winked at Ben. He was playing with Ben. There was a split second when Ben thought he'd give Thibodoux some of the same. Instead, Ben averted his eyes to the back of the courtroom. To his surprise, Mary Esther Thibodoux was seated in the rear, quietly taking in the events transpiring at the counsel table. When Ben looked back at Thibodoux, the bailiff was behind him, securing the hand restraints. His expression of swaggering bravado had disappeared. In its place was anger. Shock and surprise seemed to burst from the man. Ben wondered at Thibodoux's self-control, since it was obvious that he was practically vibrating under the skin.

Something was happening. Something triggered by the fact that his daughter was in the courtroom. Ben motioned to the bailiff to hold off for a moment in taking Thibodoux back to the lockup. Ben removed the picture of Erin Dailey that he kept in his file. Her parents had given it to him. It had been her last school photo. He headed toward the back of the courtroom, careful to let Thibodoux get a good look at the photograph. Mary Esther stood when he reached her. Ben gently put his arm around her, holding the picture for her to see.

"This is a picture of the girl that was killed," he whispered. "I want you to think about the face, and I'll ask you later whether you remember ever seeing this face before. Do you understand?" Mary Esther nodded her head. Ben could see that the young girl recognized the face, but was still doubtful that she'd ever admit as much in open court. "You needn't tell me now," said Ben. "Just think about it."

Ben held the picture a few feet from the teenager's face. He was cognizant of the fact that their conversation was being closely observed, though unheard, by Ezekiel Thibodoux.

Ben said, "Just think about it, okay?" Mary Esther nodded once more, her head moving up and down as he pointed at the face in the photo. Ben smiled, looked up at Ezekiel Thibodoux, and winked. Then, with the cockiness of a world-class athlete, Ben strode confidently back to the counsel table, still careful to let Thibodoux see the photo. He tossed the photograph onto the counsel table for everybody to see, and motioned to the bailiff that he no longer needed the defendant's presence in the courtroom.

Ben was still smiling when from the other side of the closed lockup door, Ezekiel Thibodoux could be heard yelling for his lawyer.

Ben hadn't expected his little trick with the photograph and Mary Esther Thibodoux to yield such quick results. He'd done it as if on a dare, legal gamesmanship, Thibodoux's cocksure attitude getting the best of him. Ben had just wanted to get even. A game, a trial tactic that he hadn't expected would really accomplish anything. But it had.

He was seated in the attorney interview room downstairs in the Criminal Courts Building. All the custody defendants from the various courtrooms were being rounded up and placed in lines to go onto the buses that would take them back to the central jail for the evening.

Ben could see Thibodoux, standing off to the side, his hands cuffed together at his waist in front of him. Ben had been informed by the bailiff that Thibodoux was demanding to speak with both his attorney and the prosecutor. An unusual request, at least the prosecutor part. Had it been any other inmate, Ben figured, the bailiffs would have told him to shut up and save his requests for the next court appearance.

Ben informed the sheriffs in charge of the downstairs lockup to keep Thibodoux off the bus, but out of the interview room until the presence of Antoine LeDoux was secured. Ben was not about to hold a conversation with a defendant he was prosecuting without the presence of counsel. In fact, he figured he was probably wasting his time. That when Lucky LeDoux heard of his client's request, he'd quickly put the brakes to any sort of three-way conversation which included the prosecutor.

"What the fuck is going on here?" LeDoux had just been buzzed through the security door. He held his suit coat over his shoulder and had already loosened his tie. Ben's first thought was that it was the only time he recalled seeing Lucky LeDoux less than perfectly attired.

"Ask your client. Seems he wants to talk."

"Well," said LeDoux, huffing and walking toward the glass that separated the lockup from the attorney area of the interview room, "we'll see about that. Ben, will you excuse us for a moment?" Ben moved to the back of the room, out of earshot. He watched as the conversation between LeDoux and Thibodoux became increasingly animated. LeDoux normally exercised a good deal of control over his clients. They trusted him and paid dearly for his advice.

But Ezekiel Thibodoux was different. As Ben looked on, it appeared that Thibodoux was doing most of the talking, and LeDoux the listening. Finally, shaking his head in disgust, LeDoux swiveled on the wooden stool and motioned for Ben to join them.

"My client wants to talk to you," said LeDoux. His expression revealed his exasperation.

"You sure that's what he wants?"

LeDoux didn't answer. He merely looked at his client, who was nodding in the affirmative.

"And you have no objection?"

"Of course I have an objection," said LeDoux. "Except Mr. Thibodoux says he wants to talk to you. That he doesn't care that I have advised him not to do that. He doesn't care that anything he might say to you could be used against him at his trial. He doesn't care that by talking to you he might be signing himself right into Folsom, or worse."

Ben asked, "Is that right, Mr. Thibodoux?"

"I need to talk," said Thibodoux.

Ben went through the Miranda litany, just for the record. He called a sheriff's deputy over to witness the advisement and Thibodoux's waiver of rights. Throughout the entire advisement, Lucky LeDoux looked like a man who'd just been told he had only two days to live.

"All right," said Ben, having completed the advisement and obtained the appropriate waivers. "What is it you wanted to tell me?"

Thibodoux positioned himself upright on the wooden stool. There was a plate-glass window between them, and their voices were amplified through a speaker system incorporated into the window. The speaker system made the voices sound tinny, like a cheap radio. It reminded Ben of when he was a kid and used to listen to his parents' conversations from his bedroom by placing an empty glass against the wall.

Clearing his throat, Thibodoux said, "I have some information that I believe might be of interest to you."

Ben looked at LeDoux, who shrugged and turned the palms of his hands upward. "What sort of information?" asked Ben. "And what do you want in exchange?"

"We can talk about the exchange later," said Thibodoux, "when we get to the specifics." Thibodoux's bad eye went off to the side, giving his bearded face an eerie, almost frightening appearance. Ben wasn't sure whether he was being observed with the good eye, or whether Thibodoux had changed the focus of his expression to Lucky LeDoux. It didn't matter, though. Because the words that next came out of Ezekiel Thibodoux's mouth froze Ben motionless in time and place.

"I know who killed your daughter," said Thibodoux. "I know who killed Julie."

CHAPTER 16

Claire started her fingers spider-walking down from his stomach, her face gently nuzzling against his shoulder. Softly she caressed him, fingering the sensitive mound just below the head until he grew hard in her hand. Then she alternated, her hand moving quickly, gently massaging, then making quick up-and-down motions with her thumb and forefinger in a circle. Ben groaned and turned his face to kiss her on the forehead. His breathing became faster as he lifted his hips to meet her.

When he was almost there, Claire got onto her knees, bending over him. Her tongue darted around the head, flicking in lizard-like motions. Her other hand extended downward between his legs. His separate breaths became as one, and his entire body writhed in pleasure until, at last, he came.

Claire rested her head on his stomach, listening to the noises from inside, absentmindedly fondling him.

"If you plan on fucking me to sleep," he said, "I don't think it'll work." Then he quickly added, "But it's definitely worth a try."

Ben had told her about Ezekiel Thibodoux's bombshell. They had discussed it over dinner at home. What he should do, if anything. Whether it was worth entering into further discussions with Thibodoux. Whether Ben now had the most obvious and blatant conflict of interest and should withdraw from the case. Claire wished she could take the weight from his shoulders, make it easier for him.

"You need to sleep on it," she said. She knew that Ben would have to make the decision himself. He could talk to her and to Francis Powell about the pros and cons of proceeding against Thibodoux given this unexpected turn of events. About his second thoughts, his self-doubting. But in the end, the decision was his to make.

"LeDoux's talking about withdrawing," said Ben. "Says he didn't get paid enough to take the case to trial anyway. What I think is he feels almost as uncomfortable as I do with his client. You should have seen the look on Lucky's face when Thibodoux told me about Julie. You would have thought it was *his* daughter."

"He'll get another lawyer," said Claire. Her mind was beginning to drift with the onset of sleep. She wished she could take Ben with her, if just for the night. "There's bound to be someone out there who'll take the case just for the publicity."

"Lucky thinks Thibodoux will represent himself. Jesus . . . That's just what I need, a goddam *pro per* in a murder case!"

"Are you going to talk with him?"

"If he's *pro per,* I've got to. He'll be his own lawyer. I'll be forced to deal with him. Thibodoux's damn cagey. He would have realized that."

Claire could feel him starting to harden again. She continued to massage him.

"Why tell you now?" she asked. "Why not wait until he was sure of conviction?"

Ben thought of his little ploy with the photograph of Erin Dailey. One small legal gambit—a cheap lawyer's trick, for ego gratification more than anything else—had unleashed an unpredictable series of problems.

"He must have felt that his daughter would testify against him," said Ben. "That she'd identify the picture of the Dailey girl as the same person she'd seen in the Polaroids her father possessed. That, and the history of sexual abuse to his children, would just about nail shut the lid on any chances Thibodoux had of beating this thing. He knows what he's doing. Most guys in his position would deny the reality and try and tough it out. You have to remember that Zeke Thibodoux's been through this scenario dozens of times. He's seen lots of guys go off to prison for the rest of their lives because they were either too stupid, or too stubborn, or both, to see the writing on the wall early on. I guess Thibodoux's decided to try and limit his downside risk, thinking that we have him cold anyway. Guys do and say strange things when they're looking at the death penalty."

Ben paused. He had lost track of what he'd been saying. "You are amazing," he said, sighing with pleasure. "Where'd you learn how to do that?"

Claire giggled. She got up onto her knees beside him and pulled her top over her head, keeping her arms raised for a few moments so that her breasts were displayed to advantage. He reached over and caressed her nipples as she looked down, watching him. She could see him, hard and throbbing. She felt herself stiffen with his touch, first one nipple, then the other.

Ben gently brought her to him, kissing the colored circles of her breasts, like pale orange suns, holding the tips gently between his teeth. He supported her as she straddled him, her breasts brushing against his face, his lips. She slowly put him inside. She was already wet, and her first tentative thrusts further moistened them both. She extended herself fully, then back again, for a split second straining at the tip. He felt himself tingle as her body quivered. She brought herself downward, grinding against him, forcing him to fill her. Ben watched her, her eyes closed, rocking up and down. He gently guided her, aware that she was near, wanting her to finish before he did. He thought of other things, of Thibodoux and Julie, of the decision that he had to make. He thought of his confusion. Anything to keep his mind off his pleasure. Finally, the pleasure became too much to bear. She came in shallow soft screams, a rhythmic chanting noise. And he let himself go, sealing them both in the sticky warm residue of passion.

The next thing he knew it was dark, and from the window, a faint shaft of moonlight illuminated the bed in an uncertain glow. The clock read two A.M. At six, he would dress and head for the office. Claire was pressed up against him, her body filling in the contours of his, leaving no space in between. Ben listened to her faint snores of sound sleep, pleasant dreams. He stared at the ceiling, wondering if he could bear to pass the next four hours rehashing his decision.

"Lucky LeDoux's throwing in the towel." Francis Powell stood at the door to Ben's office. He sipped on a cup of coffee. "Heard about it first thing this morning."

Ben crossed his arms, rocking gently back and forth behind his desk. "Can't say as I blame him," he said. "Probably what we all should do."

"Listen, Benny. We had an agreement. But once this thing with Thibodoux and Julie happened, the rules were changed. Hell, the rules got thrown out the damn window! I wouldn't blame you at all for bailing out. Shit, a lot of people would say you had an obligation to pull out, conflict of interest and all."

Ben knew Powell was trying to make it easier. Unfortunately, his efforts were having just the opposite effect. There was something he felt, besides his desire to see a child-killer behind bars, that didn't want to give in to Ezekiel Thibodoux. If he pulled out now—and nobody would blame him for doing that—it would be like conceding victory to Thibodoux. And, Ben thought, more importantly, it would be giving in to himself. A recognition that the emotional turmoil he'd had to endure over the years since Julie's death had, in the end, gotten the better of him. It was this last factor, Ben knew, that would ultimately tip the scales in his decision.

"Unless you or someone else has an objection," said Ben, "I'm going to stick with the case, at least for now. Thibodoux may be all bluff on this thing. We won't know until he gives us some specifics. And in order to get that, he wants me to cut him a deal. And I'm not about to do that. If Zeke Thibodoux knows something about Julie's death and wants to come forward, with the understanding that it's totally voluntary, no promises, and that a judge could look at it later in determining sentence, then that's fine. But no deals for this guy. Never. I phoned Lucky

LeDoux early this morning. Woke him from his beauty sleep. He said he'd tell Thibodoux that we weren't dealing, no matter what. I guess it'll be Lucky's last official act as Thibodoux's counsel of record."

Powell took a careful sip from the rim of his cup, smiled, then gave Ben a mock salute. "I'll take care of the brass on this one," he said. "Hell, they gotta do what I say, right?" Both men smiled. "LeDoux's supposed to go public with his decision this morning. I guess the court will either allow Thibodoux time to hire another lawyer or appoint one for him."

"Or allow him to represent himself," Ben added.

"*Pro per?* He'd be crazy to represent himself."

"I don't know," said Ben. "It just might give him the sympathy factor that he's looking for. And the man certainly knows his way around a courtroom."

Powell nodded. "And it would mean that you'd have to talk directly to him, no lawyer as middleman." Powell seemed to consider what he'd just said. "There's no reason the media should find out about this, Ben. That is, unless LeDoux mentions it."

"He won't," Ben quickly added. "Lucky'll probably say that he has irreconcilable differences with his client which have forced him to withdraw. Which is probably true, except it wouldn't be the first time that he'd had client control problems. That normally isn't a good enough reason for Lucky to pass up a big fee."

"Julie?"

"Yeah. I guess Lucky doesn't really care much for his client. And he doesn't want to get in the middle of this thing between me and Thibodoux. Thibodoux's tried to play him like he's trying to play me."

As Powell was about to leave, Ben's phone rang. Ben pressed the speakerphone button. The receptionist's voice crackled into the room, announcing that it was Mr. Thibodoux, calling collect from the jail, and would Ben accept the charges.

"It's starting already," said Powell.

"Put him through," said Ben, lifting the receiver. He waited to hear Thibodoux's voice. Powell came into the room and took a seat opposite Ben's desk. After a few moments of listening, Ben said okay and hung up the phone.

"He wants another meeting," said Ben. "He's representing himself. LeDoux's got the matter placed on calendar this morning to withdraw as counsel, and Thibodoux's agreeing with the whole thing. He says he knows there's no deal, but that he still wants to talk."

Powell smiled his sly little smile. The one not for public consumption. The one Ben had seen only behind closed doors when Francis Powell contemplated some Machiavellian move against one of his political opponents.

Powell said, "The plot thickens, eh? Be careful, Benny. Real careful."

CHAPTER 17

In all the years that Ezekiel Thibodoux had been around jails and jailers, he'd never actually stepped inside a keep-away cell. A small room, more like a cubicle, the length of one narrow platform bed, and the width barely large enough to accommodate the bed and one brown-stained toilet mounted on the wall in the corner. At night, unable to sleep, he'd inhale the sour ammonia smell of the toilet and it would make him think of when he was small, with his parents, inside the house where he grew up. They'd be in his dreams, his father and mother, and he'd be doing to them what they made him do, what they convinced him he liked to do. *Softly, gently,* his father would tell him. *A little harder now, child, that's it.* He remembered how they would both hold the back of his head and guide him, their fingers playing in his soft curly child's hair. Even when he started to choke, unable to breathe, their hands would pull his head home as if he were less a human child than a piece of machinery, a convenient device for their pleasure.

His plan with the lawyer hadn't worked. It was his first plan, though. He had almost convinced himself not to go for the whole thing, demanding a deal in return for the information. But what did he have to lose? He'd seen stranger plea bargains struck in his time. There was always the chance that he might hit just the right chord at the right moment. He had hoped to talk with Ben Green, just the two of them, alone. To get inside the man's head. You never could tell what might happen then.

But now he'd shot his wad. Or almost, anyway. It was time for plan two, which was really what he expected would happen all along.

Thibodoux leaned back against the wall of his cell, sitting on the bunk, extending his feet out into the middle of the cubicle. There were people who still believed he was innocent; unjustly accused of this horrendous, almost unbelievable crime. A smile came to him, along with the memory of the little girl. She had deserved it, he thought. He had done her a favor. Done them all a service. He'd made a mistake, though, with his daughter, and now it was coming back on him. He saw himself, his image, for a moment, in the face of his daughter, Mary Esther. Then in them all. And it angered him to see himself this way. Anger like a white-hot rod thrust into his stomach, punching and twisting upward to his chest. It was part of what he felt when he was with the girl. Part of what *they* had done to him. How could he be to blame? He was only simulating, recreating. Recreating himself. Over and over again.

He felt himself trembling. He watched as his legs jumped up and down, as if from an electrical shock. Inside his head he heard a voice asking him if he was all right. The voice was that of Dr. Hirsch. What the doctor always said, calming, soothing. Not like the anger. And the voice pulled him away from the anger for a moment, making him think of his father, and that one moment at the stream. He'd been very little then. His father was placing his arm around his shoulders and showing him the stringer made of nylon-coated rope with the sharpened metal point at one end. He flashed back to the present, thinking that the stringer had been put to good use. The thought made him realize that his worlds were crossing over one another. Thibodoux thought for a moment, even hoped, that it had all been made up. That the girl had not been with him inside the cave, that he had not done what he imagined.

Thibodoux thought of his father with him at the stream, speaking softly, slowly. As if, for some unknown reason—

and despite all that he'd done and would continue to do to his son—his father thought him special at that moment. The knife had been given to him that same day, down by the stream. It was a picture that Thibodoux had little trouble conjuring when he was younger, but which had all but disappeared in recent years. It had come to him once in Dr. Hirsch's office, though. The voice had done it, brought the picture from somewhere deep inside to that space right behind his eyes, where Thibodoux could almost touch the stringer, and the knife. Where his father's voice was barely audible, but there, all the same. Like a black-and-white photograph of something from long ago where the names and the place and the colors are missing. Thibodoux had to imagine those things, and over time his imagination had failed him. The image had become dim, and the voice was but a faint echo.

What he could always conjure up, though, were the hideous souvenirs of recollection. The beatings administered by his father. His mother in another room. Thibodoux the child could hear her crying, whimpering. But she never came in, never interfered. Thibodoux recalled, like it had just happened, his father coming into his room at night and lying in his bed. The smell of the man, his body and breath so close, as if the odor came from inside himself and not from the man who lay next to him with his stubbled face nuzzling between two shivering stick-like child's legs. That smell never left him. Even now, with the children, that same smell was there. Like the toilet in his cell.

"You got a visitor," said the deputy, clanging the ring of heavy metal keys against the bars of the cell. The young sheriff's deputy yanked on the gate, sliding it open, then made a motion for Thibodoux to turn around and face the wall. Thibodoux was familiar with the routine. All inmates were. The deputy patted him down, cuffed him, then guided him from behind, with one hand firmly gripping the handcuffs, down to the attorney-conference holding tank. Thibodoux did exactly as he was told. He didn't want to say or do anything that might anger the deputy. These guys, he told himself, were young, usually straight from the academy. Not all that bright. Tough guys, or so they envisioned themselves, who hated being inside the jail all day having to smell the inmates. Thibodoux didn't want to risk that this young deputy walking behind him might get jumpy and call off his attorney visit, but not before shoving his face into the nearest wall.

No, this visit was very important for Ezekiel Thibodoux. This might be his last shot with Mr. Benjamin Green.

Ben waited inside the glass-enclosed interview cubicle. A call to Lucky LeDoux had confirmed that LeDoux had been substituted-out as Thibodoux's attorney of record, and that the court had accorded Thibodoux *pro per* status. Ezekiel Thibodoux was now his own lawyer.

The man the deputy brought into the attorney conference room was not the same person Ben had seen at the preliminary hearing. The cocky, self-assured bravado that Thibodoux had put out for public consumption in court had been replaced. Now, Ben thought, Thibodoux looked stooped over as he checked in with the deputy at the desk, completely deflated, beaten. His hair disheveled, his beard untrimmed and growing wildly in wisps of black at his throat and around his ears, Thibodoux looked more like a vagrant who should have been pushing a shopping cart of junk and cast-off clothing down the street than the confident, physically imposing police detective of recent memory.

Thibodoux nodded to Ben, almost apologetically, as the deputy removed his handcuffs. He rubbed his wrists before sitting down. Ben could see the bracelet of rough reddened skin around each of Thibodoux's wrists.

"I've brought a tape recorder," said Ben. He pointed to the cassette recorder on the desk between them. "I want everything on the record here." Ben started the tape before Thibodoux had a chance to answer.

"Now," said Ben, "this is Benjamin Green speaking with Ezekiel Thibodoux in the attorney conference room of the Central Men's Jail." Ben went on, stating the date and time. "Mr. Thibodoux has requested this meeting, isn't that correct, Mr. Thibodoux?"

Thibodoux nodded, then said yes.

"The record should also reflect that Mr. Thibodoux's former attorney, Mr. Antoine LeDoux, has been relieved as counsel, and that Mr. Thibodoux is now proceeding *in propria persona* as his own counsel. Is that correct, Mr. Thibodoux?" Again Thibodoux said yes. Ben continued to advise Thibodoux of his constitutional rights under Miranda, making special note of the fact that any statements Thibodoux might make, even though he was representing himself, could, and would, be used against him should they be incriminating.

"I understand my rights, Mr. Green." Thibodoux spoke slowly and evenly. Without anger. He had listened to Ben's comments, his setting the scene on tape, almost without interest, answering only when requested. "As you have stated, I understand and waive my rights. It is my desire to speak with you." Thibodoux rested his elbows on the desk, the fingers of his hands interlaced, with his chin resting in the pocket that they formed.

"Mr. Green. I do not foresee the need of this tape in the future, but I can understand your concern, and therefore will speak to you while the tape is running." Thibodoux was speaking without emotion, as if reciting from memory. "As I have previously indicated, I am in possession of certain knowledge concerning the death of your daughter. How I came into possession of this knowledge I will soon relate to you. Suffice it to say that I am convinced that I know the name of the person responsible for your daughter's death."

Ben tried to evince no visible sign of emotion. He figured that Thibodoux had determined to tell him what he knew, without holding out for the deal that he'd previously demanded. Whatever cards Thibodoux had earlier concealed, he was now intent on showing them. There would be some sort of *quid pro quo,* Ben knew that. Only from Thibodoux's downtrodden expression, and Ben's refusal to deal with him on his terms, Ben now felt that it was he who would call the shots.

"I have," said Thibodoux, "done a good deal of thinking since we last spoke. I have decided—and I know you'll be skeptical of my motives here, but believe me, what I am about to tell you is the truth. I believe that the best course of action for me is not to withhold this information from you. It has nothing to do with my case. Especially in light of what I am going to admit. Perhaps this information will be of some help to you. I'll tell you right now that I wish I had not been in the position of having to offer this information in trade." Thibodoux shuddered, then turned his head to the side, away from Ben. Ben wasn't sure whether Thibodoux was in fact touched emotionally, or whether the ex-cop was in the process of one of his finest performances. Ben had seen plenty of defendants turn the tears on and off, like lawn sprinklers.

"As I was saying . . ." Thibodoux had arrived at a degree of composure, though his hands were tapping nervously, unconsciously, on the surface of the desk as he spoke. Ben noticed that Thibodoux's nails were extraordinarily long, and the cuticles were stained a dark brown. While not a flashy dresser by any means, Ezekiel Thibodoux had always been fastidious about his appearance. Some people bit their nails to the quick from nervousness, but Thibodoux, Ben surmised, was not one of those people. His fingernails, like curved claws, tapped out a high-treble beat as he spoke.

Thibodoux continued, "I have come to the realization that I have done much that has been wrong. Evil. That there is nothing that I can do now to reverse that evil. I have been involved in things that no moral person could or should accept. For this, I am sincerely sorry. I know that God will be just, but will exact his punishment." Ben watched as Thibodoux rubbed the palm of his hand across his eyes. Tears welled up, then trickled from each eye, but Thibodoux continued to talk, his voice cracking.

"At one point in my life I had an interest in photographs. Photographs of nude children. I used to collect such photographs, trade them with other collectors. You might be surprised to learn that there are worldwide organizations made up of people like myself. People whose primary reason for living is the enjoyment, the sexual enjoyment, of children. There is a very brisk market in such material. I am aware, though not from personal experience, that through such organizations one can actually obtain the services of a child or children. There are even parents who advertise in the magazines published by such organizations, offering to sell the sexual services of their children."

Ben felt as if he were in a dream. Not because of the content of Thibodoux's information, but because Ezekiel Thibodoux had so easily rolled over on his case. This information, Thibodoux must be aware, would eliminate any hope he would ever have of obtaining his freedom through the courts. He was guaranteeing his own conviction. Thibodoux was being remarkably—shockingly was more like it—candid in his admissions. For Ezekiel Thibodoux to come this far, Ben thought, must have taken a good deal of soul-searching. Maybe the man was being sincere. Perhaps he had weighed the evidence against him, examined his own motives, and determined to come completely clean. With Thibodoux's religious background, anything was possible. Such things did happen.

"A picture came to my attention," said Thibodoux. "It came to me from a source, a person, I had previously dealt with. This person had purchased from me certain photographs, and in return, had sent to me photographs for me to purchase. In one of those pictures, I saw a teenage girl. There was a man in the picture, and . . ." Thibodoux stopped. His mouth turned up to the side, as if he was hesitant to continue. "Well," he said, "there was a man in the photograph. He and the girl were together. I later learned that the man in the photograph was the one who had sent the picture to me. I kept the picture. There was something about the expression on the girl's face that intrigued me." Thibodoux paused, mistaking the confusion on Ben's face for anger. "I am sorry for that. I am telling you the truth. In my case, the truth is not always—in fact it is hardly ever—pleasant. It is what I must do, though.

"I didn't realize," said Thibodoux, "who the girl in the picture was until the newspapers carried the story of your daughter's death. There was a picture of her. I immediately recognized her face. I didn't think it was possible, you know. I thought the girls, the one in the photograph and the one in the newspaper, were merely similar in appearance. Except I couldn't get away from the fact that the faces were identical. And then when the paper said that her body was found in Barstow . . . Well, I knew. You see, Mr. Green, this person who sent me the picture lived in Barstow. I knew the girl in the picture was your daughter, Julie."

Ben wasn't sure how long it had been since Thibodoux had become silent. His mind, like a movie camera on a dolly, was slowly panning over the scenes of Julie's funeral, his identifying her body in the morgue, the highway patrol officer at his front door . . . It was all starting to fall into place, scene after scene, with this little scene, himself and Ezekiel Thibodoux, coming in toward the end of the movie. Even then, sitting opposite Thibodoux in the cramped glass-enclosed interview cubicle, Ben knew that this was not to be the last scene. That the last scene would have a desert landscape. A wasteland, stark and barren. Without life.

"What do you want in exchange for his name?" Ben asked. Ezekiel Thibodoux seemed to have taken on a peaceful calm that went deeper than the skin. It made Ben uncomfortable, because his own skin was crawling with anticipation.

"I want nothing," said Thibodoux. "What comes to me from disclosing this information will come to me anyway, free of deals or obligation."

Thibodoux could see a relaxing of attitude in the prosecutor's face. Green's demeanor was no longer adversarial. An inquisitiveness, an interest in what was being said and why, was evident in the way Green held his head to one side, pursing his lips in thought.

"Understand one thing, Mr. Green. I have made my peace with God. That is what is most important to me. Whether I spend the rest of my years in prison, whether I receive the ultimate penalty . . . those are earthly concerns that my faith in God will help me deal with." Thibodoux lowered his eyes, or at least gave the impression that he was deep in thought. He was carefully observing Ben's reaction, though.

"The name you're interested in," said Thibodoux, "is Stacey Fagan. He's in his early forties, I would guess, though I never actually met him. Just talked on the phone a few times. And, of course, he was in the photograph. There's a Barstow address. I've written it down for you." Thibodoux removed a small piece of paper from his shirt pocket and held it over his head for the guard to see. Once the paper had been inspected, Thibodoux handed it across the table to Ben. "I have no idea whether the address is still good. It's been over three years since I last had any dealings with the man. But it's yours, and for what it's worth, I hope it turns out for you, the way you expect, I mean." Thibodoux made a tent of his fingers, covering his mouth. He waited for Ben to make the next move.

"I've got to ask you," said Ben. "Don't answer if you don't want to. But why now? Why do this to yourself now?"

A smile came to Thibodoux's face. He shrugged, looked away momentarily, then back at Ben. "Even if I were concerned with the legal part of this case, you'd have to admit that with my daughters testifying against me, and that Gordon kid, you've got a damn good case. And that's without any of the psychiatrist's records or what the lab boys might turn up. I've handled a lot of cases over the years. Talked to a lot of guys looking at doing big chunks of time behind bars. The thing that always got me about most of them was that they never knew when to give up, when to throw in the towel and face facts. There will come a time, no matter what I'm convicted of, when I'll have to face a judge and tell him why I shouldn't be executed, or why I shouldn't spend the rest of my life in prison. He probably won't listen, and there will probably be a whole slew of reporters and community leaders clamoring for my skin. But you see, by doing what I'm doing now, I know that I'm doing the right thing. It might not matter, but it's better than stupidly toughing it out. I'd be lying to you if I told you that I didn't care what happens to me. I'm not a fool, Mr. Green. I've made my peace with God, I'm not afraid of death. But I'd prefer a few more years on this earth, if it's all the same to Him."

Thibodoux changed gears for a moment, speaking to Ben as if giving advice to a friend. "You know, we're not that much different, you and me. At least professionally. We're both scavengers, Mr. Green. We're used to thinking of scavengers as animals, the vulture picking clean the dead carcass. But the original meaning of the word referred to those who were employed by society to remove the dirt and debris from the street. Like garbage collectors and junk men. Isn't that what we are, Mr. Green? Aren't cops just that? Collectors of human garbage, trying to keep the streets clean of the unwanted, the human waste produced by our society."

Thibodoux had a faraway look, as if what he'd said had brought to mind some deeply personal experience. After a while his attention returned to the conversation. "Forgive me, Mr. Green. So many unusual thoughts come to mind when one is in my position."

"I can't make any deals on sentencing," said Ben, thankful that that discretion was not his to exercise. He had initially been surprised, thrown off guard, but was now accepting the new Ezekiel Thibodoux. Thibodoux had given up so much and had demanded nothing in return. "I can make a recommendation," said Ben, "but I can't guarantee anything."

"I understand."

"And, uh, well, I'd have to talk to some people first. You understand that?"

Thibodoux nodded.

"If there are any concessions to be made, I'll inform you directly."

"That's fair," said Thibodoux. He stood, readying to leave, then added, "There is one thing, though. It's no big deal for you, but they've been keeping me in solitary since the arrest. The high-power tank. I eat and sleep alone. Hardly get any exercise. If you could see fit to say something? No special treatment or anything, just maybe some library and canteen privileges. Maybe a little exercise on the yard in the sunshine. It would help."

"I'll see what I can do," said Ben, then watched Thibodoux return to the inmate corridor, thinking that that was precious little for a condemned man to ask.

CHAPTER 18

"He's a missout." The bailiff in the master calendar arraignment court blurted this out for Ben's benefit, then went back to his phone conversation.

Ben sat inside the railing that separated the audience section from the rest of the courtroom, in one of the chairs just behind the counsel table. The bailiff had the phone pinned to one side of his face and was scrutinizing a computer printout while conversing with the Central Men's Jail.

"Yeah, I'll bet." They were joking with each other now, the bailiff and someone in Sheriff's Transportation. "You better find that sucker," said the bailiff, chuckling. He placed the phone back on the hook, looked up, and said, "He DFO'd." Then seeing Ben's confused expression, the bailiff added, "Done fell out. He missed the bus. They're trying to find him now. They'll put him on the next available transportation." The bailiff went back to staring at the thick pile of computer paper that littered his desk.

This was not such a bad thing, Ben thought. Defendants with court appearances often missed the morning bus or were mistakenly sent to the wrong court. If the sheriffs changed the location of an inmate inside the jail, it often took time for the computer to catch up. Thibodoux was probably resting somewhere inside the jail, wondering why he hadn't been summoned. It wouldn't be like Ezekiel Thibodoux to go wandering around inside the jail. Every jail had its share of wanderers, inmates who, without permission, surreptitiously moved from one location to another, confusing their jailers and wreaking havoc with the computerized court transportation system.

Besides, Francis Powell was holding a press conference this morning, and Ben, while not wanting to be there, was interested in seeing how Francis handled the recent developments in the Thibodoux prosecution. Not only had Lucky LeDoux withdrawn as Thibodoux's counsel of record, but the press had somehow gotten hold of the Stacey Fagan information. There had been an article in the *Times* about the plea negotiations with Thibodoux, speculating whether Thibodoux would continue to act as his own attorney, and whether it would be appropriate for Ben to withdraw as prosecutor given these latest developments.

Ben could see the illumination from the bright TV lights as he stepped off the elevator. He'd made the short walk from the Criminal Courts Building to Parker Center. The press conference room was off to the side, but when it was filled with reporters and cameras, as it now was, it filled the entire adjacent corridor with light and the insect-hum of activity.

Ben positioned himself in the back, out of sight. He could hear Powell's amplified voice, and could just barely make out most of the questions. Only a portion of Powell's head was visible. Powell was in the process of answering reporters' questions, and looked as if he were about to terminate the press conference.

"Over there," said Powell, gesturing to a reporter whose hand was punching the air in the back of the room, like an anxious student with the right answer.

"Chief, Antoine LeDoux has withdrawn from this case, claiming conflict of interest. He and the prosecutor, Mr. Green, are friends, and apparently, Mr. LeDoux had something to do with the case a few years back that led to Mr. Green's emotional breakdown. My question to you, Chief, is that if Mr. LeDoux has seen fit to withdraw, why is Mr. Green still prosecuting this case?"

Ben felt something slide from his chest into his stomach, where it seemed to bubble momentarily, then subside.

"What Antoine LeDoux decides to do is none of my

concern." Powell looked confident; his voice was assertive. His dazzle-them-with-bullshit approach. "I can't practice law for Lucky LeDoux, and wouldn't want to try. Mr. Green and I, along with the A.G.'s staff, have examined this issue carefully and have arrived at the conclusion that there is no conflict of interest that would prevent Mr. Green from continuing as prosecutor in the Thibodoux case, as long as he desires to do so, which he does." Powell pointed to a woman seated in the front row.

"Well, Chief, don't you think that these recent developments with this person—" She referred to her notepad. "Fagan, Stacey Fagan . . . and his purported involvement in the murder of Mr. Green's daughter, are bound to affect Mr. Green's handling of the case? I have two young daughters, and if, God forbid, they were attacked or murdered, I know I would be very interested in capturing their assailants. Interested enough, I daresay, to do just about anything to bring them to justice."

"This, ladies and gentlemen, will be the last question." Powell paused a moment, collecting his thoughts. "As I have already stated, Mr. Green and I have discussed this issue thoroughly. Mr. Green is a professional. I have full confidence that if he felt that his emotional involvement would get in the way of his duty as a prosecutor, that he would be the first person to request removal from this case. The information that you have regarding Mr. Fagan, if there is such a person, is highly speculative at best."

"But you are checking it out, right?" Again the woman reporter slipping in one last question.

"Of course," answered Powell. "Just like we'd investigate any lead in a homicide."

"But Chief . . ." The woman was standing now, sensing she had Powell on the ropes. "This just isn't *any* homicide. And our sources tell us that the information concerning Stacey Fagan was provided by Ezekiel Thibodoux himself. Is that correct? And if so, will Thibodoux's supplying of that information have anything to do with your decision whether or not to seek the death penalty in his case?"

Ben felt sorry for his friend, but was glad it was Powell up there and not himself. This was Powell's turf, and despite the constrained look of gastric pain that was now creeping into Powell's face, Ben knew that Powell would tiptoe his way through.

"First, let me address your question about the death penalty. Generally, the district attorney makes the decision in each homicide whether to seek the death penalty against an individual defendant. In this case, Mr. Lanier, for reasons previously stated by him, has chosen not to become involved in the prosecution of Mr. Thibodoux." That's it, thought Ben, throw off some of the blame on the D.A. "The decision on death in this case will be determined by us after evaluating Mr. Thibodoux's record as a police officer, his community involvement, the facts of this case, and hundreds of lesser, more intangible elements. It is, in such cases, always a subjective judgment call. But believe me—or, as our president would say, 'Read my lips'—when I say that our decision here will have nothing to do with any information provided to us by Mr. Thibodoux. There will be no 'deal' with Mr. Thibodoux.

"Mr. Thibodoux," said Powell, gathering his papers and signaling to his support staff that he was about to leave, "has merely requested that he be allowed some additional exercise time while in jail, and that he also be removed from the high-power tank periodically. Given the fact that he has been kept segregated from the rest of the inmate population for his own benefit and not because he poses any sort of threat himself, we went along, to a limited extent, with his request."

Powell strode toward the exit door. The door led to a small hallway, which opened into the security corridor outside his office. Ben went around the other way, through the waiting room. He could hear the reporters buzzing, still yelling questions even after Powell had left the conference room.

When Ben found Powell, he was already inside his office, his tie loosened, seated behind his desk, his legs crossed on top, sucking on a cigarette and blowing smoke slowly from his nose. Like some sort of urban dragon, was Ben's first impression.

"Great performance, Francis."

"You caught that, huh?"

Ben plopped down in a chair opposite Powell's desk. "Part of it." He gazed away from his friend, feeling that, like the cigarette smoke, there were words left unspoken, clouding the air between them. "Tough going for a while in there."

Powell waved him off. "No big deal. Those guys are always looking for a story. It's their job, right? It'll all blow over. I don't think the public really gives a shit about conflict of interest. Hell, most of 'em don't even know what it is. What the public wants is for the bad guys to be punished. They want to be able to walk the streets at night without getting robbed, send their kids to school and back without having to worry that some pervert is going to chop them up. The public has no sympathy for men who diddle children. They want them off the street and behind bars forever. That's what we're doing, right?"

Ben didn't answer. He watched the plumes of white smoke stream like car exhaust out of Powell's nostrils, curving upward where they gathered in a thin smoky pancake cloud at the ceiling.

"Thibodoux's record alone would be enough to opt against giving him the pill. Hell, I've seen Lanier's boys not go for death on a lot worse cases. Religious man with a family. Deacon in the fucking church! A jury might have a hard time giving that guy a death sentence. On the other hand, there's the little girl with her head cut off . . . Who knows?" It seemed to Ben that Powell was trying to pump himself up, convince himself of one side of the argument or the other. So far, they were still seeking the death penalty, the pill, for Ezekiel Thibodoux. There was still time, though. They wouldn't be forced to make their final decision until jury selection for the trial began.

"This thing with this Fagan character," said Powell, "is big news now." He shook his head in disgust, stubbing out his cigarette. "You don't think LeDoux was behind breaking that story?"

Ben rejected that. "It's not his style."

"Yeah," said Powell. "I would have thought not. Except, if not LeDoux, then who?"

"Thibodoux's the only other one. I'm not sure if Lucky even knew about Fagan's existence until that day in the interview room. Even then, Thibodoux didn't mention Fagan by name."

"Why would Thibodoux call the press? What would he have to gain?"

Ben thought for a moment about Powell's question.

"It might not have been Thibodoux. You know what happens over there. Some other inmate gets wind of the story, maybe asks Thibodoux about it. Then he goes to his lawyer trying to cut a better deal for himself. Or maybe he calls the press directly, for the money, or just for the glory. Shit, that place is full of rumors and half-truths being whispered by liars, thieves, and psychopaths to anyone with an open ear."

"Like I told you before, Ben, I'd be happy to put a couple guys on it, see if they can turn up anything on this Fagan character."

Ben gestured with his hand. "Let me try it first," he said. "It's Friday. I have the weekend to get myself to Barstow and check it out. If I need help, I'll let you know."

"Okay," said Powell.

Ben had the feeling that Powell was not as unconcerned as he was making out.

"What happened in court today with Zeke?" Powell forced a smile. "Do we have another budding cop-turned-defense-attorney on our hands?"

"He didn't show. A missout. They're trying to locate him now."

"Jesus, it's amazing anyone ever gets to court at the right time. That fucking place is bursting at the seams with bad guys, then you consider all the outlying jails that are sending guys to court . . . Shit, it's like being an air-traffic controller with about a thousand planes all trying to land or take off at once." Powell's phone buzzed. He punched at the lighted red button, using the speakerphone.

"A message for Mr. Green," said the receptionist's voice. Powell lifted the receiver off the hook and handed it to Ben. It was the bailiff from the arraignment court.

Ben listened with disbelief to the message. After a moment, he placed the receiver on the desk. A scratching electrical sound, pops and clicks, could be heard coming from the tiny speaker.

"What?" Powell had been in the middle of lighting another cigarette. He now stared intently at Ben, waiting for an answer. He was waving the match out with his left hand in slow motion.

"It's Thibodoux," said Ben, still numbed by the message. "He's escaped."

It was his custom on Saturday morning to sleep late. Then, often, he would make the casual three-block walk from his apartment to the Grand Allée. There, he would have his choice from among the multitude of restaurants and sidewalk cafés in which to enjoy a leisurely lunch or late breakfast, *petite déjeuner,* as it was called by the predominantly French citizens of Quebec City.

Jonathan Racine couldn't help but think that the Grand Allée, the Champs-Élysées of Quebec, with its tree-lined streets and sidewalk eateries, would be the last place anyone would think of looking for him. Especially the goons from L.A. and Miami. It had been his final stop on a rather circuitous journey from Los Angeles, with preliminary stops in Toronto and Montreal, to put any possible trackers off the scent. He'd liked both Toronto and Montreal. To his surprise, they'd put him up at the Four Seasons in both cities. The fallout of a Republican administration, he'd thought. In each place, he was able to find a quiet area where he thought he could be happy. In Toronto, a small residential community of stately houses with well-kept gardens called Rosedale appealed to him. In Montreal, he could see himself holed up in some minor estate in the French enclave of Outremont. As it turned out, though, the United States government never had any intention of relocating him in either city. The G-man they'd assigned to ensure his safety, his disappearance, had convinced him that living in a big city, even a Canadian city, would be asking for trouble.

Someplace more off the beaten track, the FBI agent had

suggested, with that tone of voice that told Racine that he was just being nice by sounding like it was a suggestion, and in reality, there was no choice in the matter. Of course, Jonathan could have told the G-man where to shove his suggestion, but then, it was always nice to have the FBI interested in keeping you alive, especially when the mob had the opposite goal in mind.

So he'd ended up in Quebec City, in the "new" city, a couple of miles outside the eighteenth-century fortifications of Old Quebec, in an area called the Petite Quartier. They'd found an apartment for him, and a job working in a used-book store inside the walls of the Old City. It wouldn't have been his first choice of residences. It was much too cold for him in the winter, and the humidity could become stifling during the summer months. And his French was almost nonexistent when he arrived—he could ask where the bathroom was and little else. He had also been concerned about sticking out, being obviously American in a city that was so dyed-in-the-wool French.

But after nearly a year, his French was coming along. And the town was so full of tourists, speaking everything from German to Spanish to English, that he had stopped worrying about his accent bringing undue attention. This was a vacation town, a tourist center, where Canadians and Americans brought their spouses, their families, to walk the cobbled streets of Old Quebec and taste a little history, in addition to perhaps the best French cuisine on the continent. If the wiseguys found him here, they'd find him anywhere. And this place sure as hell beat living on a farm somewhere in Podunk, Iowa.

Jonathan found a table outside, at a place called Le Tops. He was hungry, and the restaurant with its umbrella-covered sidewalk café specialized in a breakfast of eggs, ham, bacon, sausage, baked beans, hash-brown potatoes, French toast, a crêpe, and a muffin. Just seeing the food made him ravenous. After finishing it, he opened his newspaper and felt the warm contented feeling that having the rest of the day totally unoccupied always provided. He slurped at his coffee, spreading the paper on the table, catching up on the latest news from the States.

He was on his third cup when he spotted the first familiar name. It made him pause, thinking of Danny and their life together before his death. He scanned the balance of the column, quickly at first, to get the gist of its meaning. Then he was forced to pause once more, unexpectedly recognizing a second name. The police investigator from L.A., the one who read poetry. Hard to forget, that.

The waitress stood at his side, speaking in French, asking him if he wanted another refill. *"Merci, non,"* he whispered, not removing his eyes from the paper. He read the article three times, then leaned back in his chair, feeling a sense of discomfort coming over him. The cars on the Grand Allée slowly snaked their way past, honking and revving their engines. Across the street, at Auberge Louis Hebert, an elderly couple was being seated at a table by a black-jacketed waiter.

At that moment, sitting thousands of miles away from Los Angeles, with a new life of his own—a protected federal informant—Jonathan Racine had a sense of what he was about to do. Looking back on that moment, he would later say that he hadn't yet decided to risk breaking his cover. That possibility had consciously come to him sometime later. But there had been a deeper, untouchable sense of direction that had taken over, there on the Grand Allée, while sipping coffee and listening to the soft whispers in French at the tables around him. Racine would later say that he felt, even then, that something was compelling him to go to the aid of Benjamin Green.

CHAPTER 19

He didn't know whether to feel depressed or relieved. After a little over two hours at a constant sixty-five miles per hour on Interstate 15, Ben stood at the address in Barstow given to him by Ezekiel Thibodoux. Even at nine-thirty in the morning, the desert heat was suffocating. He felt like a cookie just warming in the oven, ready for someone to crack off a piece and take a bite.

The Barstow Palms had been a two-story structure consisting of eight one-room apartments. It was located on the edge of town, on the Las Vegas side. A sign, taller than the structure itself, still remained. Red rusting metal with faded white script, on two poles extending above where the roof of the building had been: THE BARSTOW PALMS, ROOMS FOR RENT, DAILY RATES, ADULT ENTERTAINMENT. On the bottom of the sign were the words TRIPLE X-RATED.

Stacey Fagan no longer resided here. The building's only residents now were the insects and lizards that had crawled in off the desert seeking some shade. From what Ben could see, a fire had gutted the structure, leaving only a small portion of charcoal roof rafters to cast lattice-like shadows across the concrete slab floor. Broken glass and pieces of drywall littered the interior of the burned-out hulk, along with assorted hamburger wrappers, beer cans, tumbleweeds, and used condoms.

Most of the interior walls were no longer existent, though Ben could see, from what little remained, that the rooms had been small, one room serving as both living and sleeping quarters, with a tiny closet-sized bathroom, and an equally minuscule cooking area. The second floor was completely gone. The only evidence of its existence were the charred wood beams in the corner that precariously supported the roof.

Ben tried to tell himself that perhaps Thibodoux had confused the numbers. That maybe Fagan's building was on another block of the same street, and that Thibodoux, in his concern over his own situation, had inadvertently transposed the numbers. Maybe Fagan's actual apartment was closer to town? Yet there was nothing but desert stretching out to Las Vegas on the other side.

Ben drove back into town and did something he normally never did. He stopped at a McDonald's, the largest in the world, or so they claimed, and had a cup of coffee. He had left L.A. without breakfast, and the first mild rumblings of hunger were coming over him. He figured he'd start with the coffee, then see how he felt. If the hunger persisted perhaps he'd live dangerously and order breakfast.

Inside the restaurant it was downright chilly, as a battalion of air conditioners pumped frigid air into the glass-enclosed space. At his table in the corner, Ben sipped his coffee. The cars in the lot, along with the trees and the service road in the distance, seemed to undulate from the heat. He was mesmerized by the mirage-like tableau. He'd experienced the same sensation on the highway driving out, the concrete appearing and disappearing in a wave, like a far-off shimmering stream coursing in and out of his vision.

He'd been tricked. Duped. He should have known better. Except Thibodoux had been so damn convincing. That business about making peace with God. Jesus, how stupid could you get! Ben poured another of the small containers of half-and-half into his cup, watching the caramel-colored liquid lighten with white swirls.

Thibodoux was gone. According to the sheriffs, he'd slipped out after his high-power restrictions had been relaxed. They were still trying to figure out how he had escaped. It was probably something as simple as sneaking out inside one of the service trucks. It wouldn't be the first time it had happened. A guy as cagey as Thibodoux was already probably miles away, making himself permanently scarce. It was amazing that they'd discovered his absence as quickly as they had. Every weekday morning more than two thousand inmates boarded one of forty or more buses and a dozen vans to travel to twenty-seven courts scattered within a fifty-mile radius of the main jail. The magnitude of this transportation of humanity was such that only three jails in the country held more inmates than Los Angeles County put in transit every day. The central jail itself, with more than 6,500 inmates, was the largest in the free world. Recently, four inmates awaiting trial for a gang-related murder had escaped and their disappearance hadn't been discovered for three days. Too many bodies, doubled up inside already overcrowded cells, sleeping on the floors of dayrooms and in the hallways. The population constantly changing, new arrestees coming in, others being sentenced and shipping out. A sea of constantly changing faces.

But what had Thibodoux to lose by giving him the right information? Perhaps Thibodoux had known this Fagan character, and perhaps the address, at one time, had been accurate. It had been years since Thibodoux had communicated with Fagan. In the interim, Fagan could have moved. He would have had to move when the building burned down. Maybe the escape had nothing to do with it. Thibodoux, Ben thought, could still have been telling the truth. Sure, that was it.

Ben tried telling himself that he wasn't Ezekiel Thibodoux's dupe. That Thibodoux hadn't been planning the escape all along, and hadn't used him to ease his custody restrictions to facilitate his getaway. Ben had started out that morning with mixed feelings. He half-hoped that Thibodoux's information would be a dead end. He thought that he'd already put all that behind him. He wasn't at all anxious to bring it to the surface again. Yet following the lead was something he had to do. If he didn't check out Thibodoux's information, it would stay with him, gnawing, questioning, filling him with regret.

What he should do, Ben told himself, was to accept the fact that he was at a dead end. Accept the reality that Ezekiel Thibodoux had escaped, due in part to the easing of his restrictions. Whether he had planned the escape all along, or whether it had come upon him only after he'd been released from the high-power unit, was irrelevant. Thibodoux was gone, probably for good unless they got real lucky. Whether the information about Fagan was true or not, there was at this point no place for Ben to go, nowhere else to look.

The finality of his situation imparted to Ben a certain uneasy sense of calm. He finished his coffee, and decided to call the office before heading back to L.A. The receptionist at Parker picked up the phone on the sixth ring.

"Just a minute, Mr. Green. The chief wants to speak with you. Very important."

Ben leaned against the wall adjacent to the telephone. It was right outside the entrance to the restrooms, and flocks of parents with screaming children in hand were migrating from the restaurant to the bathrooms and back again.

"Ben, I'm glad you called." Powell sounded out of breath. "You find anything out there?"

"Just a burned-out building. No trace of Fagan, or any other occupant for that matter. The place looks like it's been that way for a while."

"You think Thibodoux gave us the runaround?"

"Either that, or he hasn't talked to the guy in a while. Either way, there's nothing here. Anything new on him?"

"Still looking. You know the jail, everyone's pointing the finger at somebody else. Nobody wants to take the blame. We'll find him, sooner or later." Powell seemed to change gears. Ben could hear him take a deep breath before speaking.

"I received a very interesting message this morning. You remember our friend Mr. Jonathan Racine?"

"Yeah." Images of Racine and the Arnie Rosen murder quickly passed through Ben's mind.

"The call's from him. Racine wants to talk with you, Ben. He says he's got information on Stacey Fagan."

"Fagan? How the hell does he know about that?"

"How should I know, Ben? Just because the guy's gone undercover doesn't mean he can't pick up a newspaper.

That shit about you and Fagan and Thibodoux was front-page stuff in the *Times.*"

"What'd he say?"

"Not much. Just that he needs to talk to you in person. Telephone is too dangerous. He wants you to go to him."

"And where might that be?" said Ben. He heard Powell chuckle.

"Quebec City," said Powell, still laughing. "That's in fucking Canada, Benny."

"Quebec City! Jesus, why can't we just fly him out here?"

"Something to do with his passport. I had a meeting with the feds in charge of the Witness Protection Program. They're pretty closemouthed, but apparently Racine has contacted them about this. They've given him a new name, changed his identity. The usual stuff. Except they've had a little problem recently. They think the bad guys might be onto the new name. It's too late, and too much trouble, to change Racine's passport. They'd have to give him a whole new identity, and they're not about to do that just so he can fly into the U.S. to talk to some cop about a local homicide."

Quebec City? Ben was conjuring up in his mind a map of North America, trying to remember exactly where the province of Quebec was located, and wondering whether Quebec City was there or in some other province. He remembered that Canada had provinces instead of states, and that they stretched along the northern border of the U.S., but little more.

"Air Canada has a flight out of LAX first thing tomorrow morning," said Powell. "I booked you a seat in economy. We're still working on the hotel."

"The city's footing the tab on this one?"

"Why not?" said Powell. "It's a murder investigation, right? There's no statute of limitation on murder. You talk to Racine, Benny. See what he knows. Then you and me will catch this Fagan asshole and bring him to justice."

A father and his young daughter were standing in front of Ben. The daughter was just old enough that she could no longer accompany the father into the men's restroom, but young enough that she felt uncomfortable going into the women's by herself. Ben could hear Powell's slow, controlled breathing on the other end. He thought about the young girl, hesitating in front of the door, her father telling her to go ahead. Most of Ben's memories of Julie were of her at an older age. It was only from pictures of her as a toddler, and her first day of nursery school, that he had any recollection of his daughter as a small child. When Julie reached adolescence, Ben had promised himself that as a grandfather, he would not let that happen again. He had told himself that he would carve those precious early memories of his grandchildren into his mind forever. But that was never to be. It was ironic, he now thought, how certain things worked out.

"Thanks, Francis," he said. "I'll call you from Canada."

The geometric wedge of glass and concrete seemed to spring up out of nowhere, completely unexpected amidst the romantic sidewalk cafés of the Grand Allée and the quaint nineteenth-century brick houses that filled the predominantly residential Quebec City neighborhood. Hotel Loews Le Concorde occupied the corner of Place Montcalm and the Grand Allée at the end of the stretch of sidewalk cafés. It overlooked National Battlefields Park and the St. Lawrence River. It was where Francis Powell had booked a room for Ben, and where Powell had communicated as much to Racine, through intermediaries.

Ben's room on the twentieth floor overlooked the Citadel, with its star-shaped eighteenth-century fortifications against attack by way of the St. Lawrence River and beyond. A passage in the hotel's guidebook briefly narrated the history of the park, where in 1759 General James Wolfe won the battle and lost his own life on the Plains of Abraham. What had survived in the over two hundred years since were a series of bastions and cannon-guarded batteries set amidst the pastoral splendor of wooded parkland and beautifully landscaped gardens.

It was to one of those gardens, a rectangular parcel of land about a block in length, across the street from the hotel, that Ben had been directed. A message, left with the concierge at the hotel's front desk, and delivered a few moments after he'd been shown to his room, advised Ben of the time and location of the rendezvous. After making a quick trip to the revolving restaurant atop the hotel to kill a little time, while taking in the panoramic view of the city, Ben made his way downstairs and across the street.

In the early-evening twilight, couples strolled along the stone paths that formed the perimeter of the garden. The focal point was the large statue of Joan of Arc sitting atop a horse. In layers around the garden's outer edge, annuals and perennials displayed their seasonal splashes of color, each color cascading over the other. Ben took a seat on a wood bench near the statue, taking it all in, thinking that the city must be very liberal in its maintenance budget for such a place. The planting scheme showed taste and a knowledge of horticulture that he was not accustomed to seeing in Los Angeles.

Ben scrutinized each passerby, without appearing to scrutinize, wondering if Jonathan Racine's appearance had changed so much that he wouldn't recognize him. Racine's message had merely stated that he would meet Ben in the gardens across the street, near the statue. Ben looked around, wondering if there were other gardens or statues that might qualify. Most of the area was wooded parkland crisscrossed with paths tailor-made for joggers and sightseers.

He was looking out, away from the direction of the hotel, over a grassy knoll at the St. Lawrence when he heard the voice.

"Had a good trip, I hope?"

When Ben looked up, a slightly heavier Jonathan Racine stood opposite him, smiling and extending his hand. Racine had a book of poems under his arm, and to the casual observer looked like an average Quebec citizen taking an early-evening stroll, perhaps filling his senses and his mind with the beauty of the gardens and the poetry. Even with the added pounds, Racine still appeared slender, well-muscled, and in better than average shape. His raven-black hair was combed back, away from his face, and neatly trimmed.

Racine sat on the bench next to Ben. He placed the book—a volume of Robert Frost poems, Ben saw without surprise—on the bench between them.

"I never thanked you for the book you sent," said Ben, lifting and examining this book of poems.

"Well," said Racine, "we were both pretty well occupied with our own concerns. I know I was. When the feds found out I sent that to you, they almost flipped." Racine smiled, as if he found the memory bittersweet.

"You're costing the city of Los Angeles a good piece of change, having me flown all the way up here just to appreciate these flowers and talk about poetry and old times."

Racine rested one leg on the seat and draped his arm over the back of the bench. "I read about your predicament," he said. He looked around as if he expected someone might be listening. "I have some information that might help you. I am familiar, in a roundabout way, with Stacey Fagan. I don't know him personally—in fact, have never met the man." Racine paused. What he was about to say seemed to pain him.

"Danny . . . Danny Villapando, that is, knew the guy." He waited until Ben nodded, acknowledging the name of Racine's now-dead lover. "The way I remember it, Fagan was into the mob for about ten grand. Supposedly, he was going to open up some sort of porno store in Vegas. Danny met the guy on one of his trips to Vegas. It was Danny, I believe, who arranged the loan. When Fagan didn't pay up, it was Danny who went out there to light a fire under him."

The events of the past were starting to fall into place for Ben. Racine had been Danny Villapando's lover. They'd met each other during a stretch in Dannemora Prison. Danny, unbeknownst to Racine, had maintained his criminal contacts after his release, providing muscle for a group of West Coast mobsters. By the time Racine found out, Danny had been diagnosed with and was dying of AIDS. After spending thousands of dollars in an effort to find a cure—thousands of dollars of mob money—Danny died, leaving Racine to pay back the debt. Instead, Racine had turned State's evidence, providing the testimony that put an East Coast mob boss behind bars. For this, Racine was placed in the Federal Witness Protection Program, given a new identity and a new life.

"After the loan was made," said Racine, "but before Fagan disappeared, Danny would get letters from Fagan telling him how good the business was in Vegas. He'd usually enclose promotional stuff, crude flyers, you know, pictures and form letters that he was sending to his . . . customers. Apparently, Fagan had a pretty good little business, sending pornography through the mail. Naked men and women, kids even. It was the kiddie porn that was apparently his calling. There are groups of these guys across the country, believe it or not, who correspond with each other, sending one another pictures of naked kids. Lewis Carroll Collectors' Guild, Wonderland, the North American Boy Lovers Association, and the Pedophile Information Exchange in London, to name just a few. Child pornography has been estimated at anywhere from a multimillion- to a two-billion-dollar-a-year industry, and most of it is distributed through these pedophilia networks.

"Occasionally, when I had the bookstore, and afterward when I ran the business out of my home, I'd get that sort of crap in the mail." Racine paused, pursing his lips as if he were having second thoughts about what he'd said. "I know that I'm hardly the one to throw rocks because of someone else's sexual preference. But it does seem to me that this is different. No matter what people think about being gay, it's still consensual activity between two adults. But with kids too young to understand, it's different." Racine shuddered. "Ben, if you could see the look on some of those faces in the pictures . . ." He looked away.

Darkness was washing over the garden, muting the colors. The exterior lights of the hotel had been turned on, giving the wedge-shaped building a sort of Christmas-tree effect.

Ben gently grabbed Racine's arm. Both men were silent for a moment, each lost in their own recollections.

"I had an address in Barstow," said Ben. "It turned out to be a burned-down flophouse. A dead end."

"Fagan?"

"Who knows? He could be anywhere."

Racine nodded. "You're on the right track," he said. "What I mean is, Fagan used to operate out of a porno store in Barstow. A place call 'The Child In All Of Us.' " Racine nodded, acknowledging the disbelief on Ben's face. "Yeah, I know. A lot of these guys are very public with their beliefs. From what I gather, this store in Barstow specializes in kiddie porn. The stuff on the shelves pretty much spans the gamut of smut. But it's the material that's sold under the counter and through the mail that's the real reason they stay in business."

"And Fagan? What's his connection?"

"Not sure. He might have worked there, he might own part of it. I don't know. I do know that when he met Danny, it was there, and when he sent stuff to the house it was from the store. There was a woman, I think, who at the time was involved in the kiddie-porn thing with Fagan. I don't know if she's still there or not. Her name was Harrold, Geneva Harrold. If she's still around, she might know where to find Stacey Fagan."

"That's it?"

Racine nodded.

Ben was silent for a few moments, pondering what Racine had just told him. Then he turned to Racine. "Ya know," he said, "it would be a shame after flying all this way not to experience some of that superb French cooking that I'm always hearing this place is famous for."

"I have just the place," said Racine, smiling.

Racine led the way down the Grand Allée into the walled city. Near the Hotel Frontenac, which stood atop the bluffs overlooking the waterfront, was the beginning of the Breakneck Stairway leading down to the Quartier Petite-Champlain. At the foot of the stairway on the Rue Petite-Champlain in an unpretentious, centuries-old fieldstone building was Le Marie-Clairisse, where Ben and Racine spent the evening eating lobster and eel, and even, to Ben's surprise, stingray, all marvelously prepared and painstakingly served.

They talked about their previous meetings, and what had transpired in each of their lives since. Ben filled Racine in on the Thibodoux case, his wild-goose chase to the Barstow Palms looking for his daughter's killer, and Thibodoux's escape from jail.

"You don't blame yourself for that, do you?" Racine said. "He might have been using you, maybe not. Either way, his escape should not be on your conscience."

"Maybe not," said Ben. "In any event, they should catch up with him soon."

"And then what?"

"Then? We'll prosecute the bastard." For the first time in a long while, Ben was thinking about the case itself. In the previous weeks, most of his waking time had been devoted to the investigation and prosecution of Ezekiel Thibodoux. But in the last few days, since Thibodoux had come forward with the Fagan information, the actual trial had become secondary. It struck Ben that perhaps the reporters had been right. Perhaps Lucky LeDoux had the right idea in withdrawing from the case.

On the way back from the restaurant, filled almost to bursting, Ben and Racine opted against retracing their steps up the Breakneck Stairway and, instead, took the funicular car to the upper town. The two men walked silently past the restaurants and cafés that lined the streets. Past the displays of local artisans and craftsmen, the throngs of tourists and vacationers taking in the bustling nightlife. At the Hotel du Parlement, just outside the gates to the Old City, Racine stopped.

"This is where we part, my friend." Racine shook Ben's hand, then extended the small volume of poetry. "I want you to have this."

"Another gift," said Ben. He took the book, gently rubbing his fingertips across the cover.

"Until the next time," said Racine. He started to back away into the shadows. Ben didn't move. He stood, holding the book at his side, watching as Racine waved once more, then turned and headed down the hill. As he turned toward the hotel, Ben heard a voice in the distance. He looked back to see Jonathan Racine standing under a dimly lit lamppost. He had one arm extended, his body weight supported by the palm of his hand which was resting against the lamppost. His legs were jauntily crossed, and his jacket was draped over his shoulder. It made Ben think of the Frank Sinatra impersonation that everyone did. All that was missing was the fedora.

"What?" Ben had to yell due to the noise from the cars and people on the Grand Allée.

"You make sure you get that bastard," Racine yelled back. He waited a second, then waved once more before walking out of sight.

"Okay," Ben said, barely above his normal speaking voice. Racine was now a mere speck among many in the twilight. "Damn right I'll get him."

CHAPTER 20

After touching base with Francis Powell and learning that Zeke Thibodoux was still on the loose, Ben rented a car at LAX and headed straight for Nevada.

The Child In All Of Us turned out to be a P.O. box in Barstow. The box, from what Ben observed, was shared with other businesses of the same ilk. *Eros Inc., Double-D Cup, Inside & Hot,* along with sundry other nudie magazines, all received mail at the same location. After some questions and a few well-placed twenties, Ben was able to trace the ultimate destination of these "adult" publications to a reconverted gas station about a half mile from the edge of the Barstow business district. The station's gas pumps had been removed, and the office area had been enclosed and reinforced with iron bars over the windows and a permanent steel door over the garage opening.

Inside, in what would have been the station's office, there was a small desk, behind which was posted a sign saying that you have to be over eighteen to enter the store.

Inside the garage were row after row of unfinished wood shelves containing magazines, some inside plastic sleeves, other open to view. On the walls around the perimeter of the garage were additional shelves of magazines, paperbacks, and, in one corner near the sales counter, a glass case containing a selection of sexual devices. Just to the right of the sexual devices was an elevated counter, behind which sat a middle-aged man wearing a bleached pair of Levi's, no shoes, and a T-shirt with faded lettering that read IF IT MOVES, FUCK IT. The man was poring over a Technicolor centerfold, staring at the air-brushed body as if he expected the young woman in the picture to spring to life at any minute.

Ben approached the counter, and for a moment looked over the man's shoulder, gazing at the pictures and reading the copy. On the sales counter were similar magazines, stacked haphazardly, as if each were to be thoroughly reviewed by the salesman before hitting the shelves. *Busty, Forty-D Cup, Big Breasts, Juggs,* and a dozen or so more with various titles, each referring to the grossly enlarged portion of female anatomy highlighted in vivid Technicolor photography on the pages inside.

"I'm a leg man myself," said Ben.

The man with the magazine looked up, pointed to the far side of the store, then returned his attention to the magazine, saying, "Legs are on the far wall, between Asses and Beavers."

"I suppose," said Ben, "that if I wanted a certain type of woman and a certain part, that you'd have the exact magazine."

"Depends." The salesman turned a page, then another, still not looking up. "We got white asses and black asses. We got white women with black women, and black men with white women. We even got Oriental women in bondage, though there's not much call for that. We can order anything you don't see on the shelves."

"I'll bet." Ben's gaze wandered to the sexual devices. A glass-enclosed case with a few of the products displayed prominently on top. Dildos of every size, shape, and color, some electric, others windup models. Inflatable life-size dolls, "with simulated operating genitals," or so read the claim on the front of the package.

"I'm looking for a woman by the name of Geneva Harrold," said Ben. The salesman still didn't look up. Nor did he answer. Ben pulled out his L.A.P.D. identification and held it in front of the salesman's face, blocking his view of the page-filling breasts. "It's important," Ben added.

The salesman picked up the phone and punched in three

numbers, then told the voice on the other end that the cops were here. He put the receiver back on the hook, saying, "She's in the back." He pointed to the general area he had before. "Through the door that says 'Employees only.' " The salesman then went back to his reading, or his ogling, as if the presence of an L.A. cop were a daily occurrence, nothing to become particularly riled up about.

The EMPLOYEES ONLY door opened to a small storeroom. At the rear of the storeroom, a back door led outside. Behind the store, in a fenced area, was a small patio covered with wood lattice. Ben found himself standing on a square of concrete that divided the store in front from a smaller, newer structure in the rear. The patio was surrounded by tubs and hanging baskets of colorful flowers. Overhead, the stained wooden trellis provided a pleasant filtered sunlight. Graceful long clumps of fragrant violet-blue flowers, wisteria, hung from above. The air felt motionless with the thick perfume of flowers. Ben was aware of a low-pitched buzzing, bees laterally shifting from flower to flower, apparently so content with their foraging that they didn't see him as a threat.

In the far corner of the patio, sitting in a large rattan chair that was suspended from the wooden crossbeams of the trellis by a heavy metal chain, and swinging gently back and forth, sat a grossly overweight black woman, smiling contentedly, stroking a creamy-white cat that rested on her lap.

"This isn't a professional visit, if it, Officer? You've strayed a little outside your usual jurisdiction, wouldn't you say?" The woman did not get up. She continued gently swinging in the rattan chair, silently taking him in. Ben's eyes were drawn to the metal chain that supported the hanging chair. The chain rose from a steel support at the top of the chair and connected with a similar support bracket at the joists of the trellis. Despite the substantial support beams, Ben was concerned that the swinging weight of the woman might bring down the entire structure.

"Please," she said, partially extending her hand toward a small wicker settee just opposite her chair. "Make yourself comfortable." Her entire attitude was one of minimizing effort: eyes that looked only mildly interested; a dull, lifeless monotone to her words; the gesture with her hand as if it were a monumental effort that she found physically draining.

Geneva Harrold was not what Ben expected. She was camouflaged in a garish floral short-sleeved shift of the tropical island variety. The soft chocolate-brown skin of her face gave her the sort of youthful healthy look that many overweight, but attractive, women possess. Her arms, like thick brown anacondas, wrapped around the ball of creamy fur, stroking with short, stubby, pink-tipped fingers. The cat seemed content to rest in her lap, motionless, while she caressed it absentmindedly.

"Would you care for some iced tea?" she asked, her voice betraying a Southern accent of some sort. Ben looked at the small serving table within arm's reach of the hanging chair. On the table were two tall glasses filled halfway with crushed ice, and a pitcher of dark brown liquid in which floated slices of lemon. Two bees perched precariously on the rim of the pitcher.

"No, thank you," said Ben. He watched one of her fleshy brown hands reach for the pitcher and deftly lift and pour the liquid, then gently place the pitcher back onto the table. Even though she projected an economy of movement, Ben knew that the full pitcher of iced tea was heavy. The ease and obvious strength with which Geneva Harrold had lifted and poured the tea, using only one of her hands, did not escape him. She took the cover off a small china serving bowl containing sugar, spooned three heaping measures into her glass, and stirred. She then returned the top of the china bowl to its rightful place and put the spoon back on the table.

"Well," she said, sipping her tea, "let's get on with it, shall we?"

Ben watched as the bees that had been perched on the edge of the pitcher, and had moved to the table when the pitcher was lifted, carefully made their way toward the sugary puddle of tea and sugar where Geneva Harrold had deposited the spoon.

"Ms. Harrold," he said, "I'm looking for a man by the name of Stacey Fagan. I am an investigator with the Los Angeles Police Department, and Mr. Fagan's name has come up."

"Come up as what?" She eyed him warily, still sipping on the rim of the frosty glass. The cat raised its head momentarily, letting out a muted screech, apparently at one of the bees that had buzzed too close by. Geneva Harrold baby-talked a question to the cat about its comfort, then resumed stroking its head.

Ben decided to be straight with the woman, and if that didn't work, to threaten her. "He might be a suspect in a murder. We're not sure. I need to question him, and your name was given as someone who might know his whereabouts. I've already been to the burned-out apartment. That's the last address we have on him."

Geneva Harrold continued running her hand through the cat's fur. With her toes, she gently swiveled the chair back and forth. Ben could hear the beams creaking overhead.

"I should have guessed it," she said. "He had a streak in him, that one. We used to run this place together, for a while. But Stacey, he wasn't much for business." She laughed. "Unless it were monkey business you'd be talking 'bout. From your look, I bet it is."

"Do you know where I might find him?"

"Find him? Why, child, I imagine he's at the same place he's been for the last few months." She smiled, and Ben grew increasingly impatient.

"And where might that be?"

"Why, I woulda thought you boys woulda known all that by now. He's in the hospital. The nuthouse, if you wanna know. Stacey done lost his mind, child. Crazy, nuts, loony as a fruitcake."

The confused look on Ben's face eventually registered. Geneva Harrold added, "He was hit over the head with a baseball bat. Some irate father found out Stacey was having fun with his little girl. The child was only seven. I told Stacey 'bout that sorta stuff. That it wasn't no good. But that boy just never listened! I knew something like this would happen, and, sure 'nough, it did. Might say he had it comin'—Stacey, that is. The man did a real job on ol' Stacey's head. Lordy be, that boy ain't never gonna be the same. One good thing come outta it, though, I guess. They couldn't try ol' Stacey for what he did, him bein' so crazy and all. The docs, they put a metal plate in that ol' boy's head. Got the brains of a five-year-old, or so they tell. Don't think you're gonna get much information outta Mr. Stacey Fagan." She laughed, and took another sip of her tea. "No sirree, ol' Stacey's off in his own little world now. That man sure did a number on that poor boy's head, sure 'nough."

"Where is he now?" asked Ben, his voice showing his disappointment.

"They had him at Patton, last I heard. You know, the state hospital. Don't know whether he's still there. Imagine he is, though, since the way I heard it, they gotta keep him there 'till he's sane enough to stand trial, which, from the way they tell it, ain't gonna be no time soon."

Ben thanked the woman and headed back toward the shop. At the back door he turned for one last look. Geneva Harrold had swiveled the chair so that she was facing away from him, though he could still hear her voice. "Where's my little fur ball?" she said. "Come on, baby, come to Momma." The cat was rubbing itself against a damp, cool clay pot in the corner. It eased its way over to her, low-slung and not in any particular hurry. Effortlessly, it sprang into her lap, lowering its head beneath her hand and luxuriating under her caress. Geneva Harrold whispered, "That's a good baby." The cat stretched itself slightly forward with every stroke of her hand. "That's one messed-up white boy, ain't it, baby." Geneva Harrold continued stroking the cat's fur as she spoke. "Yes sirree, one messed-up white boy."

Back on Highway 15, returning to Los Angeles, Ben luxuriated in the air-conditioned rental car. Just the whooshing sound of the blast-furnace wind pounding the hood and windshield of the car. Time to think.

Where was Thibodoux? Had he planned this all along? Was he himself just another one of Zeke Thibodoux's victims? Had he been used? Ben wished he had the answers. All he had were questions. And the questions kept repeating themselves. He could turn on the radio, except out here there weren't a lot of stations to choose from and, in the end, he knew that radio babble, even music, would not do the trick. No, he had to think this one through.

Suppose that Thibodoux had been lying. That he made up the whole story about Stacey Fagan. If that were the case, Ben thought, then he had wasted his time and the city's money. He'd also taken his emotions on an unnecessary roller-coaster ride. But he'd get over that part. What would be harder to overcome was the knowledge that Thibodoux had duped him, had cleverly used his emotional attachment to Julie's memory for his own ends.

But was the connection between Racine, Danny Villapando, Fagan, and Thibodoux mere coincidence? Or was Thibodoux telling the truth? Could Fagan be Julie's killer? If he were, then Ben was at another dead end. If Geneva Harrold was right, Fagan was a vegetable, and would spend the rest of his life rotting away inside Patton State Hospital. Yet to know this for sure . . . to be certain that this, in fact, was the ultimate ending to the mystery . . . That's what Ben decided he needed to find out.

Was Ezekiel Thibodoux shrewd enough to know about Fagan's background, his residence in Barstow, where Julie's body had been found, and then to hold on to this information for years until it became of some use to him? It was possible. Difficult to believe, but definitely possible. Zeke Thibodoux was tricky, he'd proven that much already.

But something inside Ben told him that there was more than mere coincidence and the cunning mind of Zeke Thibodoux at work here. There was some kernel of truth in what Thibodoux had said. Enough to make Ben believe that Stacey Fagan knew something about Julie's death, even if he wasn't her killer. It was that belief—mere hope was more like it—that caused Ben to turn south off 15 onto 215 and head straight for the California Department of Corrections Mental Facility at Patton.

* * *

Varnished pine cabinets lined the walls of the small waiting room. They were streaked with grime from thousands of sweaty hands. Small black holes, cigarette burns, spotted the wood and the linoleum floor. The cushions on the sofa were vinyl, in an institutional green, ripped and patched at the corners. A picture of George Deukmejian, covered in glass with the glass covered by protective metal bars, graced the wall opposite where Ben sat. On another wall hung a paint-by-the-numbers Western scene of a wagon train heading off into a heavy-handed sunset. The room reeked of disinfectant, chlorine mixed with the faint odor of human waste. It was where they had brought Ben for his meeting with Stacey Fagan.

Ben had stopped thinking about all the possibilities. It was consuming him, and the effort was proving useless. On sensory perception now, he awaited the arrival of Stacey Fagan, wondering what the man looked like, but thinking of little else. A cockroach at work in the corner of the room occupied Ben's attention. Ben watched, waiting for the shiny black shell to move. It jumped, then scurried beneath the baseboards when the door opened.

"This is Mr. Green," said the large male attendant who had accompanied Stacey Fagan to the interview room. The attendant guided Fagan, who was dressed in loosely fitting cotton pants and matching shirt, both with the name of the hospital stenciled across the front. Fagan was not handcuffed, and appeared at the door, smiling and bobbing his head up and down, like one of those dolls you see in the back windows of cars. On first sight, Ben knew that Geneva Harrold had been right. Stacey Fagan had little idea where he was, or how he'd gotten there.

"He likes candy," said the attendant, handing Fagan a stick of Jolly Rancher cinnamon gum. "I'll leave you two alone. I'll be right outside if you need me."

Ben said thanks, and waited until the attendant closed the door.

"Ray-mond says that you're a po-lice-man." Fagan's speech was on the level of a four- or five-year-old. Slow, deliberate, with the emphasis often on the wrong or nonexistent syllable.

"Yes," said Ben. "That's true. I've come to talk with you, Stacey. Is that okay with you?" Ben went right into his Department 95 simpleton approach. He was accustomed to speaking with mental patients from the cases he'd handled in Mental Health Court.

"Do you have any can-dee?"

"Uh, well. Not with me. No. But maybe after we talk, I could get some for you."

"I li-i-ke can-dee." Fagan smiled. A small globule of saliva formed at the corner of his mouth then rolled down his chin. Fagan made a sucking sound, but didn't wipe at it.

Ben's expectations were quickly fading. "Stacey, do you know a man named Ezekiel Thibodoux?"

A look of confusion crossed Fagan's face. He seemed to ponder the question for a split second, then shrugged and smiled. "Ray-mond says that I eat too much can-dee."

"Yes, well, uh . . ." It was obvious to Ben that further questioning of Stacey Fagan would be fruitless. He tried one last question. "Did you ever send someone a picture of yourself and a girl, Stacey? When you were living in Barstow? Do you remember anything about that?"

"Pic-ture? I like pic-tures, Mis-ter Green. I have lots of pic-tures. Pic-tures of hor-ses, and pic-tures of pee-ple, and pic-tures of chil-dren . . ."

"What pictures of children?" Ben leaned forward, as if he could will an intelligent answer from Fagan.

"You know. Pic-tures. From mag-a-zines." Fagan smiled with a new thought. "Do you have any can-dee?"

Ben gave up. He opened the door and motioned the attendant back inside. "Here's a dollar," he said, handing the bill to the attendant. "Buy him some M&M's on me."

He almost decided not to bother. He'd seen Stacey Fagan, or what was left of him. Even if Fagan were Julie's killer, there was no chance that, in his present condition, he'd ever be brought to trial. And little purpose, Ben thought, in doing so anyway.

Arising from the feeling that once he left Patton he would probably not ever get back, Ben requested Fagan's legal file from the hospital administration. He also placed a call to Francis Powell, leaving a message that Powell should check out Fagan's criminal history on the computer. Ben took the thick folder to a bench in the waiting area and leafed through the documents. Most were the usual commitment paperwork, a partial rap sheet listing prior offenses, social studies prepared to aid the court or the hospital, and medical charts listing the patient's daily activity.

Toward the back of the thick sheaf of papers, Ben came upon a stack of police arrest and investigation forms pertaining to some of Fagan's earlier court cases. Run-of-the-mill stuff, except for one L.A.P.D. report which caught Ben's eye. He followed the listed information on the first page of the report down to the bottom, where, to his surprise, Ezekiel Thibodoux was listed as the investigating officer. A misdemeanor child-molestation case five years back, during a time when Fagan had been in Los Angeles. Thibodoux had handled the investigation, but there was no information in the file as to the resolution of the case.

Ben put the file to the side for a moment. Thibodoux had mentioned nothing about this connection with Fagan. It surely was something that he wouldn't have forgotten. So Ben figured that Thibodoux had intentionally omitted any mention of this when he told his story about Stacey Fagan. And why, other than wanting to hide something, would Thibodoux have left all this out?

An idea began to form, coming to Ben in quick flashes that individually were confusing but together painted a rather disturbing picture; the connection between Thibodoux and Fagan was the arrest. The relationship, if there was one that extended beyond officer and arrestee between the two men, originated with Fagan's arrest. Thibodoux would, by way of his position, have had knowledge of Fagan's whereabouts, his activity, even after the arrest. Thibodoux could keep track of Fagan easily, know his comings and goings. And if the two men were, as Thibodoux had claimed, exchanging kiddie-porn photographs only through the mail, perhaps Fagan didn't realize he was dealing with his former jailer. Perhaps Thibodoux eventually held this over Fagan's head, threatening him with exposure, extorting him for some unknown purpose.

Ben looked carefully through the most recent social study. Fagan's landlord was listed. He had been interviewed by the social worker as part of his background workup. From a pay phone in the corner, Ben asked for Barstow information, then gave the name of the landlord. Ben dialed the number they gave him.

"Yeah?"'

Ben introduced himself, and asked the landlord if he knew Stacey Fagan. The landlord, sounding tired, groggy, and more than a little hung over, grudgingly admitted to knowing Fagan, but quickly denied any affiliation with him.

"He's a fucking nut," said the landlord. "Stupid fucker ran off owing me two months' rent."

"I'm not interested in that," said Ben.

"Well, I sure as hell am!"

"I can appreciate that." Ben was trying to maintain his patience. "Let me ask you something. Did Fagan leave any property lying around the apartment? Anything you might have kept until he returned?"

"Shit, mostly. Just a lotta junk, if that's what you mean. I shoulda thrown that crap away, the whole lot of it."

"You mean you still have it?"

"Yeah. It's stored out in the garage."

"Could I take a look at it?"

"Don't see why not. You said you're with the cops, right?"

"That's right."

"Well, if it'll get that bastard more years behind bars, then look all you please."

Ben told the landlord that he was two to three hours away, but that he was on his way. He didn't mention that the issue of increasing Stacey Fagan's custody time was irrelevant. Ben was anxious to get a look at Fagan's property, and, at the time, would have said almost anything to keep the landlord happy.

It was starting to get dark as he pulled back into Barstow. He had stopped for gas along the way, noting the increased mileage he'd added to the rental car. He figured he'd find a place in Barstow to spend the night before returning to Los Angeles.

The address the landlord had given him was a dilapidated one-story apartment building on a side street, a few blocks from the main drag. The landlord's unit was in the front, facing the street, with a flashing VACANCY sign over the door. After some small talk, the landlord, wearing a sweat- and grease-stained T-shirt, followed his enormous beer belly down the row of splintered doorways to a small garage area in back. The landlord carried a flashlight, which turned out to be a good idea, since all the exterior lighting of the apartment appeared to have been broken or shot out.

"Here's where I keep all the junk, the stuff the tenants leave." He flashed the light on a locked wooden cabinet. From his pocket, the landlord fished out a small key and opened the padlock. "There you have it," he said, stepping back and shining the light inside.

Ben's first sensation was not of sight but of smell. The stench from the opened cabinet was almost too much to bear. It smelled like a small animal had crawled into the cabinet a few months earlier and died.

"Gets a little stinky," said the landlord, his beer belly, like Jell-O, shaking with laughter. Ben grabbed the flashlight and began poking around inside. He began to pull the various items of clothing, broken toys, car parts, and old furniture out of the cabinet. The two men stood looking down at the pile of junk at their feet.

"Like I said," said the landlord, "a lotta garbage. Not worth the trouble of saving, and not worth the hassle of standing out here this time of night." The landlord headed back toward his apartment. "Leave the flashlight by the door when you leave."

Ben kicked at the pile with his toe, not knowing what he was looking for, what he expected to find. A shoe box, torn at the corners, had tipped over when removed from the cabinet. Its contents, assorted keys, paper clips, Scotch tape, used envelopes and papers, spilled out onto the pavement. Ben kneeled to get a closer look, splashing the flashlight across the pile of junk. His eyes came to rest on a packet of photographs, rubber-banded together. Six in all. Thirty-five-millimeter camera, Ben thought, probably mounted on a tripod and placed on a timer from the look of them. He examined the photographs one by one. Fagan appeared in some of them, but never alone. Each picture depicted a young girl, naked or barely dressed, along with Fagan or some blurred photographic rendition of him. The photos were all slightly out of focus, but it looked like that same shit-eating grin on Fagan's face, the one Ben had seen in a different light at Patton.

Ben was disgusted with what he saw and depressed at encountering yet another dead end. And because of this, he almost failed to closely examine the last picture. But the light from the flashlight found the familiar face in the photo. At that moment he knew that he'd found his killer. The girl in the picture, standing next to the shadowy male figure, was Julie.

Still shaking, holding the picture of Julie in his hand, Ben dialed Powell's home number. "Francis, it's me," he said.

"Benny! Where the hell are you?"

"Still in Barstow. I found something, Francis. Thibodoux was right about Fagan, Francis. It was Fagan who killed Julie. I have the picture of them right here. He's the one, Francis. He's the one."

"Benny, something's happened." Ben could hear the agitation in Powell's voice. "It's Thibodoux," said Powell. "He's killed them all. His entire family. They found them inside the house. They've all been shot through the head."

"Jesus . . ."

"It has to be Thibodoux," said Powell. "Eliminating any loose ends. Jesus, I can barely believe it."

Ben's mind was switching gears. He was having a hard time focusing, his thoughts hopping back and forth between the picture in his hand and Thibodoux.

"And Benny," said Powell, with a note of practiced caution in his voice, "you asked me to run Fagan's record. The whole thing, including prison commitments? Well, I have some bad news for you, or maybe it's not bad news, depends on your point of view. Benny, Stacey Fagan couldn't be Julie's killer. He was doing a year for burglary in a Nevada State prison at the time."

CHAPTER 21

Just two cops, parked out in front. Like they were advertising the damn thing. Daring him to try something. Well, if that's the way they wanted it . . .

Thibodoux had already driven past the Gordon home twice. Seen the two cops in the unmarked police cruiser sipping coffee and eating doughnuts. Now he was a block down the street. The Toyota he'd stolen was pointed away from the cops. He watched the cops eating and talking inside the car. He couldn't see their faces in the dark, except when they cracked the door and the dome light went on.

He'd wait them out. He was good at that. Patient, that's what he was. Very patient. And he knew cops. Knew that they would have assigned two guys straight off patrol. Knew that these guys probably hadn't slept much in the last few days, because whoever assigned them to protect the Gordon kid probably didn't care that they'd just gotten off a month of early-mornings. Thibodoux knew that either one of them would fall asleep, or they'd drink so much coffee that they'd need to urinate. That's when he'd make his move. In the darkness, when the odds were in his favor.

So he waited. For a moment, he remembered what he had told Green, and wondered what the prosecutor had managed to turn up. Fagan was a punk. Whatever he got he deserved. Wild. Not careful enough. He'd told him that. He'd told Fagan how he would end up if he kept on doing that shit the way he did.

Thibodoux felt that the conflict that had raged inside his head was fading. He thought he'd changed. Become whole. That the forces pushing him toward action were now united. For a moment, he wondered about his other self. But only for a moment. As if by some finely honed defense mechanism, the new Ezekiel Thibodoux had pushed out all remnants of doubt, destroyed all thoughts that might weaken his resolve. He thought of Dr. Hirsch, but not in the same way as before. The calm, soothing voice had disappeared. Hirsch's face traveled through his memory as one-dimensional, without substance or meaning. The new Thibodoux was seeing to that, controlling his thoughts, dictating his acts. Just as it had done with Mary Esther and the rest of them. Weakness was not tolerable, and needed to be cut out, lest it spread its self-doubting cancer as it had before.

Thibodoux saw himself smile in the rearview mirror. It was time. The dome light of the police car had popped on. One of the cops got out of the car and was stretching, arms poking the night sky. Of course. He was tired.

The dome light stayed on for a few moments. Thibodoux watched the stretching cop motion to the one behind the wheel, then start on foot down the block. There was a small strip shopping center about a block away. Thibodoux knew that because he had carefully cased the neighborhood after his first meeting with Josh Gordon. Perhaps he had known, even then, that this moment would come.

When the stretching cop was about a block away, Thibodoux started the car's engine—just a quiet hum, barely noticeable, the Japs were great that way—and slowly U-turned, heading back toward the cop car. He lifted the gun with the silencer from the front passenger seat. Nice and easy, he told himself. His left hand was on the steering wheel, while his right cradled the gun on his lap. His driver's window was rolled down. He saw the cop look up, a cup of coffee in his hand. He didn't realize what hit him. Two shots, the car barely moving, and the cop's head slammed back and then disappeared inside the car. Thank God for shatterproof glass.

Thibodoux didn't stop. Just kept on down the street, slowly. He made a turn inside the parking lot of the shopping center, just outside the 7-Eleven, then parked on the street, the Gordon kid's street, looking back toward the house. He let the stretching cop get about halfway back before he pulled alongside to ask directions. And when the cop bent over, framing his face in the Toyota's passenger window, he gave him another small eye right in the center of his forehead.

Thibodoux parked right in front of the house. A long circular driveway distanced the house from the street. He'd do the rest on foot. Two lousy patrol cops! They had paid for underestimating his power. He slammed a new clip into the gun and headed for the house. They would pay, all right. All of them.

The images of Thibodoux and Fagan and Julie took center stage in Ben's thoughts and dreams. He had driven back to L.A. thinking of little else. Almost had two accidents, not paying attention to what he was doing. Closing in on Julie's killer, at last. The emotional high caused by the discovery of Fagan's photographs would not leave him. Ben forced himself to push it aside. There was much that still needed doing. He knew he would need a clear head to finish his job.

The problem was that Ben knew there was some nexus between Thibodoux and Fagan. More than Ezekiel Thibodoux was letting on. The discovery that Thibodoux maintained his relationship with Fagan long after Fagan's arrest was what triggered the process in Ben's mind. Erin Dailey's body had been buried in Newhall, but there was no trace of her head, and no evidence that she'd been killed in the same place. The SID boys told him that the actual killing, the torture, had taken place elsewhere, and that she'd been dumped in Newhall afterward. Then there was Julie's body in Barstow. But that had happened over three years ago. The lapse of time was what prevented Ben from seeing it sooner: Stacey Fagan was in Barstow. Thibodoux had contact with Fagan. Thibodoux knew of Julie's death *in Barstow*—though he could have read that in the newspapers . . . Still, it was consistent with his theory that Thibodoux was likely involved with Fagan at the time of Julie's death, or shortly thereafter, since he had seen the photograph of Fagan and Julie and had matched the face with Julie's picture in the paper.

Ben had the strong feeling he was right, despite the lack of factual support. He'd spent the time between one and three A.M. sifting through some of Thibodoux's old arrest reports, looking for the link. He was amazed when his gut suspicions proved true. What Ben had found both shocked and gratified him. If he was right, the Thibodoux case was much bigger than anyone suspected.

Ben picked up the phone, rubbing the sleep from his eyes. He looked at the clock, seeing that he'd gotten only a little over an hour's worth of slumber. It was still early, and when Francis Powell answered, it was with a bearlike growl.

"Francis, I think I've got an angle on Thibodoux and the Dailey girl."

Powell didn't answer. Ben could hear him yawning on the other end, then the phone was dropped.

"Sorry," muttered Powell.

"Listen, Francis. Where did Thibodoux dump the Dailey girl's body?"

"Is this twenty questions or something? Jesus, Benny, it's fucking four-thirty in the morning!"

Ben continued, not really listening to Powell's complaints, "In Newhall, right? And Julie's body was discovered in Barstow. Fagan lived in Barstow. Thibodoux had arrested Fagan. There was a relationship there."

"Benny, tell me something I don't already know."

"The place in Newhall where the little girl was found. Thibodoux arrested a guy a few years back. That same guy buried the body in almost the same place as the little girl. Thibodoux arrested Fagan, Fagan lived in Barstow, Julie's body was found in Barstow. What I'm saying, Francis, is that I bet if you check over Thibodoux's cases, the ones where the suspects buried the bodies, you'll find a connection."

"I still don't follow."

"Thibodoux, Francis! He's burying the bodies of the kids in the same places as his suspects. That's the connection with Fagan. That's what that madman's doing!"

"But there's only the one girl. You don't think . . ."

"Francis, it's the same guy that wiped out his entire family. It's the same sicko asshole that chopped off that girl's head. This isn't his first, Francis. I'll bet on it."

The line went silent for a few seconds. Then Powell's voice returned. "I'll have the cases pulled first thing. It'll take a while to sift through them, but I'll put someone on it right away." Both men heard the double click on the line. "Hold on a sec, Benny." Powell switched lines of his call waiting. He was off the line for a little over a minute. When he returned, Ben could hear the sadness in his voice.

"Benny, Thibodoux got to the Gordon kid."

Ben saw a mental picture of himself during that split second. He was mouthing the word *What?* but no sounds were coming out. He felt his heart racing out of control, wanting Powell to tell him more, and at the same time not wanting to hear it. The grief over Julie that he'd managed to suppress exploded in him like a gusher.

"He killed the two surveillance men we put out in front. The Gordons had stepped out for only an hour or so, but Josh was home with a baby-sitter. The sitter is dead."

"And Josh?"

"Critical. He's at West Hills Hospital, that's all I know so far. I sent a unit over there to keep an eye on things. We'll set up a twenty-four-hour surveillance. West Hills is pretty good about that." Powell paused, waiting for Ben to speak. "Benny, you still there?"

Ben could hear Powell's voice, a tinny vibrating sound coming from the telephone. He'd placed the receiver on the nightstand. Sitting on the side of the bed, Ben had his head in his hands, aware of Powell's muted voice in the background. It was exploding. Everything was breaking up, disintegrating before him. That feeling of guilt and helplessness he'd thought had been banished, had in those few seconds returned with a vengeance. It was happening all over again. Thibodoux and Fagan. And Julie in Fagan's pictures ... *What had they done to her?*

Ben knew he needed to get control of himself, that he needed, now more than ever, to be able to think straight. But knowing and doing were two very different things.

"Get a goddamn grip," he muttered, smacking the sides of his head with his hands.

Murray Rosenthal had been jogging the paths of the Santa Monica Mountains near Topanga for years. After his heart attack and his bypass surgery, and fifty-five years of eating and drinking whatever he damn well pleased, Murray Rosenthal had been forced to see the light. As his doctors had told him—after showing him the bright red slash in the center of his chest, the most recent addition to the new and improved Murray—if he cared anything about living a few years longer, he'd better start eating right, stay off the cigars, and get some regular exercise.

Murray's first thought was to tell the docs to go fuck themselves. But then he thought of his three little grandchildren. He threw away the rest of his cigars, giving his expensive handmade humidors to his neighbor. No more red meat, only fish and chicken, and he'd cut out the booze entirely. All losses that pained him dearly. He'd even started exercising. Walking around the block at first. Then jogging. He was up to five miles a day now. He'd never felt better. He would walk a little, then run, walk, then run. The mountain paths, especially in the morning, were cool and pleasant, and a lot less boring then running the streets. When he had the time, Murray would drive up Mulholland Highway, park the car, and set out up one of the sloping dirt roads into the hills.

So seeing a stray coyote or two wasn't something that shocked Murray. He'd seen them before, heard them howling in the early-morning twilight. Shadowy gray figures, like four-legged morning ghosts, in the hills, shifting in the uncertain light behind rocks and bushes, looking for food. Murray soon discovered that the coyotes were more afraid of him than he was of them. And someone had told him that as long as he didn't meet up with a large pack of them, he had little to fear.

This day, though, he was less than certain about that advice. Three coyotes, larger than he had seen before, yelped and growled at each other, fighting over some small morsel on the ground. Murray watched as one of the animals deftly picked up the scrap in his teeth, letting it dangle over his lower jaw, then scurried back up the hillside out of sight. The other two followed, yelping and scrapping with one another.

Once the sounds of the animals disappeared, Murray felt it was safe to emerge from the boulder behind which he'd placed himself out of harm's way. He inspected the area where the coyotes had been feeding, noting the trail of blood in the dirt, along with a few small scraps, rubber band–like, of what he took as animal carcass. The coyotes, in their fighting, had dislodged a large bush nearby. Murray walked closer to inspect the damage. What he discovered was that a section of vegetation appeared to have been cut, then restacked alongside a large outcropping of rock. A colony of giant red ants busily made their way, battalions of uniform lines, across the face of the rock, disappearing into a seam cut into the face of the stone. Murray pushed on the stone near the seam and could feel that is was not secure. He pushed harder, feeling some small movement. His curiosity got the better of him, and with a concerted effort, he was able to dislodge the large stone from its resting place. To his surprise, Murray found that the stone had been covering the entrance to a small cave.

The inside of the cave was dark, and smelled of decay and moisture. And there was another smell. One that surprised him. A familiar odor that didn't seem to fit, way up here, away from human habitation. It was but a few seconds before he placed the odor. Bleach. Chlorine bleach. But surely he was mistaken. There would be no reason for using bleach up here . . .

It was too dark to see much inside. Even close up, the light that trickled in from the outside, in the sun's present position, barely illuminated the entrance to the cave and little more. Murray stepped slowly, not knowing what he might encounter. After his first two steps, he stopped, thinking that he'd be better off returning later with a flashlight. He was a city boy . . . Who knew? This might be the home of some sort of bear or other dangerous wild animal. Then he told himself that there were no bears in these mountains. But there were mountain lions. People had seen them. Small children had been attacked by what the rangers thought were mountain lions coming ever closer to civilization in their effort to stay alive.

Just about to leave, his hand came to rest on a large stone in the center of the cave. His hand brushed something on top of the stone, and he recognized the object as a pack of matches. With both hands, feeling his way along, he removed a match and struck it, illuminating, for a few seconds, the inside of the cave. During those first few seconds, Murray confirmed that he was in fact standing inside a small natural cave carved into the side of the mountain. Just before the light from the first match went out, he thought he saw something in the corner of the cave. He lit another match, and held it up in front of his face, in the direction of the corner. What he saw he did not believe. Mesmerized, hypnotized by disbelief, he forgot about the match. The flame quickly burned down, burning his fingertips.

"Damn it," he blurted, but immediately struck another, unable to believe what his eyes had told him. It was there, though. In the corner. Someone had been here, inside. Someone had collected those . . . *things.* Murray only hoped they were animals, and not what he thought they were. He lit the last two matches in the pack, because he still couldn't believe what he'd seen.

When the matches were gone, Murray ran down the hill to his car, faster than he had ever run before.

CHAPTER 22

It was something she liked to do during the summer. Get out of the mess that her condo had become and spend the weekend getting a little TLC at the Marriott in Warner Center. Twenty-four-hour maid and room service, no phone ringing off the hook with patients, catch up on that novel she'd started too many months ago, and a chaise longue by the pool with her name on it. Sure it was a luxury, and more than a little decadent, but so what! She needed the escape, and besides, she could never totally get away from being a psychiatrist. Like this afternoon, lying around the hotel pool, sipping on a tropical drink, taking in the finer points of around-the-pool social etiquette.

A young couple, she guessed not married, were setting up a few yards away. He was of average appearance, not particularly good-looking but not what the kids these days would term a geek. She, on the other hand, was an absolute knockout, and from the few inches of fabric she wore under the guise of a swimsuit, the young woman was clearly aware of her God-given attributes. Beth found it interesting to observe how the boyfriend handled the attention that their little spot around the pool was getting. It seemed as if every adolescent and postadolescent male in the area made it his business to stroll by the young couple. Some were creatively discreet, keeping their distance, acting as if they were on their way to some other destination and had merely stopped within gazing distance of the micro-bikini by pure coincidence. Others, usually in pairs, took up positions nearby, smiling and giggling and grabbing the crotches of their swimsuits as they leered at the young woman, hoping that she would move around or at least turn over to reveal more of what they'd come to see.

The boyfriend, by the look of him, must have been through this before. After bringing her a tall pink drink from the bar, he conscientiously spread suntan oil on her back, very carefully avoiding any contact with the X-rated areas, apparently oblivious to the small crowds that had gathered around them. Beth had the feeling, though, that he was anything but oblivious. His girlfriend was too much of a knockout for him to remain unaware of the attention. Beth figured that he'd just gotten used to the gawking of strangers. It was a trade-off, to be balanced against whatever emotional pleasure or ego gratification he received by having such an attention-getter in his company.

Fun though it was, Beth decided she was going nowhere with this clairvoyant psychiatrist routine. She had just returned to her novel when her pager went off. She found the hotel phone, on a table near the bar.

"I didn't recognize the number," she said, after hearing Ben's voice on the other end.

"So how's my favorite headshrinker?" said Ben. "I'm calling from Parker Center, downtown. I got an office here for now. Back working for the good guys again."

"Erin Dailey," she said. "It's been in the papers." She hesitated, wondering whether to bring up the bit about Julie and the criticism of Ben in the media.

"Hard to miss, I guess. But this isn't a personal problem. At least, not what you think."

"Oh, and you're an expert in telephone mind-reading these days?" She heard him laugh.

"I need a quick profile. You've probably followed the Thibodoux case."

"He's on the loose, right? The one that killed his family and went after that little boy."

"That's why I need some quick answers." Ben paused, trying to organize his thoughts. The first reports on the discovery of the cave had just come across his desk. He'd just come from the scene himself. His head was filled with questions, and confusion. His worst fears about Ezekiel Thibodoux were coming true.

"Okay, shoot. I warn you, though, I'm in my mini-vacation mode, and I've just finished a little number the bartender here calls a Bermuda Triangle: two kinds of rum and about a half dozen multicolored liqueurs. I think the pineapple on the top was the only ingredient less than eighty proof."

"What I have," said Ben, "is a violent pedophile. Tortures the kids, sexually molests them—I'm not sure of the order, if it matters—then kills them, removing their heads."

"Delightful."

"That's not the really weird part."

"You've been doing this too long."

"The really weird part is that he saves the heads. Keeps them on a stringer. A fishing stringer, for like . . . fish, you know. These little heads, all lined up on this stringer inside a cave."

"Jesus . . ."

"I'm pretty sure the cave is where he tortures his victims. Oh, and he takes pictures of the kids, Polaroids, which he also saves. We found a bunch of them in the cave, along with some cassettes. You won't believe what's on the tapes."

"You're probably right."

"It's the guy doing his number on the kids. He actually tapes himself torturing his victims."

"Do you really need me to tell you what this guy is?"

"And then there's the semen."

"Semen?"

"Yeah, little vials of the stuff, with names and dates penciled on the top. I guess the guy didn't like to part with it."

"This is Thibodoux, right? The cop?"

"Ex-cop."

"That gives me a very reassuring feeling. I thought they screened those guys."

"They do," said Ben. "In the academy. Psychiatrists. *Experts* in their field."

"Okay, so what is it exactly that you want from me? You've got a violent pedophile who is also a homicidal killer. You're familiar with the basic literature in the field. Most of these men were abused themselves as children. Often the father was both violent and sexually assaultive. It's not uncommon for the child, in an effort to turn away from the father, to seek the solace of the mother. That can lead to further molestation by the mother. When the child matures, he goes out and does the same thing himself, either with his own children or with strangers."

"What about this cave thing? The semen and the tapes?"

"There you're talking about something separate. Most pedophiles, thankfully, are not violent. Only a small percentage of male pedophiles physically force themselves on their victims. Even a smaller percentage resort to actual violence. The great majority of these men are childlike themselves, identifying with the children they molest, molesting them by working into positions of trust, as opposed to relying on physical strength.

"My guess," said Beth, "is that this cave is a religious place for this guy. Based on what you've told me and what I've heard, Thibodoux probably killed his victims in the cave as a sort of ritual sacrifice, with heavy sexual overtones. He saved parts of them perhaps as a form of talisman or amulet. To prolong the experience, perhaps relive it later. I'm guessing here."

"And the semen?"

"Not sure. Many pedophiles are overly fastidious about themselves and those around them. It could be that. I'm not sure. I'm not sure about any of this. What you should remember is that you're dealing with someone for whom sex and the attainment of power go hand in hand. Physical aggression becomes eroticized for these individuals and sexual satisfaction is achieved only when the child has been hurt or humiliated. The sadistic pedophile sees the child victim as a representation of everything he hates about himself as well as the dreaded memories of his own childhood."

"No remorse, no guilt?"

"It's like this: the molester is able to compensate for childhood feelings of helplessness, powerlessness, and terror through his acts of molestation. Psychosexually, he is in a position of strength and command over his young victims. And the more he does it, the more comfortable he becomes. It's like when you're a kid and you go to a horror movie. The first time you see it, it scares you silly because you don't know what will happen next. But if you go to the same movie a second time, you're in control. You know what's going to happen every minute. It's not nearly as frightening."

"How is this guy likely to react when he learns that his sacrificial place has been discovered by outsiders? Let's say, the location and its contents are discussed in detail in public?"

"I think you know the answer to that one. My guess is that Thibodoux will react violently. He's already on a violent rampage, striking out at those he feels are against him. If his secret place is violated, he'll undoubtedly strike out again at those he holds responsible." She paused. "Ben, what are you thinking of doing?"

"Nothing," he said, his mind elsewhere. He thanked Beth Mellnor and hung up. Pausing only a few seconds, he lifted the receiver again and dialed the number of the *Los Angeles Times.*

Thibodoux could see the hospital from where he was, inside the car, looking through the space between the floors of the parking structure. The boy was on the second floor. That could be a problem, except now it no longer mattered. Thibodoux placed his hands gently on the explosives that were strapped around his waist. Where the boy was would not be a problem. Not once they saw him. Not once they realized that with one slight movement of his hand he could blow the entire floor to smithereens.

And he would, too. For what they'd done to him, and to his place, and, most of all, to his children. His treasures, touched by the hands of others. Impure hands. The thought choked him, constricting his throat. Sadness and anger bubbled inside. He started sobbing, unable to control the flood of tears. Sobbing and blubbering his love for his children, and his hatred for those who had defiled him. It was Green. Green who was behind this. Green who had disclosed the story to the press. Green who had treated him as he would some lowly animal.

Thibodoux had brought the newspaper with him. It lay on the front seat, open to the story inside. He'd underlined the parts that were important. Slashed them with his pen so that now he could barely read the words. But he didn't have to read them. He knew the words exactly. They'd been etched in his mind and had scarred his heart. *Zeke the Freak.* That's what the newspapers were calling him. And they'd told of his children, and his pictures, and the tapes ... *All gone forever* ... They didn't understand.

The rage was steadily building. The boy would be first. Then Green. Green was part of the cancer, like the others. Green didn't understand. None of them understood the new Ezekiel Thibodoux. They mocked him, as Christ was mocked. *Zeke the Freak* ... It was his destiny. He'd known that all along. And now, with these acts, he would realize that destiny. And all would behold his power and pay homage to the new Ezekiel Thibodoux.

Even now, this far along, like a sliver on an otherwise smooth piece of oak, Thibodoux was pricked by the memory of his parents. He swiftly plucked the offending thought, crushing the intrusive image then discarding it. The old Thibodoux raising one last gasp of self-doubt before forever fading into death.

The boy is on the second floor, he whispered to himself as he emerged from the car and entered the dank, malodorous, urine-scented stairway.

First the boy.

CHAPTER 23

It was like all the doctor shows he'd watched on TV over the years. Dark-screened monitors with just a single electronic line moving from left to right, horizontally across the center of the screen, beeping small triangular-shaped mountains every so often, then disappearing into darkness. A rubber bellows-type contraption moved rhythmically up and down, pumping something—perhaps air, he thought—into the young boy who lay motionless underneath the clear plastic tent.

Ben was alone in the room with Josh Gordon. The doctors had provided their doom-and-gloom prognosis, not willing to go out on a limb as to the young boy's chances of survival. Lots of medical terms hidden behind, but what it boiled down to was that the boy had been seriously injured by Ezekiel Thibodoux: internal injuries for which surgical intervention might be helpful, but not until the patient stabilized.

So Ben, along with the parents, who had stepped outside to have a moment to themselves, along with the uniformed officer seated just outside the door to the boy's room, along with the two plainclothes cops reading the paper and drinking coffee in the main floor lobby, were forced to wait. All were waiting for different reasons, though. The parents had little immediate concern with the capture of Ezekiel Thibodoux. Though Ben knew that revenge would raise its spiteful head as soon as the boy's condition took a turn for better or worse.

For the cops outside, theirs was the old waiting game. Keep the eyes and ears open. Try not to let the daydreams get the better of them.

For Ben, seated next to the young boy covered in clear plastic sheeting, the waiting was a bit of both. But also an opportunity to gather his thoughts, contemplate his next move. Prepare himself for what he knew would soon be coming. Thibodoux was out there. Ben wondered how close. He wondered if Thibodoux had yet devised a plan, and if he'd be prepared for whatever it was. Ben went through the options. He'd already surveyed the avenues of escape, the elevators and stairwells, and placed men at key points to intercept Thibodoux if he should appear there.

And he used the time to think about his own situation. He'd never find out whether Stacey Fagan had anything to do with Julie's death. He knew that Fagan couldn't have done it himself, not from behind prison walls. Fagan may have known something about the murder at one time, though. But in his present condition, what he had once known was as irretrievable as a single grain of sand at the bottom of the sea. Fagan would never improve. If he knew anything about Julie's death, that knowledge would die with him, forever buried in his childlike mind.

It would just be another loose end in a life of perpetually dangling threads, a garment . . . *perhaps a shroud?* . . . that for better or worse would remain incomplete. Ben didn't blame Fagan for that, or even Thibodoux. He didn't even blame himself any longer. What good was blame? Would it bring his Julie back? Would it explain or ameliorate his past actions, or failure to act? Would attaching blame eliminate his nightmares, the scenes that ran periodically through the magic lantern of his mind?

What good was attaching blame?

None that he could think of, sitting at the side of Josh Gordon's hospital bed, watching the miracle of modern medicine, the electronic beeps, and monitors, and gauges and dials.

Still, he wanted to know. He'd have given almost anything for that knowledge. And despite what he kept telling himself, it was Julie's killer that remained in his consciousness, lurking there in the back, just behind his eyes, waiting to torment him.

Somewhere between torment and longing, Ben became aware of the loud noise just outside the door. Voices, and shouting. And what sounded like chairs or other furniture being upturned. He took two steps toward the door when the door burst inward, toward him, crashing back against the wall, then swinging closed again, only to be stopped by the shoulder of the tall, lanky figure who had stepped inside.

"What a nice surprise," said Thibodoux, stepping quickly inside the room, his hands resting on a large canvas belt that he had strapped around his waist. A small black box was attached to the belt. A switch. Thibodoux's fingers rested on the silver toggle protruding from the box.

"Tell them to stay out," he barked, jerking his head toward the sound of voices on the other side of the door. He raised his hand over the switch to show he meant business.

Ben yelled that he was okay, and for the others to remain outside.

"Before you try anything stupid, Green, I believe you know what this switch is for. You try anything cute, and believe me, I won't hesitate to pull it. Rest assured, I have very little to live for."

The steel-gray of Thibodoux's eyes, the unblinking stare, the madman's countenance made a true believer of Ben. He couldn't take the chance, not with a crazy man ready to pull the switch on what seemed a very large amount of explosives.

"Plastic," said Thibodoux, grinning like a hyena. "Ideal for this sort of thing. Enough to make little pieces of us all." He quickly glanced around the room. "Now, now," he purred, moving closer to the motionless young boy. "What do we have here? It seems that I was less than totally effective." He curled his lip in a half-smile, half-snarl. "It won't happen again."

"You'll never escape," said Ben. It sounded stupid coming out. Like something from a movie he'd seen. But it was the only thing he could think of saying. He needed to do something. To talk. To buy time. It was obvious that escape was not foremost on Ezekiel Thibodoux's mind. A trade seemed out of the picture. Ben had to believe that Thibodoux was willing to go down with the ship, willing to play the kamikaze pilot on this one.

"You're scared, Green. I can smell it on you. Your cheap courtroom tricks won't do you any good here. Just you and me." He turned toward Josh Gordon and smiled. "And, of course, the boy."

Ben thinking, words coming out of his mouth before the thoughts were completely formed: "I met with Stacey Fagan."

Thibodoux paused. His hand rested at the corner of the plastic sheeting. The other hand still hung loosely on his belt, just inches from the switch. Thibodoux seemed momentarily confused, then a smile came to his face and his eyes sparkled with recognition.

"You did that, did you?" Thibodoux chuckled. Then great belly laughs. He even threw his hands in the air, taking his fingers off the switch, making himself vulnerable. But then, quickly, as if this were a movie and the intervening scenes had been spliced out, Thibodoux grimaced and his eyes sharpened. The moment for attack had been lost.

"You're even more stupid than I thought, Green. Let me tell you something. And I may as well tell you now, watch you twist and squirm before you die. That stuff about Fagan was pure bullshit. Sure, I knew the guy. That part was true. And we traded pictures, just like I said." Thibodoux paused, seeming to enjoy the look of pure dread on Ben's face. "But that's not the good part, Green. You wanna know what the good part is?" Again the smile, the unblinking stare. "I did it, Green. You got that? I was the one that killed your precious Julie. It was me all the time." The belly laughs again.

Ben was shocked into paralysis, his mind caught up in what Thibodoux was saying—admitting. The shadowy figure in Fagan's pictures came to mind. *Thibodoux . . .*

"You look surprised, Green. Don't be. It was easy." Thibodoux walked back around the bed, closer to Ben. He seemed almost conversational in tone, as if discussing the weather. "Didn't really plan it that way. It just happened.

She got in the way. Saw some things she shouldn't have seen." Thibodoux snickered. "Now I couldn't afford that, could I, Green?"

The paralysis was still there, mind and body unable to move. Ben was digesting Thibodoux's words, one by one, in slow motion, still in disbelief of their meaning. He saw the man, the monster, standing opposite him, grinning that wild grin, throwing it in his face. Go ahead, he was saying, do something. Do anything! You can't. You can't because you're weak. Because you're so fucking tied in knots at the thought that you'd just as soon stand there, slack-jawed, looking stupid.

When the movement came it was sudden, eruptive. As if his muscles were some enormous dam, straining to hold back the waters, and finally breaking. Ben lunged for Thibodoux and caught him momentarily off guard, surprised. Ben hadn't thought of options or consequences. Hadn't reasoned his chances. Hadn't considered odds. He moved like a wild animal awakening from slumber to find an enemy within striking distance.

Within moments of his attack, Ben found himself on the ground, his head throbbing with a stinging ache. Reflexively, he touched his forehead, feeling the warm blood ooze from a place just over his right eye. Just as quickly he got to his feet, only to see Thibodoux a few feet away doing the same. Ben dove at him, knocking him to the ground. The cart on which the monitor rested slid wildly to the side, yanking cords and wires loose. Ben, in that split second, was aware of the absence of the electronic beep. In that moment, he knew that Josh Gordon needed attending to. But Thibodoux was still there, in front of him, groggily getting to his feet.

From outside the door came a crashing noise, and the room suddenly filled with people. Ben turned to see Frank Chen and two others pushing their way through the obstacle course of medical equipment. When Ben turned back, it was already too late. What he saw—his last vision of Ezekiel Thibodoux—was the back of his body, poised in a crouch at the window's edge. Thibodoux was in movement. Leaping through the air, using the window ledge as leverage. Ben saw him as if he were stopped in time, slow motion. Then there was a deafening crash of glass as the picture window cracked into millions of splinters.

Thibodoux was gone.

CHAPTER 24

Ben rushed to the window, his shoes crunching in the sandbox of broken glass that lay on the floor. Thibodoux was nowhere in sight. He could survive it, Ben thought. Though he was sure that Thibodoux would have sustained some injuries, broken bones, torn or strained ligaments at least. But Thibodoux was gone.

As if he and Frank Chen had been thinking on the same wavelength, both men immediately started for the door, quickly running toward the stairwell, barking orders as they moved. The stairs led to a side exit which opened onto a small grassy area. Just to the east they could see a portion of the parking lot. Adjacent to the lot, traffic moved slowly toward Sherman Way. In the distance, a few cars back from the traffic light, they saw Ezekiel Thibodoux limping down the sidewalk. Thibodoux turned and spotted them. He then hobbled between two cars, approached the driver's door of a late-model Acura sedan, opened the door, and yanked the woman driver from her seat. Within a few seconds, the Acura swerved out of the traffic lane, through the red light, and up Sherman Way out of sight. The woman, totally dumbfounded and in shock at being torn from her car, stood screaming in the middle of the street, while the remaining drivers looked on.

"He's heading toward the freeway," yelled Frank. Both he and Ben ran for their car. Once inside, Frank gunned the engine, the tires squealing as he pulled out onto

Sherman Way in pursuit. Ben broadcast the chase over the police radio, arranging for Thibodoux to be intercepted. The problem was that they weren't sure exactly where he was headed. Ben and Frank quickly moved through traffic on Sherman Way, following the two-lane highway to the intersection of Valley Circle Boulevard.

Still no Thibodoux.

"Turn left," Ben yelled. He had a feeling that Thibodoux would be heading toward the freeway, opting perhaps for one of the canyons that he was familiar with. A few blocks further down, they eventually caught sight of the Acura moving along the sidewalk, past a waiting line of cars.

"There," said Ben, pointing.

"Fucker's driving on the sidewalk," said Chen, pulling his vehicle over the curb to follow. "Doesn't he know that's against the law?" Chen flashed a quick smile and kept driving. He was enjoying the chase. "Just like on TV, eh, Benny?"

They followed more slowly now, over the sidewalk and curb, past the cars waiting to enter the freeway. Thibodoux was visible a couple of blocks ahead of them. Overhead, the police helicopter whirred and flapped, hovering in circles.

"We got him," said Ben. The sound of sirens wailed in the distance. Red flashing lights and parked patrol vehicles blocked the Hidden Hills entrance to the freeway.

"He's stopped," said Chen, slowing the car, watching and approaching carefully.

"No, he hasn't," said Ben. Both men watched as the Acura slowed, then stopped. Then suddenly accelerated toward the roadblock, swerving to the right, over the shoulder of the road and around the parked black-and-whites.

"Damn!" yelled Ben. Thibodoux had successfully avoided the roadblock and was now speeding away from them on the Ventura Freeway. Ben, along with the patrol cars that had formed the roadblock, went in pursuit. A few miles north, at Las Virgenes Canyon Road, the Acura turned off the freeway and headed toward the ocean. Las Virgenes, like Topanga Canyon, was primarily a two-lane road, one lane in each direction. It swerved and snaked its way through the mountains to ultimately terminate at Pacific Coast Highway, near Malibu.

Traveling quickly on the winding canyon road was difficult. Switchback after switchback forced them to have to ride the brake. One wrong turn, one curve taken too fast could result in the vehicle careening off the road and down the side of the deep, and quite deadly, canyon wall.

The helicopter had followed them. Ben and Frank could hear the officers in the copter barking out warnings to Thibodoux over the loudspeaker. At the same time, they monitored the observations of the pilot, along with the other black-and-white units, over their car radio.

They were halfway through the canyon, at a place where the side of the road dropped off suddenly to a bottom that wasn't visible unless you stood at the edge and hung over the side looking down. On the other side of the road, the face of the mountain rose almost perpendicular, leaving little room for driver error. It was there, around a hairpin turn, that they lost sight of the Acura. It was no longer on the road. Ben looked at Frank, who slowed the car, peering into the distance. They could see the empty road ahead. Seconds passed. They had no idea where the Acura had gone.

Then they heard the explosion, at about the same time that the aerial report came over the radio that Thibodoux's car had gone off the road over the cliff.

Frank pulled a quick U-turn and both men got out of the car. Off to the left, about fifty yards up the canyon, they saw the place where the metal traffic restraint had been mangled. From below, all that could be seen were billowing clouds of gray-black smoke coming from the canyon floor. The first explosion was followed shortly thereafter by a second one, greater than the first.

"The plastic explosives," said Ben.

Chen looked to Ben, then back at the smoke.

"Millions of little pieces," Ben whispered, then smiled.

Frank Chen seemed confused. "What?"

"Nothing," said Ben. He looked up to see the helicopter hovering where the plumes of smoke began to dissipate into the blue canyon sky. Over the radio, the pilot was giving his report of the damage. The total destruction, as he put it, of the car.

"No sign of life," yelled the pilot. "Burned to a crisp."

Ben headed back to the car. A dozen units were already at the scene. Fire fighters were carefully making their way down the side of the canyon, using ropes. A fire-department helicopter had come into the area, dropping water and chemicals to prevent the flames from spreading.

Ben sat on the edge of the passenger seat, his legs stretched out the open door. He reached for the microphone, then stopped. He didn't know what to say. He wanted to speak with Claire, or Francis, or someone who would appreciate what he was feeling. The only voices over the radio were those of strangers. Nobody who could really understand what was going through his mind at that moment. Nobody who could tell him what to do next, how to handle the knowledge that he had so craved and now possessed. Thibodoux was Julie's killer. Thibodoux's reign of terror was finally over. The madman was dead.

CHAPTER 25

Claire had kissed his wounds, making a big deal over what amounted to a purplish bruise and small gash over his eye. The ER doctors had managed to close it with three stitches and a butterfly bandage, so that now he looked like one of Rocky Balboa's sparring partners.

They were together at his place, which was just where he wanted to be. Alone with Claire. Nightfall was coming with the first few cloudy swirls of fog and a jagged line of illumination, the sun's bright shadow, along the ridge of mountain. The serrated edge of light made Ben think of the monitor in Josh Gordon's room, its electronic life-light severed during the fight with Thibodoux. Josh had survived. With a little luck, he'd live a long and healthy life.

"This is the best time," he said. They were walking together about thirty yards from his house, along a narrow path that irregularly wound its way through the canyon, just below the extended outdoor decks of Ben's fellow canyon-dwellers.

"It's cooler," said Claire, not absolutely certain what Ben had meant. He'd been quiet during the days since the incident at the hospital. Francis Powell had filled her in on what had happened there and the subsequent chase. Ben's first words to her had been that he was fine, and that Ezekiel Thibodoux was dead. He finally seemed relieved, and she thought it best to leave it to him to pick the time for further explanations and descriptions.

The sun dipped and then was gone. The electric outline

of mountain ridge was but a faint shadow, barely enough to distinguish the mountain from the black night. Patio lights twinkled behind the houses, and in the distance, the neon of Ventura Boulevard played visual counterpoint with the hum of evening traffic.

But the canyon was for the most part shrouded in nightfall, playing for Claire and Ben its own music: the howls of stray dogs, perhaps coyotes, and the chirping of crickets, stopping then starting again as they passed.

Three stones, almost rectangular in shape, appearing to stand on end, marked the place where the path dipped down into a small gully. It threw Ben for a moment, those stones. He'd traveled the path scores of times before and hadn't noticed them, at least not the way they appeared now. Ominous in the indistinct moonlight. Like headstones. Grave markers protruding from the ground. He half-expected to find something inscribed on their faces, like *Here lies So-and-so. A good father, husband, and . . .*

Seeing the stones caused him to think of Julie. He hadn't heard anything more from his ex-wife. He assumed that the cemetery defacement was an isolated incident, or at least had not yet occurred again. He remembered that he had thought of Julie that afternoon, sitting in the patrol car, watching the smoke billowing up from the canyon floor. He had wanted to tell somebody that Thibodoux was dead, and exactly what that meant to him.

"Why don't we head back," said Claire. She stopped and faced him, and in the moonlight the soft features of her face appeared as if in a dream. The entire scene, their two bodies barely illuminated in the shadowy light, the cool fog-laden breezes rolling their way through the canyon in waves, seemed illusory, unreal. Like something idealized in a painting.

"All the cases checked out," he said, his eyes focusing on something over her shoulder, the children's faces still painfully clear in his memory. "Skeletons in shallow graves. Forensic's still going over them." He paused, blinking hard, fighting back the tears. "Francis said it'll take a few more weeks. You know what he called them? 'All the milk-carton kids . . .' "

His eyes were glassy pools, staring into the darkness. Claire caught the reflection of the moon and part of herself in them.

"You got him," she said, gently lifting a finger to his chin and locking on his eyes. She brushed a tear from his cheek, then gently took him into her arms. "The killing is over, Ben. It's over."